THE MARRIAGE OF VIRTUE & VICIOUSNESS

Vampire: The Requiem, Book 3

By Greg Stolze

WORLD OF
DARKNESS
www.worldofdarkness.com

Earth Baines took the stairs two at a time, thinking that maybe tonight he'd ask Julia to take it up the ass. No, just tell her. Demand it.

Bitch is halfway in love with me, he thought. *She's all doped up on the blood loss. She'll do anything I tell her to.*

He knocked on the hotel-room door, heard the click as someone inside turned the lock, and pushed inward.

"Yo, trick," he said, and then stopped short as he realized the figure before him lacked Julia's voluptuous curves and cascade of dark, fragrant hair. Instead, this figure was bald, scarred, and definitely male.

Oh snap, he thought, and then Solomon Birch's eyes hit him like a runaway train as the Bishop of Chicago said, *"Freeze."*

Baines heard the sound of the closing door but stood stock-still as Solomon stood before him again, putting those killer .44 caliber eyeballs in Baines' view once more.

"Sit on the bed until I'm done with you."

Fuck that bitch-ass buggity bullshit, Baines thought, but his feet toddled him over regardless. He not only sat, he folded his hands politely in his lap.

The leader of the Lancea Sanctum looked at him with his head tilted to the side.

Chapter One

Steve Quartermain stepped from cab to curb and bee-lined toward the Jade Room. *Sexy,* he thought. *Very sexy. Be very sexy.* He focused his mind on it like a Zen koan. Steve was wearing black pants and pointy-toed shoes. He hoped no one would look at his shoes. His shirt was green, but not just green, it was a medley of greens, a shimmering, subtle weave of dark and darker, and here and there just a brief glint of something pale.

He had spent far too much money on it, but it was a hot shirt. He wore it half-tucked into his black pants belted with a silver buckle and he looked as by-God good as he knew how to.

He looked neither left nor right but went into the club, like a man on a mission.

Backstage at the Jade Room, Velvet tuned her slap bass and thought it was funny how things turned out. She'd started out playing violin, classical violin, but somewhere along the way she'd drifted into jazz. Her group was called the Velvet Four, though Velvet was in no way its leader. The first time they'd played, a music reviewer from *City Pages* had interviewed them after the show, and he'd been ditch-water drunk. The article the next day had been full of misquotes and half-accuracies, and stuff he'd apparently just made up after looking, sober, at his drunken notes. One such made-up fact was that the bass player was called 'Velvet' and that the band was named after her. Before that article, she'd used her name, 'Violet.'

She tuned carefully and thought about classical music, which she really preferred, but jazz fed her. She had perfect pitch and when her instrument matched it, she wandered to the backstage door and looked out.

She saw a man in a green shirt with a shaved head and a goatee enter the room and scan around, looking like a lion on a high place over the savannah. She didn't know him, but she knew as much as she needed to. The sweep of his gaze moved over her body, in the dim by the door, and paused. She felt it. Something trembling and familiar, but always new, every single time, new. She didn't know if it was weakness or strength she felt, but she knew she would obey.

The man moved toward the bar and a woman came into the club.

Aurora Graham wore a tight sundress printed with red and orange hibiscus flowers, bigger than real ones. It had a plunging neckline and, at the lowest dip of her cleavage, a pair of mirrored sunglasses jumped and jiggled, the stem stuck in her décolletage. The entire effect was like a pair of silver balls hung too close to the tip of a Christmas tree branch. She had open-toed shoes with medium platforms, and she moved on them like she'd been wearing high heels since before her first period.

Aurora was not tall and she was not obese by any reasonable standard, but there was a fullness to her body that would have embarrassed many other ladies. Her hair was a rusty red that had been pushed past normal limits by spray and coloring and teasing. Like her figure and her clothes, there was a lushness to it that bordered on caricature.

She had strong features, full lips, brown eyes and a cigarette. She took a drag, squinted around, and looked for an ashtray as she exhaled. Seeing one on a small, round table, she sat and ashed and caught the eye of a cocktail waitress with ease.

Aurora had come to the Jade Room for a reason, and it was not to hear bluesy be-bop.

The Jade Room was quiet and smoky and close before the music started, even without many people present. Steve knew he'd gotten there early, that he was being eager, that eagerness wasn't cool and that uncool wasn't sexy, but sitting at home listening to "Sketches of Spain" again just made him jittery. He needed to get out. He needed to *go*. He needed. He knew that need wasn't cool, either, but he hoped that he'd get to the bar, relax, pay far too much for a variant martini and maybe bore himself enough that when the time *was* right, when the crowd *was* there, he'd be able to work it right, play it proper, isolate one doe-eyed target from the herd and close in for the kill.

He sat behind his drink and tapped his fingers and thought about how finger-tapping wasn't cool.

More people drifted in, women and men, mostly in pairs and a few groups—work cliques, gangs of friends, aging hipsters, married couples or daters. Steve sat turned sideways with his eyes going nowhere in particular. Many clubs had a big mirror over the back of the bar, but not the Jade Room. It had a mural of jazz greats dead and gone, drawn by Alfonse Nazzario back in 1987 and then—sacrilege!—colored by some yahoo, some house-painter pal of the owners who'd needed work in the winter months. Students from the Art Institute sometimes came by even now to sniff at it, even though Nazzario had stopped being cool sometime in the 1990s and even though the artist himself had said he thought it looked fine with colors, shit, it was just some sketches he did for fun, he knew they'd get smoke-stained anyhow, and Christ, why did people have to make such a big deal out of everything? Then in 1998, he OD'ed and the mourners had come to the Jade Room after his funeral. The owners had done good business that night.

Steve hadn't been in the Jade Room for Nazzario's funeral, but he knew all this stuff. Steve picked up facts, back-stories and trivia the way a white car collects mud. He had all this at his fingertips, along with a witty comment about how some of those Art Institute people were still coming to the club to hear *music* now. He had charming commentary prepared. Steve Quartermain was all loaded up and ready to fire at the right target, the right person.

Any minute now.

As he turned the stem of his martini glass, his eye wandered again to the woman in orange. She was, he realized, the only person in the club who was not wearing a single item of black clothing. At least, nothing visible.

Steve quirked an eyebrow and imagined doing a full check.

A man walked in. Most of the people present didn't notice or didn't care, but the way this particular fellow carried himself, the subtle clues of his dress (leather blazer, aggressive belt, well-worn sneakers that had cost more than Steve's entire outfit) shouted to anyone paying attention that this here was a *man*, a man's man, a ladies' man, and that 'ladies' was in the plural possessive because it's more than one lady but if they get possessive he's outta there, he can't be tied down because, ladies, he's a *man*.

The only people paying attention were Steve and Aurora. Velvet was backstage, muttering a few last minute things, musical minutiae, to the rest of the Four.

Steve thought, *Oh no.*

Aurora thought, *Oh shit.*

Neither had met the stranger, but each felt they knew him by type. Aurora's dismay was not that of prey for predator, but more that of a hunter who spies an animal that isn't worth a bullet. Steve, on the other hand, very much perceived him as a challenge, and never more so than when he went directly for the table of the only obviously unaccompanied woman.

"Hey," he said to Aurora. She didn't reply. Nor did she make eye contact, choosing instead to pull a compact from her big brown purse and powder her nose.

"Oh, you don't have to gussy up for me," he said.

She turned a flat look on him that, if it conveyed anything, sent the message, *What kind of man under the age of 60 says 'gussy up'?*

"Is this seat taken?" he asked.

"That one isn't," she said, pointing her chin at an empty table.

"But the view there isn't as nice." He pulled up beside her. "What are you drinking?"

"What am I *drinking*?"

"That's what I asked," he said, signaling the waitress.

"You really want to know what I'm drinking?" Aurora asked again.

"I am *dying* to know what you're drinking," he said.

"I'm drinking alone," she said, and turned her back on him.

Steve didn't hear the conversation, but the body language was enough. The guy looked around as if to broadcast, *What's with this crazy bitch? Am I right, fellas?* But, like Steve, everyone studiously ignored him. He seemed shrunken, shriveled, a teenager dressed in his hip older brother's cast-off clothes. The victim of a professional-grade blow-off, he exited gracelessly to try his luck elsewhere.

Then the curtain opened, and without a word of introduction the Velvet Four began their set.

───

They started out with the Dave Brubeck tune "Truth," but where Brubeck initially composed something wise and hopeful and lively out of its minor tones, this version was mellow, slow, and resonated with a sadness absent in the original. To Steve, his favorite recording of "Truth" (off *We're All Together Again for the First Time*) had always seemed to be about someone who'd been around the block and seen the evils of the world, but who remained convinced of essential goodness nonetheless. The Velvet Four took that and changed it into a melancholy but not dispirited resignation—a dreamy recognition that things were bad, but even at their worst not without moments of pleasure.

They segued into an original tune after that, "Bottomless," which the trumpeter, Mitch Michaelson, announced as one of his own compositions. Steve liked the way he said it. He didn't brag and there wasn't false modesty, he just said, "I wrote this song," the way a mason might say, "I built that wall." It was all right, Steve felt. A sophisticated piece that was almost showy, but that didn't take itself too seriously and thereby avoided seeming overblown.

Two more covers followed: Chet Baker and Miles Davis. Steve wasn't exactly a jazz purist—in his opinion, being a purist was contrary to the spirit of the music—but he set high standards for Miles, and the Velvet Four didn't quite meet them. Rather than concentrate on perceived flaws, he let his eyes drift around the room. Inevitably, they settled on the woman in the orange dress.

She looks bored, he thought. She was sitting at her table, lightly rubbernecking the room, fiddling with her sunglasses.

Then another song began. Michaelson introduced it as "The Ghost Light," and it was good enough—new anyhow—that Steve's full attention returned to the performers.

"The Ghost Light" had a lot of tempo changes, a lot of surprises and movement, but it returned at unexpected intervals to the same hard-cornered melody. Steve found himself smiling, and as the band members soloed one by one, he relaxed. For the first time that night, he relaxed.

When Velvet started her bass solo, with just touches of snare drum or piano accenting her in the background, she turned right to Steve. Her face held no expression, her body was coiled around her instrument and intent only on it, only on playing, but her eyes caught his and held them. He gazed back and saw promise, potential and more... something he'd never seen before.

Steve didn't go out every night, he fought it off, but when he broke down and put on a too-expensive shirt and bought too-expensive drinks, he was looking for something. He was a hunter with an eye for cheap intimacy, even false intimacy, but looking across the room at Velvet, her eyes seemed to tunnel through the blue smoke and darkness to offer him something he'd never dreamed of, something he'd always secretly wanted even when he couldn't name it. He felt briefly that she might be unique, special, the one who could set him free and end his searching.

But didn't he always feel that way?

"The Ghost Light" was a long song and he applauded loudly afterward. He went to the restroom and when he returned, Velvet was lounging at the bar.

———

"That was a great set," Steve said, returning to his stool. The bassist had taken the one next to his, right by his empty martini glass.

"Thanks," she said.

"Buy you a drink?"

"Already got one," she said, shaking a half-empty cup of something clear with ice in it.

"Cool," he said, and for a moment they were quiet. Inside, Steve had anecdotes, jokes, commentary cascading through his head, but he'd learned the hard way that sometimes you just have to shut up.

"You staying for the second set?" she asked. "It's different."

"I might," he said.

"I'm Velvet, by the way," she said, extending a slim, pale hand.

"Steve," he said.

"Whoops!" said the woman in orange. She'd come up to the bar, had teetered on the edge of one shoe's platform, and had splashed Velvet's black broomstick skirt with something syrupy and garish, a drink that nearly matched her hibiscus flowers. "Oh, I'm so—"

Steve didn't get a chance to hear if she was going to say 'Sorry,' because the bass player had leapt up off her stool and hissed.

"My bad, my bad," the woman in orange said, and started patting at the stain with a napkin from the bar.

"Yes, everyone knows whose fault it is." Velvet shoved the woman's hands away.

Reaching for more napkins, she knocked over Velvet's drink, too, and only a second quick leap kept the musician's shirt dry.

"Ah, I'm all over the place here."

"Would you *quit* it?"

"I apologize, it's—" She kept dabbing.

"Just *shut up!*"

"That's gotta be really cold, frozen daiquiri mix. I don't think it'll stain."

"Get *off me* you fucking *sow!*"

The woman in orange stopped. So did the conversation in the rest of the room.

Velvet straightened herself and took a deep breath.

"I'm going to go to the ladies' room," she told Steve, her back to the interloper.

"Do you want me to come with?" the lady in orange said.

Slowly, Velvet turned and the two women locked eyes.

"I beg your pardon?" the bassist asked.

"I mean, to help you out." But now the woman in the orange dress didn't seem so clumsy or apologetic. She met Velvet's gaze, cool and level. "I feel so bad about spilling my drink on you. Helping you clean up is the least I can do." She lipped a fresh smoke from the pack and held the box out toward Velvet.

"No thanks," Velvet said. Her voice was hard as granite. "Good way to die."

"Sorry?"

"Cigarettes."

The other woman shrugged, dull-eyed, and lit her smoke with an insolent flick. Velvet twitched.

"If you're sure," the smoker said.

"Dead certain."

"Okay then."

Velvet turned with a swirl and stalked two steps toward the bathroom. Then she paused, turned back and put a hand on Steve's forearm.

"I really hope you stick around for the rest of the show," she said. Her voice softened until it was positively silky.

"Um…" Steve said, but before he could think of anything worth saying she was gone.

"Whoa. Hope I didn't piss off your girlfriend there," the other woman said.

"She's not…" Steve let it drift off and kept watching until Velvet was out of sight.

"Yeah well, she seemed pretty mad."

Steve turned back, something in her tone drawing him. Something heavy and wretched.

"Um…"

"Maybe she's right. Maybe I'm just a fat, klutzy cow." She bowed her head and stabbed her cigarette out in an ashtray with more force than was needed.

"Well, I'm sure she didn't… She was just startled, you know, and… cold, I guess."

"Is everyone looking?" the woman whispered. "God, I'd hate to think I humiliated myself in front of everyone here."

Steve swiveled his head. Most of the people had turned back to their friends or spouses or life partners when Velvet had made her dramatic exit. Almost against his will, he found himself wanting to console this woman, who sounded like she might start crying. "No. Nobody's looking."

"Are you sure?"

"Hey, it's Chicago. People are blasé. If we want drama, we'll just go to a city council meeting."

She gave a little laugh. "Thanks, pal." She turned to him and swept her hair back with a hand and a head toss. "I'm Aurora," she said.

"Steve."

"What do you do, Steve?"

He glanced at the stage, where the curtains were still closed, then looked back at her. "I teach," he said. The first few times he'd been asked that question by women in bars, he'd said, "I'm a teacher," but he'd decided a simple "I teach" sounded more classy. He thought about lying, but he wasn't at that stage yet.

She smiled and Steve blinked. It was a very nice smile, nicer than any he'd gotten in months, from anyone.

"What do you teach?" She signaled to the bartender.

"Music, actually. I work at a school and do some private tutoring."

"Yeah? Is that how you met your girlfriend? Oh, wait, you said she wasn't…?" She rolled her eyes and turned to the bartender. "Let me replace that dumped drink," she said.

"It was just water," he said.

She gave a short laugh. "Maybe a little gin in it would help her lighten up." She flicked a glance at Steve as she said it. When he smiled weakly, she smiled back. As if they were now complicit.

"Why don't you get me another?" she said, gesturing at her empty cup. "And one for Steve here. Unless you were going...?"

"I thought I might stick around for the second set," he said.

"Yeah? They're not doing much for me. But, you know, I'm not a real jazz sophisticate." She raised an eyebrow. "Not like a music teacher. I bet you're pretty good, huh? What do you play?"

"A little bit of everything, really—some sax, some piano. Nowhere near as good as those guys, though."

"Yeah? Maybe you can tell me what I'm missing."

Initially, she'd seemed a little too much to Steve—too garish, too vivid, too *something*. But there was that smile again and the chance to be an expert in front of her, and she laughed at his jokes and showed interest in his stories. By the time the curtain went up again, he was flushed and her calf was gently touching his shin.

From the stage, even across the blinding lights, Velvet could see that they were together. She gritted her teeth, dropped a beat and had to concentrate to recover.

After his third martini, Steve figured it out. He was having a harmonic convergence. His horoscope, his biorhythms, his lucky numbers—they must have all lined up. That was the only way to explain getting attention from *two* women. At first he'd thought it was some kind of competition thing for them, that seeing one wanting him made the other want him too, but this was too strong for that. Aurora was giggling and leaning on him and seemed awfully eager to get him to leave the club, apparently before Velvet could get offstage. Steve found himself resisting every time she asked to go. Not because the jazz was that great (though it was certainly pretty good, he especially liked a song called "Night of the Hunter" and wondered if it was inspired by the Robert Mitchum movie), but because he wanted to prove to himself that he could resist her and she would stay interested.

As for Velvet, she found herself thinking about an item she kept hidden in her bass case, but no, it was a bad idea.

Why did I have to lose my temper? She asked herself. *Everyone saw me get mad at her. Shit.*

In the middle of their last song, she saw the other woman lean over and whisper something in Steve's ear. She couldn't see his face because of the footlight glare, but from the change in his posture she knew he'd been galvanized.

The applause at the end was moderate and before the curtains had even swept closed Velvet was scurrying into the darkness and pulling out her cell phone.

———————

"C'mon, let's go," Aurora said to Steve, fluttering her eyelashes for all she was worth.

"You're sure you want to...?"

"Leave? Yeah, I'm sure. Sorry to trounce your jazz fix, but I think I can make it up to you."

"No, I mean... we just met and everything and, um, we've both had a few and..." At one level, Steve couldn't believe he was cock-blocking *himself,* but everything had gone so on-script tonight, he'd gotten so much that he just couldn't resist a little more.

"I'm a big girl. I know what 'consent' means, okay?" She put a hand on his arm to soften her words. "You're sweet, though. Really. That's why I think I might..."

Then she leaned in and whispered in his ear some more. That was the end of the debate. He was up off the barstool and headed out the door thinking, *The guys will never believe this.*

Aurora certainly was into him—at least it seemed that way to him as she pulled at his arm, urging him toward her car. "C'mon, not far, just down this street."

Even in her tall shoes she seemed sure-footed, while Steve's three plus-sized martinis made every surface feel sloped and uncertain. He stumbled and crashed, shoulder-first, into a lamppost. "Whoa," he said, "Hold on."

Aurora giggled and came to his side. "Whoopsie!" She snugged an arm around him and offered support. Maybe it was the booze, but she seemed unusually stable to Steve.

"Let's just… just take a minute here. I gotta catch my breath."

"Don't keep me waiting," she crooned. He didn't see her eyes slide down the road toward the Jade Room, and didn't see her scan the alley outlet that led behind it. He didn't see what her eyes were doing because she was kissing him. His eyes were closed as she looked over his shoulder.

She pulled back.

He grinned. "That won't help me get my breath back," he said.

"Oh you," she replied and gave him a playful swat on the chest. Oh boy, he was ready. He was kissing her again when the cops showed up.

It started with a loud, sharp, "Woooo!" from the patrol car's siren, and then red-and-blue light strobed his eyelids. He popped them open just as the officer hit the spotlight.

Aurora winced and threw up a hand as a sharp, metallic voice came over the loudspeaker. "Break it up, kids."

"What the…?" Steve blinked at the car and then blinked again at the woman.

Bright light was not kind to Aurora. In the spotlight's harsh glare he could see the grit of makeup on her face, and see the cobweb-fine lines radiating from her eyes and bracketing her lips. Away from the shadows and smoke of the Jade Room, her hair looked brassy and fake. The blinking red and blue threw the veins in her hands and forearms into high relief and seemed to make every sag, wrinkle and fold stand out like a mountain or chasm.

In an instant, each of her beguiling artifices had been stripped away.

"What's the big idea?" she yelled, turning to the car with her hands on her hips. For a moment her boldness lent a trace of her old charm.

"What seems to be the problem, officer?"

The cop got out—a middle-aged man, gray in his moustache, beef-bellied and stout-looking. He ignored Steve completely.

"C'mon honey," he told Aurora. "I asked you off my beat nicely and here you are again."

"What are you talking about?" Steve demanded. The cop's eyes served him a cocktail of pity and contempt.

"I don't like tricks getting turned on my beat, sir," the cop said.

"What?!" Aurora screamed. That was it as far as Steve was concerned. The romance was dead. "That is fucking *bullshit!*" she continued.

"Sir, did she solicit you in any way?"

"Solicit... er, you mean...?"

"He means did I ask you for money," Aurora said, glaring at both men with equal wrath.

Steve tried, drunkenly, to project some dignity, tried to take control of the situation. "She did not, officer. We just met at a bar—"

"The Jade Room, right? Christ, at least change it up sometimes, huh?"

"I am not a prostitute!"

"Do you really want me to haul you in and see if the D.A. buys that?" By now a small crowd was forming and it occurred to Steve that covering his face—discreetly—might be a good idea. Thanks to the top-shelf liquor coursing through his veins, he was less subtle about it than he might have liked. But hiding one's face from a crowd that's watching you talk with a cop about prostitution is difficult to do with dignity, even at the best of times.

Preoccupied with his own problems, Steve didn't see Aurora clutch her large purse close to her, the way unrehearsed criminals often do when there's a cop around and something felonious in a bag.

"Don't you dare arrest me," Aurora said, but her voice was less confrontational. "You've got nothing. You've got the wrong woman. There's no case and you know it. I'm just getting in my car to drive off and you're lucky if I decide not to sue you."

"Uh huh," the cop said, voice flat.

"I'm memorizing your badge number!"

"You do that. Sir, you going to call a cab?"

"Uh... yeah. Sure. That's probably a good idea. I'll just..." Steve gestured to a Starbucks, thinking that getting some coffee would help, and would certainly be preferable to standing out on the street being stared at.

Aurora drove off in a huff, and shaking his head, the policeman left right after.

Steve sat and for a moment just stared into the dark whirls of his coffee, wondering what had happened to his harmonic convergence. Then he became aware that someone was standing next to his table.

He glanced over at a black broomstick skirt with a sticky patch barely visible, if you knew where to look. Medium-heel granny boots under it, gray silk blouse above and at the top the cream-white face, hazel eyes and chestnut hair of Velvet the bass player.

"Hi," she said.

"Hey there." Steve blushed.

"You were out of the Jade Room in a hurry."

"Well that... um..."

"That woman?"

"Yeah."

"Kind of pulled you away?"

"You could say that. I guess. It's embarrassing."

"I've seen her go to work before," Velvet said, sliding into the booth across from him. "A lot of men just aren't equipped to say no to a woman."

"Did you know she...?"

Velvet blinked. "She what?"

"Nothing, nothing. I got away from her out on the street she... um, she finally over-played her hand. A bit. I guess."

Velvet chuckled and Steve asked what was funny.

"You," Velvet said, and tucked her hair back behind her ear.

———

They talked, she declined coffee and then they went for a walk and found a closed public park, deserted and empty in the post-midnight calm. They sat on a bench and looked up at the ugly yellow glare of sodium-vapor street lights reflected on low-lying clouds. He kissed her then and it was sweet. Her skin felt unbearably smooth, so cool and flawless under his hands as he stroked her neck and her upper arms. She made a soft sound, nuzzled his neck, and when her fangs came out and she bit him—quite hard—he was lost in bliss, his hands slack.

Steve was awash in alabaster serenity. All the small things of his small life—vacuuming, changing the oil, paying the rent, getting to work on time, clipping coupons for sub sandwiches—it all swirled away, drained by an echoing vastness, something more important and more real. Maybe love, maybe death, maybe the biggest thing of all.

If Steve was rapt, Velvet was more so. As a vampire, to bite and drink was her sole purpose, her sole consolation. Undead and unnatural, the immediate act of feeding was the only time she knew respite from the nagging, burning hunger.

Both of them gave in to the sensation. Neither really wanted Steve to die, but neither wanted the feeling to stop, either.

Then, in a split second, Velvet broke off and whipped her head around. In that moment, that slender moment, Steve opened his eyes to see what had made the bliss end. Against the yellow streetlamp glow he saw fangs and saw blood, *his* blood, gleaming ruby on her lips.

He also saw Aurora slam a wooden stake into Velvet's back.

Earlier, in the bar, Velvet had hissed. This time she *yowled* and her eyes flared red like a cat's at twilight. Some instinct, some predator's sense had picked up a stray scent of hairspray or had heard the sound of a cracking twig underfoot. She'd turned partway and kept the stake from striking straight and true, but it still went in, still hurt. Velvet completed her turn and Steve felt sick, felt faint as he saw the thick piece of wood sticking out of her back, between her spine and shoulder blade.

Velvet threw her body movement into a backhand slap that rocked Aurora back on her heels. In the strange clarity of shock in which all details seem equally relevant, Steve realized Aurora had changed into jeans and sneakers and, for some reason, knee-pads.

Aurora backpedaled, a hand diving under her jacket. *When*

did she change her clothes? Steve wondered. Velvet continued the movement of her hand until it was behind her own back, down by her waistband where the blood from the stake hadn't yet dripped. *There's very little blood,* Steve thought. *Is it mine?* And then he saw a glint of metal.

The wind blew, the clouds cleared and in the sudden moonlight Steve saw a knife in Velvet's hand and a gun in Aurora's.

Over me? Steve thought. His heart hammered and his hands shook. Every nerve fired to act and yet… to do what? He had no idea, or perhaps a thousand ideas at once. Run, fight, laugh, shout, go mad. All he managed in his frozen hysteria was to muster a weak voice and say, "Wait."

Velvet didn't wait. Steve actually felt a backdraft as she blurred, and then he heard a sound like a firecracker, saw a flash and realized that Aurora had shot Velvet.

Both women were screaming. Steve saw a stream of dots in the air, gray in the moonlight, and when they hit and spattered he realized it must be blood, more blood. This time he shouted "STOP!" at the top of his lungs.

Velvet half-turned. There were no fangs, no cat-eyes, just a stricken look, but his blood was still on her face and then her jaws clenched and she turned back to slice Aurora again.

Aurora hadn't paused. She put the gun right against Velvet's belly and pulled the trigger again. Steve saw the gray blouse bloom outward as the bullet exited. He had a brief view of the sheath from Velvet's knife and then a truly inhuman wail split the night.

He had a moment to realize that the muzzle flash had set Velvet's shirt on fire. There was something like the Doppler Effect as she raced away, impossibly fast, out of sight before her knife clattered to the pathway.

Chapter Two

A woman and a man knocked on an imposing oak front door. They'd been coming here for years and they still knocked politely. They still were made to wait even though their host knew they were coming. They didn't mind. On some level, they almost enjoyed it, felt it was proper and fitting.

Beatrice Cartwright didn't look old enough to have been doing *anything* for too many years. She had the coltish, fatless physique of a college track runner. Her skin had the pallor that Americans associate with zombies and the British, and her unlined face indicated either youth or Botox to a modern eye. But her brown hair was lightly streaked with gray, and there was a solemnity to her posture, a severity to her department-store brown pantsuit that would have fit better on a 50-year-old librarian. She wore no rings, her pierced earlobes were unadorned. Her only decoration was a thread-thin gold chain with a small pendant shaped like a serpent devouring its own tail. She had a medium-sized handbag, flat-black leather, looped over shoulder and head in the approved anti-purse-snatcher position. She looked ready to pull out a Bible and start talking about salvation. Her shoes were ugly, very ugly and very sensible.

Standing beside her was a man whose age would seem easier to determine. He was barrel-chested and looked fit, but his graying hair matched a seamed and weathered face. The natural tone of his skin was a golden olive, but there was a waxy quality to it. It seemed pale and sickly and washed out, like someone with late-stage leukemia and a spray-on tan. Beyond squint-lines and deep-cut wrinkles bracketing his mouth, his cheeks carried clusters of round pock-scars, like Manuel Noriega or Edward James Olmos. He was heavyset in a blue, pinstripe Brooks Brothers suit, wing-tip shoes and a red tie. His lapel pin was a red-and-white striped elephant with a star-spangled blue head. The hand holding a well-used leather briefcase had old brawler's scars on the knuckles. He looked like he should have a slight feral reek of perspiration, but he actually smelled lightly of Lauder's *Intuition* for Men. His name was Xerxes Adrianopolous.

The door opened and a living man looked out at the two walking corpses. For those who knew the look, that's what the two guests obviously were. They could hide it when they needed to, but in this house, they did not.

"Ian," Xerxes said with a smile.

"Come in," Ian Brigman said, swinging the door wide. "He's at prayer. Emily is up in the study. I'll bring him up to all of you as soon as he's finished." The study was lined with old books and new, the new ones stripped of any bright-paper dust covers to reveal plain cloth. There wasn't a paperback present to offend the eye. Handsome walnut bookshelves had scrollwork insets labeling the subjects—Biography, History, Military Strategy, an entire case of Religion, three shelves for Philosophy and two for Theosophy/Occult/Dark Arts.

Leaning in a corner was a pretty woman, whose prettiness would somehow manage to escape notice or comment, would somehow fail to incite arousal. This was Emily and she, like Beatrice and Xerxes, was dead. She greeted them with a cordial smile and exchanged ephemeral pleasantries. She was known as the Bearer of the Mask and was one of Solomon Birch's closest associates.

Xerxes set his briefcase down by an overstuffed chair and sat, hands lifeless in his lap. Beatrice stood by the desk, idly examining a sharp letter opener, and glancing at the three books scattered on the blotter.

"I'm sorry to keep you waiting," Birch said as he entered.

"It was nothing, Solomon," Beatrice replied. Emily's smile broadened.

Solomon Birch was taller than Xerxes and not quite as bulky, though there was clearly a great deal of muscle under his loose blue polo shirt. He wore it over gray silk slacks and hand-tooled leather sandals. He had the same deathly pallor of his guests, but in his case, it was unbroken even by hair, save for a short and severe goatee.

It was impossible to ignore his scars.

Wide scars and thread-slender ones. Great, raised worms of tissue and even a few glossy dents over his cheekbone or cranium. There was no visible part of his body free of them. At first glance it would seem he'd been in some catastrophic accident, but a closer look (not that many living people cared to give the matter that much thought or attention) revealed that no one incident could have caused these results. The scars crisscrossed and overlapped. There were scars that ran under other scars, clearly showing that time had passed between them. Some seemed to have arisen from burns or abrasions, some from deep and narrow slices, some from wide hacking chops. They were, taken together, a confusing but undeniable affidavit of a long series of violent, terribly violent experiences.

Birch smiled easily over his colleagues, but his glance lingered on Xerxes. Suddenly, the shorter man flinched.

"Where are my manners?" Xerxes said, and scrambled to his feet.

"I'll overlook it this one time," Solomon said, with a wink.

"So." Beatrice gestured to the book on the desk. "Reading *Rites of the Dragon?*"

"It pays to be informed."

"You're not thinking of switching allegiances on us, are you?" She grinned widely and Solomon returned it. It was a sign of their comfort that she could joke about such a thing.

"What other covenant would have me?"

"I imagine the Invictus would find you a place," Xerxes said.

Solomon's reply was a shrug and a question. "What brings you to my home?"

"We need to talk."

Solomon sat in one of the overstuffed chairs, and Xerxes resumed his seat. Beatrice perched on the edge of the desk, a choice that made her look like she'd died young and not old.

"Nothing good ever comes after that sentence," Solomon said. "What's your problem?"

The visitors exchanged a glance, and then looked over at Emily. It was a meaningful look, but one their host chose to ignore.

"First things first," Solomon said, looking between them. "I've forgotten *my* manners. Would you refresh yourselves?"

"We're fine."

"Are you sure? Ian's daughter is, I think, ready to be shared. Frankly, I think the experience would do her good. She has accustomed herself to my kisses after some willful displays. Now would be a good time to see how deep her devotion has become."

"I'm sorry," Beatrice said. "I'd really rather... just get this over with."

"By all means, then."

Beatrice turned to the other woman. "Emily, if you'll excuse us?"

Emily looked to Solomon.

"Anything that can be said in front of me can be said before one of my bearers," he said.

"It's a very... private issue."

"That's fine," Emily said. "I don't want to intrude."

"Why don't you go fetch Margery," Solomon suggested.

"That's really not necessary," Xerxes said. "Emily, I hope you'll forgive our abruptness, but this really is a matter of great urgency."

Emily's face became even blanker as she smiled and left the room.

Solomon turned to his remaining guests and raised an eyebrow. "Your problem must be serious indeed to drive away one so close to my counsel."

"Oh it is." Beatrice looked him in the eye. "My Bishop lies under a vinculum."

There was a moment of silence.

It is important to understand how bold she was, and how trusting, to meet the gaze of Solomon Birch. There are many strains of the vampire curse, and his inclined him toward provoking unreasoning passion, affection, adulation—even love. This, along with a tendency toward vast strength and speed, made his species the most efficient of predators among the undead.

Yet Solomon had eschewed the easy path of forced affection, choosing instead to pursue a different form of power. With no weapons but a met glance and his voice, he could impose his desires on those around him. While it was a power most reliable on humans, his fellow vampires—his 'Kindred'—were far from immune.

Her words and gaze were doubly bold because Birch was known for a cruel and violent temper. Triply bold because *he* was her Bishop.

"Ah," he said.

A vinculum, or blood oath, forms when someone drinks the blood of a vampire, willingly or no. It binds the will and suffocates judgment but is most insidious for corrupting emotions. Love of family, country or creed are inevitably drowned out by the mystic blood, turned to the enslaver, until ultimately the victim can think of nothing else, care for no one else, and must spend his every waking thought on the approval of his master.

More drinks meant tighter bondage. Solomon had been forced to sip the blood of Maxwell Clarke, not once, but twice. Maxwell was Chicago's Prince of the Kindred, the secular leader of the city's vampires and once a close ally of Solomon. Now he was much more and far less.

"Solomon," Beatrice said. "Think back. Just a year ago, what would you have said about a Bishop who was under the bondage of an unbeliever?"

"Do you think Maxwell is unprincipled? He has made our beliefs—that no one shall spread the curse, that no vampire shall destroy another—into the law of the city."

"He paid lip service to our faith and then transgressed it with that Moore woman," Xerxes said. "Before your mind was fogged by unnatural love for him, you knew this. Surely your memories are still clear? I have even heard that you agitated for his ouster." Xerxes ran the church Inquisition, monitoring believers to ensure orthodox behavior. He had been in that position since before Solomon's rise to leadership, and the two were collegial but not close.

"Do not presume to teach me my own history. I'm no drowsy ancient, confused by the nightmares of decades. My mind is clear and more, my will is my own—"

"Solomon, he threw you down and force-fed you before the assembled Kindred of Chicago!" Beatrice cried.

Instantly, Solomon was on his feet and across the room. His chest thudded into her before she could react and she sprawled back on his desk as he stood between her knees, hands behind his hips, glaring down at her.

"I was there, Beatrice. I remember."

Awkwardly, she tried to get a leg around to stand, to rearrange herself. Solomon's hand came down on the table beside her scrawny hip.

"Now, if you'd let me finish my sentence?"

Mute, she nodded.

"As I was saying…" He stepped back and suddenly he was perfectly casual, an affluent middle-aged man you might see at the country club or a backyard barbecue. "My will is my own as long as I am away from his presence."

"Surely your holiness can understand how that is… not a fully reassuring caveat," Xerxes said.

"I am your Bishop by the acclaim of the church. I am Bishop by my faith and will, and though it has been twisted it has not broken. Nor will it."

"Maxwell…"

"Maxwell has me in check but he dares not strike openly against the Lancea. We are too strong, too organized. We put him on the throne and nearly took him off it, and he knows it." Solomon stood and gazed into the cold fireplace, hands behind his back. "He dares not take advantage of his bond upon me."

"What?"

"Think about it," Solomon snapped at Beatrice. "He can make me his tool, but as soon as he does, I lose most of my value. The Lancea Sanctum won't tolerate a Bishop who is the mere puppet of the Prince—"

"I believe that's her point," Xerxes said, his voice mild. Solomon glared nonetheless.

"Haven't I made my point about being interrupted?" Xerxes raised his hands and Solomon went on. "Maxwell has the passive power to stop me, but he knows that as soon as he attempts any sort of active meddling, I'll be flung down. He has no interest in seeing me fall, because I would certainly be replaced by someone less tractable. Yes, someone lacking his vinculum," he said, before Beatrice could speak. "His interest is in keeping me in power and with that we can turn even this to our advantage."

"Surely you jest."

"Do I? We negotiate with him through intermediaries. He exerts his pressure to keep me in power, and as long as I appear strong—as long as my agenda progresses, *our* agenda—I can fend off challenges from beneath."

"Such as challenges from me?" Beatrice said, her voice neutral, her eyes level.

"You, or others," Solomon said. "You don't frighten me, Beatrice. You think as I think. You just aren't as strong." He didn't say it as an insult, simply as a statement of fact. "Let me describe the *worst* outcome, Priestess. You know our church is riddled with the fat and the lazy, opportunists and hypocrites. Under the banner of 'moderation,' they could place some waffling dunce with rubbery theology in charge. I've been keeping the weak-willed in line. I've been driving for doctrinal purity and I've been the one who has made the Holy Spear a force to be reckoned with in Chicago. Remove me, and it can all unravel. Xerxes, you remember what it was like before…"

Adrianopolous nodded, though he did not comment or change expression. Solomon took it for assent.

"Numerically, the Lancea is inferior," Solomon said. "Our strength comes from unity, and unity comes from doctrine. Our weaker, short-sighted congregates would drift into the sort of equivocations that have paralyzed the Circle of the Crone and left the Ordo Dracul an inert clique of self-absorbed dilettantes. Without me, the Lancea Sanctum becomes a hollow shell—a social club with no truer philosophy than the power-worship of the Invictus or the fraudulent debates of the Carthians."

"Without you... or someone like you," Beatrice said.

"A hand-picked successor," Xerxes said. "Conferring the mantle on a new Bishop of your choosing would keep the moderates in line. It's not like you'd be *gone*. You'd remain our primary theologian and philosopher. But can you honestly say the Lancea wouldn't be better served by a leader whose opinions were not skewed by knee-jerk adoration for the Prince? You yourself would never bend knee to a thrall, you've said so!"

"It wouldn't have to be forever," Beatrice added. "As long as you... are not defiled further... his hold on you will eventually fade. How much stronger will you look for doing the right thing, even when it means sacrificing your own power?"

"Can *you* honestly say that in five years, or 10 or 20, I'll be in a stronger position, having surrendered the mask under a cloud of shame?"

"I would give it back as soon as you asked."

"But are unwilling to let me keep it now, when it's mine."

She lowered her eyes. "I meant," she said deliberately, "As soon as you were once more your own man."

There was silence, and then a gradual creaking, crunching sound intruded. It was Solomon grinding his teeth.

"I have considered your offer and decline," he said. "My assistant Hortense can show you out."

"Solomon, we don't want a schism. We don't want an upheaval. But we can't tolerate a Bishop who is not loyal, first and foremost—"

"You finish that sentence at your peril, Beatrice."

She backed up a step. "We can't tolerate a Bishop whose loyalties are strained. In your heart, you know that."

"If I am unfit, let the Sanctified remove me."

"Are you willing to show that much weakness before the Carthians? Before the *Circle*?"

"Let what must be done, be done," Solomon said, showing them the door. "If I am to fall, let me fall in the Temple. Let my own people drag me down. Not in my home. Not in some backroom *deal*."

For a moment, the three dead looked at each other with the stillness of corpses.

"As you will," Beatrice said at last.

———

"That's good, but you're missing the syncopation," Steve said, yet he was distracted from teaching. His 12-year-old student looked up, face contorted in concentration.

"Now, what's syncopation again?"

Steve had a canned explanation and he gave it on autopilot while his hands stole up to his throat again, to the wide bandaid covering two round holes. He'd stared that morning, aghast that it wasn't a dream.

"Mr. Quartermain? My reed broke again!"

He had 30 minutes to eat, and Tyler was waiting for him in the teacher's lounge.

"Hey." Tyler taught math, and his schedule was more rigid than Steve's, but Tyler had, with geometrical precision, made sure to build in 45 minutes for lunch. Steve sat beside him and opened his small cooler. "What'cha got?" Tyler asked.

"Braunschweiger."

Tyler winced and looked away.

A few minutes later, Tyler said, "Steve? Hey Steve, you even awake?"

"Sorry?"

"I asked what you thought of the game last night, and you just stared off into space."

"Oh. I, no, I didn't see it. I went out."

"Jazz clubbing?"

Steve smiled. "You know me so well."

"You're gonna go broke paying those amped-up drink prices and covers and everything."

"It's not so bad."

"You meet anyone?" Tyler was married and knew about Steve's social life, but only the details Steve had chosen to reveal.

"Um... yeah, actually, I guess."

"Oh? Another jazz fan?"

"Two."

Tyler made a derisive noise. "Pull the other one."

"No, I... honest, I met two women. Is that *so* unbelievable?"

"Next you're going to tell me you were the hinge joint in a three-way."

"Is that what you'd like me to tell you?"

Tyler considered it.

"Well I wasn't," Steve said, and gave his friend a little glower. "One of them turned out to be... well..."

"A little unstable?"

"Or something. She took off. And the other was something else altogether."

"Could you be more vague?"

"A gentleman doesn't kiss and tell," Steve said automatically.

"Oh, so there was kissing?"

I don't know what there was, Steve thought, and then Tyler guffawed.

"Oh my God, don't tell me she put a big ol' hickey on your neck?"

Steve realized he'd touched his bandage again. He said, "Um..." and blushed.

Tyler shook his head, but his expression was suspended between disbelief and admiration. "Jeez," he said. "What's her name?"

"You wouldn't believe me if I told you."

"What? C'mon man. You're not saying she was someone famous, are you?"

"No, it's just... she has a non-traditional name. That's all."

"You got a hickey from Pussy Galore?"

"You kiss your wife with that mouth?"

"Only every chance I get," the math teacher replied, slurping coffee and looking self-satisfied. "You going to see her again?"

"I don't know." Steve knew he was touching it again, knew he was staring off into space again. "I really don't know."

Across town from Steve's public school, on the grounds of an exclusive Latin School, a pretty young girl with blonde hair was stretching.

The girl, Margery, was on the track team, the honor roll and on student council. She'd just finished a run—not part of the team training regimen, it was too early in the season for that, but she wanted to keep her edge. She was pleasantly winded, her hair was damp with sweat and fine golden wisps had escaped her rubber-banded ponytail. She turned her head, caught her breath and arched her back with no sense of self-consciousness, as people do when they think they're alone.

"You're lookin' good."

She whipped her head around and straightened her posture. "Thank you, Eric," she said, and started heading briskly toward the door of the gymnasium. He stepped in her path.

"You and me, we should go out some time," he said.

"That's flattering, but I'm not interested."

"C'mon, I've got a Hummer. Bose sound system. I'll give you a ride. Where you headed?"

"I've got a ride with Elizabeth. Sorry. She's waiting."

"C'mon." This time he put his hand on her arm to keep her from going. She sighed and looked him in the eyes, her face frank.

"Eric, I'm not interested in going out with you. I'm not interested in going out with anyone right now. Sorry. That's just how it is."

"We don't have to go out," he said, stepping closer. She leaned back. "We could just go somewhere, y'know? A little privacy." The back of her head brushed the shaded brick wall. She couldn't lean any farther away from him. His arm was between her and the door. "Just a little hookup. No one has to know or catch feelings. I'm one of those guys who likes eating pussy. I'll eat it all day for you."

"How proud your mother must be," Margery snapped. "Now move your arm, please."

"Don't be like that," he whined. "I know you're not all stuck up. No one so good looking could be. I just want to see you get wild. I want your hand on my cock. C'mon—"

Margery put her thumb to his throat, to the hollow below

his Adam's apple and above the hard ridge of his sternum. She pushed in, which hurt and made him take a step back. Then she bent her thumb to probe down behind the bone. That was excruciating, and he hunched in and dropped back, instinctively shying away from the pain.

She pulled her hand back and waited for him to stand. He did, raising his hands to his neck, just as she'd expected. She squatted a little to get a good angle so that she could drive her fist up into his groin with maximum force. She stood up into it.

"You asked for it," she said, then went to take her shower. After a few steps, she turned back to him and said, "Your dad's a lawyer, right? You should ask him to explain what 'sexual harassment' is, and when it becomes 'sexual assault.' Really. I think you need to know."

Eric was curled up on the ground, clutching his groin with one hand and his neck with the other. "I... I'm sorry," he croaked. "Shit, I'm sorry."

Margery looked down at him, her face as beautiful and pitiless as a Greek statue.

"That's good," she said, then left him.

———

Margery had gone to some jujitsu lessons when she was younger, but mostly she'd learned to fight from someone who lived in her house. He wasn't a relative, but he'd been with the family a long time.

For many other teenage girls, a confrontation like the one with Eric would have been traumatizing. Even ending in physical victory, it would have frightened them, left them wondering if he'd come back with a knife or a gun, wondering if he'd sue or tell some lie or try to get revenge in some other way.

To Margery, it was simply an obstacle, and she'd dealt with it. She'd seen worse.

Margery's last name was Brigman, and the guest in her house was Solomon Birch.

On the train home, Steve shook with the movement of the car on the rails and stared at an advertisement for a discount shoe outlet. It was where he'd gotten the shoes he'd worn Thursday, the black shoes he was ashamed of, the shoes that made him exasperated with himself for being the kind of guy who's ashamed of shoes that try to be cool but maybe don't quite make it.

Today, on this commute, he wasn't thinking about his damn footwear. He was thinking about Aurora.

"Oh fuck," she'd said, looking down at her arm that night, in the moonlight. At first he thought she was upset that her jacket was cut. Then he saw the blood emerge from her cuff and start dripping down her hands, down her fingers.

"Are you okay?" Steve had jumped to his feet, and then just as suddenly collapsed onto the ground again, everything spinning, worms of light crawling across his eyes.

"Shit, are *you* okay?" Aurora came over to him and held out her right hand, the clean one. She'd moved the gun over into her crimson left.

"Yeah. I'm fine, you're the one who—"

"You've probably lost more blood than I did," she said. She tried to pull him to his feet and then they both stumbled over to the bench. She put away her revolver.

"Shit," Aurora said. She blinked hard and swiveled her head. "You think she'll come back and finish the job?"

"Huh?"

"Come back here and kill us. For Christ's sake, could you focus?"

"What would she... why...?"

"Okay, I'm sorry, just... take a deep breath. Think. Let's both think for a moment."

They did.

"What the hell just happened?" Steve asked.

"You got attacked by a vampire and I drove her off."

"No."

"Yes," Aurora said, her voice unexpectedly mild.

"No, there's no such thing as vampires."

"Okay then, you got attacked by something that ain't a vampire but that sucks blood and got shot and still ran off faster than Marion fucking Jones!" She sighed. "We've got to get out of here."

"Huh? I mean, I'm sorry to keep…"

"Gunshot. The cops are going to show up eventually, even if *she* doesn't call them. Like she did *last* time." She turned her head to glare at him. "I'm *not* a hooker, by the way. You believe me now, right?"

"Sure, I guess… er, I mean, yeah. Yeah, she must have set that up. God, what's *going on*?!" He didn't realize he'd shouted until he heard the echo.

"Vampires," Aurora said, hoisting herself to her feet. "They're real."

Steve opened his mouth to protest and realized just how foolish he would sound.

"So what do we do?" He got to his feet as well. "Are you hurt?"

"Yeah," Aurora said.

"How bad?"

"Dunno." She bent down and picked up Velvet's knife.

"Do you…? Let me take you to a hospital."

"No."

"I insist."

She looked at him and pointed the knife in his general direction. "Or what? I've got a gun, too. Remember?"

"I don't want you to die because you helped me."

Aurora's face flushed and her lip trembled and then she was crying. Just a little bit.

"Are you okay?" He took a step forward.

"No, really." She held out her bloody hand, palm out, to stop him. "Honest. I'll be okay. If I need to go to a hospital… I will. It's just that…" She stopped and made a snotty inhaling sound and then smiled at him. "What you said was… it was sweet, I guess." She craned her neck again, looking around. "You need a ride anywhere?

"I've got a bus pass," he said, and felt incredibly inane. She smiled.

"Take it easy then. Stay away from her."

"Do you think she'll come back after me?"

"Does she know your real name and stuff about you?"

"Yeah."

She sighed. "Then you'd better run. What *is* your name? Where do you live?"

"I'm Steve Quartermain. I... here, I've got a business card."

She shook her head, but she grinned and took the card.

"Lie low," she said. "I'll try and get back in touch."

That had been the last thing he'd heard from her. He'd wandered home somehow, practically in a fugue. Later, he'd tried to remember what kind of car she had.

That morning, he'd gotten up with a killer headache. Half-asleep, he showered, and when he put shaving cream on his chin and neck, he was shocked by an icy pain. Eyes suddenly wide and alert, he wiped steam from the mirror and seen the two puncture holes, about an inch apart. They were scabbed over but oozing a little, the red drops stark against the white shaving lotion.

He made himself another braunschweiger sandwich for supper. That stuff went bad fast and besides, he had a real taste for it. He'd been starving ever since...

Ever since Velvet, he realized. *Braunschweiger is, what? It's chopped liver, right? No wonder. If she really did drink my blood, I'm probably iron depleted. I should get one of those multivitamins,* he thought, and then he had to sit down and slap himself for even taking this whole vampire nonsense seriously.

His rational mind insisted that such creatures were a violation of the natural, scientific order of things and that there must be a better, more rational explanation.

He thought about the wooden stake.

Yeah, but that could just be Aurora being crazy. I mean, she's the one who said 'vampire' and if she's a nut, what else is she going to use? Silver bullets? Fuck, for all I know she did fire silver bullets. Why did I give her my card? I'm an idiot. A crazy chick who carries a gun and a wooden stake is fixated on me and I just hand over my address and phone number.

Still, there was the matter of Velvet moving so fast even when *obviously* hurt. After getting shot, for Pete's sake.

But hey, what would make you run fast, Steve, if not getting attacked by some lunatic? Maybe Aurora missed both times. Hell, maybe she was loaded with blanks for some reason.

He thought about the knife. It was not a pen knife, not a pocketknife, not any kind of cooking knife he'd ever seen. He'd only glimpsed it, but his memories were intense and he suspected that what Velvet had been carrying could only be called a fighting knife—double-edged, pointed, thin, and with a couple metal flanges to keep your fingers from slipping onto the blade. Not anything someone carries to open a tough bag of chips. Especially with a sheath hidden at the small of the back.

Okay, so maybe they're both nuts. Maybe they're co-crazies. Maybe it's all some weird fucked up sex game between two lesbian psychos who like to play Buffy vs. Barbarella with some innocent bystander guy in the middle. Maybe I am *the hinge joint.*

Deep down, though, he knew his rational side was getting clobbered. The image of Velvet's fangs in the moonlight was just too clear to smear with plausible maybes. But beyond that, there was the sensation.

When she kissed me, he thought.

No, when she bit *me… what was that? What* was *that? I've never felt like that before.*

Steve was a lonesome man and he tried. He gamely went on fix-up dates, he went on singles internet chat-sites, he smiled at strange women on the train, at the supermarket, at the Art Institute, he was always alert, always on the lookout, always ready to be helpful or polite or charming or, hell, he'd even try suave. Who knew? He might manage it, right? He did all the single stuff that single men did.

Then, he'd take it a little further. When the loneliness went beyond a sad fact that he managed and became consuming, became driving and burning and maddening, when that happened he'd go out and score. He wouldn't try to make a spiritual connection or find an intellectual peer or even make an implied social contact with sex as an element. He always *hoped* for those, for any of the above really, but when all that stuff failed him he would just lower his standards. Fresh out of college, when he'd gotten lonesome that bad, he would smile at women twice his age, chat up women twice his weight, women who were ugly or unhygienic or clearly plagued by serious mental problems. He didn't care. A woman who couldn't shut up about her recovery? Or her ex-boyfriend? Or who couldn't construct a complete sentence? Sure, whatever, he just wanted *contact*, just something, anything to satisfy that horrible skin hunger.

Now, though, he'd found another way. Now he didn't lower the standards governing which women were acceptable for a dance, or a hurried mash session in a doorway, or even a cluttered episode of mutual masturbation in the stale-smelling backseat of a 10-year-old Honda. Instead, he lowered *himself.*

Like a salesman slashing prices and going out of business, he jettisoned his scruples. Lie? Tell her he's a Libra, a Libertarian, a vegan? Sure, why not? Tell her he's a doctor, a lawyer, hell, he'd tell her he was an Indian chief if he thought she'd buy it and consequently put out. She didn't even have to screw him. She just had to *hold* him, or even just look at him the right way, look at him like he mattered, like he was real. Even though he was being false.

It went beyond dishonesty. It went into a strange sort of aggression, a mental place that he didn't like to go, a competitiveness where any weakness in his chosen woman was a reason to rejoice, was a lever, an opportunity, a chink in the armor. Beyond even deceit, he would engage in the most selfish forms of psycho-tactics. He would manipulate without conscience. He would do whatever it took to get her to submit.

Submission, of course, meant being attracted to him, even as he used strategies that repulsed him. He hated being like that, hated knowing that he could sink to that level, could be such a pushy, devious, scheming selfish *shit*. He hated himself. That was the worst.

Except for loneliness, being an asshole was the worst.

So then, what had he done with Velvet? What had he *had* with her?

Now the memory seemed cloudy, but that only made it more alluring. For just a little while, with her, he'd been free from the self-doubt and self-regard and *self-consciousness* of being Steve Quartermain. He'd been free of himself, but at the same time he *hadn't been an asshole*. No, he'd been completely naked and honest and essential somehow. He'd been *more* human than when he was being himself.

Hell Steve, half the time you try *to be yourself you fuck it up anyhow.*

With her he had been purely human and nothing else. Beyond words and thought and memory, he had been something pure, had touched something essential.

Was that a near-death experience? He wondered. *Is that what all those books are about, all that religious stuff, all those people who talk about satori or enlightenment or rapture?*

Did I touch death?

Is that, ultimately, what all humankind has in common?

Before he'd consciously thought it through, he was waving down a cab and telling the driver, "Jade Room."

Chapter Three

As the twilight dim gave way to the bright of street lights, a very different figure walked into a very different bar.

This bar was bright, almost blinding. Everything was white porcelain and brushed steel. The walls were all mirrored, but the mirrors were distorted, scoured and blurry. The entire effect was something like walking into a sterile mirage of a '70s science-fiction movie set.

The bar was named "The Discarded Image" and almost no one ever drank there. It was a Friday and the bar was close to Chicago's Water Tower Place, so it should have been hopping. But there were three customers and one man behind the bar. That was it.

There was one black man in an immaculate blue suit, conservatively cut but made of some fabric that gave it a subtle shimmer, subtle black ripples. He had a bottle of Perrier in front of him, and he had not taken a single sip.

A woman in fashion jeans and a bustier under a man's jacket rested beside him, stiletto-heeled sandals motionless as she sat with her legs crossed. Her hair was copper-red and close-cropped. She had a gin and tonic in front of her, untouched.

Another woman, in an ecru business suit, spoke with the bartender, who wore a tight black t-shirt over khaki pants. Both of them had brown eyes, so dark they were almost black. The woman's blonde hair was in a severe bun, while the man had a crew cut, bristly black. He put a glass of white wine in front of her and they continued a muted conversation as she ignored it.

All four of them were perfect.

It wasn't just that they were beautiful—in actual fact, the

redhead and the bartender were rather plain in the face. Nor was it that they had flawless physiques, though there was not an ounce of fat to mar their slender profiles. Rather, their perfection was that of a finely crafted statue, the faultless aspect of something timeless and unchanged.

Robot designers talk about something called "The Uncanny Valley." Charted by Masahiro Mori in the late 1970s, it's a mathematical function that gauges human reaction to human-like faces. At first, when faces on dolls or toys or cartoon characters aren't close, people like them the more they cleave to human norms. But past a certain point—when the face is human-like but not quite enough to fool anyone—viewers begin to dislike them, even feel uneasy around something that is manlike but not man. This dip reverses as the device or image approaches 100% verisimilitude. Then, once again, more human is better.

These perfect people rested in the Uncanny Valley. While all the right pieces were in the right places with the right proportions, it would take a hard person to see them and repress a shudder.

When the door opened, all four turned, and in their movement they exited the Valley and seemed, for a moment, to be normal people. Indeed, graceful and attractive. But when they were still again, that mannequin ghastliness settled over their features.

The man who entered could, at rest, project a small part of that inhuman stillness, but he moved more, or more naturally, or perhaps had a better instinct for camouflage among the living. Or maybe it was just that in the Discarded Image, the other four felt safe enough to let down their guard.

They stared in silence for half a moment, then the redhead leaned in and whispered to her companion. He grinned.

"No, he's real," the black man said. "I see him, too." He turned his attention to the interloper and widened his smirk. "Mr. Baines! What can I do for you?"

"Yo, homey," Mr. Baines replied and held out a fist for the other man to knock.

"Jane, my sweet, allow me to introduce Mr. Mayfield Baines.

His friends call him 'The Earth.'"

"'Sup," Baines said, barely sparing her a nod.

Easily over seven feet tall, poured and set like a cement statue of a linebacker, Earth had dressed for the evening in a blue muscle shirt, baggy silver track pants, immaculately white Reebok basketball shoes, and jewelry. Lots of jewelry.

The biggest single piece was a Mercedes logo superimposed over a globe, with tiny diamonds around the rim. It dangled against his preposterous pecs on fat gold links. On a thinner gold chain was a Chicago Cubs medallion, hand-crafted from mother-of-pearl, red jade and lapis lazuli. The shortest chain, silver, supported a plain gold letter, the capital letter "I." Matched by a high-school class ring on his left hand, a three-finger gold ring on his right that spelled out "C.R.E.A.M." with diamond periods, and topped with a humble Cubs cap, Baines' presence in the Discarded Image was like a cinder block thrown into a still pool.

"Charmed," Jane said, and blinked slowly.

Not only was Baines a giant costumed for a hip-hop video, but he was also lily-white. He had the blonde hair and blue eyes of a bona-fide Aryan, and even his voice was mellow and Midwest-steady beneath the abruptness of his adopted lingo.

"So Earth, what can I do for you?"

"Stingo, I need work."

The black man—Chris Stingo by name—spread his hands and widened his eyes. "Are there no crimes, vendettas or transgressions requiring your skills? Should you not then rejoice in the good manners of Chicago's Kindred and rest, satisfied with a job well done?"

"Chris, you know that ain't it." Agitated, the big man shifted from foot to foot while everyone else seemed comfortable with perfect stillness. "I get called in for the hound work, for punchin' an' shit, but I can do more, y'know?"

"You're admirably skilled at... punching and shit," Stingo said.

"I want better than that. You think I wanna still be hustling losers and smacking ghouls around in 20 years, a hunnert years? I gotta show I can do better, earn some respect. 'S'all I'm asking."

"You want to transcend your role as a mere thug. Why haven't you spoken to Norris?"

"Norris doesn't like anybody until he's got their balls in a vise. He gots nothing on me so he don't trust me. Won't give me no jobs but the same old thing."

"Hm. Well, your Protestant work ethic seems to be alive and well," Stingo said, earning chuckles from the others. "I have to admire that. I think I can help you out. I may have a chance for you to show your quality."

"Straight up?"

"Certainly... if you do me a little favor first."

Half an hour later, Earth Baines pulled up in front of a shitty, cheap apartment building.

Earth drove a Cadillac Escalade. It had chrome trim, a neon-lit undercarriage, tinted windows, spinners on the hubcaps and a metal-flake purple paint job. Its Illinois license plate read "IMPOR 10."

The building was home to a man named Morris Watts, who had the misfortune to owe Chris Stingo some money.

The door on the Escalade opened and anyone in the neighborhood who'd been thinking vaguely unlawful thoughts about it started, thinking vaguely uneasy thoughts about personal health, instead. Baines got out, went to the building's door and opened it without knocking. It wasn't locked, but Baines gave the impression of someone who would open it easily whether it was locked or not.

When he got to Watts' apartment, he finally knocked. Hard.

"Watts," he barked. "Open up. Stingo sent me, get his money. Open the door."

He waited a few seconds, but not many, and then put his shoulder in.

Morris Watts was sitting on the sofa in boxer shorts and a wifebeater. He was trying to stay cool with a small electric fan, and was cleaning a variety of guns. He'd been in the middle of dissembling a 12-gauge when Baines knocked, and was briefly sad that it was not ready to shoot, but he quickly decided on a Sig Sauer. It had not yet been cleaned, so it was on the left side of the table. (The clean guns were on the right.) He reached for it with his left hand while his right groped on the floor for a full clip. As Baines spoke, Watts loaded and ran the slide, and when Baines crashed through the door he was standing and aiming.

"Bitch!" Baines yelled. Then he lowered his head, reached his arms out and charged into gun smoke and the loud sound of a pistol shot.

Watts frowned, thinking that maybe he wouldn't stop this guy in his tracks and would have to wrestle his deadweight off after a second shot. *Christ, how am I supposed to move a dead guy that big anywhere anyhow?* He fired again and then Baines tackled him.

Both bodies plowed into the sofa hard enough to rock it on its rear legs. Watts' head smacked into the wall and Baines wrenched the gun out of his hand. Watts had a moment to realize that, for a guy who'd been shot point blank with at least one 9mm bullet, this big fucker didn't seem to be slowing down or even flinching. And then somehow he was upside down.

Baines had simply wrapped one arm under each of Watts' knees, pinning them in his armpits. He straightened up, kicking the table of guns and parts back out of the way. Morris' hands scraped the floor and his head was a little above the giant's knees.

"What the fuck?" he squeaked. Then Baines squatted and started banging Watts' head on the floor, up and down, like a kid on a pogo stick.

"Money!" Baines shouted. "Money, bitch! Gimme Chris Stingo's money!"

"Ow, fuck, okay! Okay, shit, just put me down!"

———

The woman in the eggshell suit had been replaced by a pair of short, skinny girls in matching red dresses. One was blonde, the other had dark hair. Like Chris and Jane, they were perfect. Each had a Black and Tan sitting in front of her. Both drinks were full up to the rim, and the beaded water condensing on the sides was evenly distributed. Not only had they tasted nothing, they had not even touched the glasses.

"You *didn't*," the blonde said. Her name was Catherine and she went by 'Cat.'

"I only needed to fool the wife for a few minutes while I got away." The dark-haired one was Katherine, nicknamed 'Kitty.'

"But the *baby*?"

"I just put it next to him and started slinking off. If it hadn't started crying, it would have worked perfectly."

Chris Stingo was on the phone as Mayfield Baines walked in. Seeing the gym bag in Baines' hand, he smiled and hung up. Jane was still at his side.

"Done an' done."

"At least something's gone right tonight." Stingo handed the bag to Jane. "Count that, would you? There should be two thousand."

Jane unzipped the bag and riffled the rubber-banded stacks of 10's and 20's with a thumb. The money whirred like cards in a shuffling machine.

But more, when she opened the bag, everyone in the bar subtly shifted posture, perhaps leaning in just a fraction of an inch, perhaps coming alert in a way that was not immediately perceptible, perhaps just flaring their nostrils ever so briefly.

Only Jane could see the speckles of blood on the money. As she handled it, the tiny droplets were fresh enough to smear.

"It's $40 light," she said. Chris turned to Earth and raised an eyebrow.

"Motherfucker put a hole in my shirt. I extracted some payment."

"And the gun stuck in your waistband?"

"He put a hole in me, too."

Chris frowned. "You didn't...?"

"What?"

"You didn't give anything away to Watts, did you? He was outside the loop, you know."

"Nah. Shit, I didn't even need any funky voodoo shit to take him on," Earth said, puffing out his magnificent chest.

"He saw you take a bullet."

"Things was hectic. He'll think he missed or had a bad round."

"Did you taste of him?"

"No!" Baines sounded genuinely offended.

"There's blood on the bills."

"At the last minute he decided to keep it real. I smacked him. That's all. No feeding. Shit, I don't do that wi' *guys*."

Stingo raised his hands, expression mild and apologetic, though he did not actually say he was sorry.

"Now," Earth said. "Bidness."

"Ah yes, your opportunity. Do you know Velvet? Violet Metzger, plays the violin at Elysium?"

"Oh, yeah. She's in the Sanctum, right?"

Chris nodded. "Last night she was attacked by a woman with a gun... and a wooden stake."

"No foolin'? Some chick in Chicago gone all Van Helsing?"

"So it would appear. Obviously, if Ms. Metzger's assailant has penetrated the Masquerade, it's imperative to—"

"Kill her ass."

"I was going to say 'contain the situation,' but, yes, we're on the same page." Chris leaned in. "Just as important, of course, is finding out if she told anyone."

Earth nodded. "No problem. What do you want me to do?"

Chris tilted his head and spread his hands. "You wanted to show your stuff, right?"

Earth shifted his weight. "Well, yeah, but..."

"Then far be it from me to steal your thunder by micromanaging your investigation. Off you go now! Have a nice time finding the vampire hunter!" He made a brisk movement with his fingers, as if shooing away a mouse.

Baines opened his mouth, then shut it, shrugged, put an insolent look on his face and stalked out the door, his exit ruined only by the giggles of the girls in red dresses.

"So?" Jane said.

"Did you see what I did?"

"I saw that the Lancea Sanctum is going to need to waste resources coping with an inept investigation into an assault on one of its congregates, while you nevertheless fulfilled your duty to them."

"Correct. Is that all?" When she made no answer (though she did manage to look stylishly amused, as if she was playing a game with him and not losing at it), Chris gently shook his head. "I also got him to accept that doing this task *for* me is a favor *I'm doing him.*"

While Baines was shaking down Watts, Velvet went shoe-shopping.

"Go ahead, Sylvia. Try them on," Velvet told her companion, a birdlike woman who was apparently in her 50s.

"Oh, I don't need any such fanciful shoes," Sylvia replied. "I leave that to you youngsters who need to catch yourselves young men." Her eyes twinkled merrily. Passersby figured them for a woman and her grandmother.

Velvet moodily picked at a pair of outrageous black stilettos. "Sylvia… something happened last night."

"I know dear."

Velvet turned her head sharply. The other woman was glancing off toward the sneakers and tennis shoes.

"What do you mean, you know?"

"Well, I knew something was bothering you."

"You didn't do a reading on me… did you?"

"Violet, my sweet, I didn't need to. Oh, what do you think of these? I think they'd look nice on you."

"Do they have a size eight and a half?"

They looked through the boxes under the display. "Just one left. It must be popular," Sylvia said, but her face fell when she lifted the shoebox.

"What?"

Sylvia's answer was to lift the lid and reveal that there was only one shoe inside. "I thought it felt a little light."

"No big loss."

"It's probably the partner of the display shoe. You could still get it, maybe even at a discount."

"Nah." They silently walked through another rib-high row of footwear racks. Then Sylvia spoke again.

"So what happened?"

Velvet glanced around, though she rationally knew Sylvia wouldn't have asked if there was a risk of being overheard. She still lowered her voice. "I got jumped by a witch-hunter," she said.

"You're sure it wasn't just a mugger?"

"She left a wooden stake in my shoulder so... yes. I'm pretty sure."

"Oh my. Have you told anyone? Besides me, I mean."

"I told Stingo." Seeing Sylvia's response, Velvet furrowed her brow. "What? You don't think I should have?"

"Stingo is a very resourceful fellow," she said neutrally, "But did you really need to go to an outsider?"

"Sylvia..." Velvet sighed.

"Fine, never mind. Forget I said anything."

"You're not that old. You still remember the separation of church and state."

"You're acting suspiciously mortal, child."

"Well, if my home was burgled when I was living, I'd have called the police, not the local cathedral."

"Hm."

"Would it be better if I'd called an Inquisitor instead?"

Sylvia sighed. "Perhaps you're right," she said reluctantly. "Do you mind if I...?" She held out her hand.

Looking to the left and the right, Velvet held her own palm up as well. Sylvia touched it and closed her eyes. For a moment, she was still, and in that stillness she looked as dead and uncanny as anything from the Discarded Image.

When she opened her eyes, she gravely said, "I saw it." Then Velvet's cell phone rang.

Sylvia discreetly moved off, though they both knew she could eavesdrop from a hundred feet away if she wanted to.

When Velvet caught up with her, she said, "Stingo sent someone to deal with it and he wants to talk to me at the Jade Room."

"Who did he send, Loki?"

"Someone named Mayfield Barnes."

"Never heard of him. Do you mind if I tag along?"

Velvet shrugged. "What's your interest?"

"Violet! I want to make sure you're safe, of course."

As they walked toward the door, Sylvia picked up a box of Nike cross-trainers. "Steal these for me, would you dear?"

When Earth Baines arrived at the Jade Room, the other two were already there. It was a Friday night and crowded, but his girth and his garb ensured a perimeter around his table.

"Ay," he said, extending his hand to Velvet. "Violet Metzger, right? Velvet? I'm Earth Baines."

"Earth?"

"'Cause I'm large," he said, then turned to Sylvia.

"Mr. Baines, this is Sylvia Raines," Velvet said.

The pair exchanged glances and for a moment there was tension, an instinctive curling of lips from suddenly prominent teeth. Strangely, it was the enormous man who flinched back and the tiny old woman who seemed to restrain herself. Both recovered their cool and shook hands.

"Raines and Baines, yo," Earth said. "You're the Sanctum scholar, right?"

"I fear you have the advantage of me, young man."

He shrugged. "I ain't done nothing special yet. I just remembered your name 'cause of the rhyme."

"And have you been a Sheriff long?"

"Uh... no," he said, shifting his eyes off her. "Not long at all."

"I feel safer already," Velvet muttered.

"You should," Earth said. "I've faced Lupines. I think I can handle one scrawny mortal with a nine in her purse."

He held her eyes as he said it and she nodded slowly.

"Who sent you, dearie?" Sylvia asked.

"Stingo. Is that going to be a problem?"

"I have no problem with Mr. Stingo," she replied. "I certainly hope he has no issue with me."

"Velvet," the bartender said, tilting his head so he could eye Baines. "Friends of yours?"

"My cousin Erasmus and my aunt Sylvia." Velvet moved to the bar and the others trailed along. "They just wanted to see where I play."

"Chocolate Box is doing the first set tonight."

"Jazz isn't really my thing,'" Sylvia said apologetically.

"Yeah, we can't stay," Velvet said. "But, hey, while I've got you here, do you remember that guy I was talking to on-break the other night?"

"Bald guy, flashy shirt?"

"Yeah. Did he leave his name?"

He shook his head.

"What about that woman he was with? Do you remember her?"

"The drunk chick who spilled on you?"

"That's the one," Velvet said, gritting her teeth just a little. "I know you see about a thousand customers a night, but... any chance you caught her name?"

He squinted and looked off in the distance, opened his mouth and didn't say anything, and then...

"'Scuse me? Can I get a house merlot and a Blue Moon here?"

The bartender snapped out of his reverie, gave an apologetic head-shake to Velvet, and went to fill the order.

"Damn," Earth muttered. "You think anyone else here has a clue?"

"No, and it's probably a good idea to move before we draw any more attention," she said, looking pointedly at his conspicuous bling.

"Is this where she sat?" Sylvia asked, her eyes closed.

"Why? Are you getting something?" Velvet leaned close.

Raines opened her eyes and shook her head. "No, sorry. It's too faint."

"Well, I've got something with a stronger impression," Velvet said heading for the door. "It's in my trunk."

"Wait," Earth said, plucking at Sylvia's sleeve—an odd gesture, his banana-like fingers clumsy and hesitant. "You do that..." He made a vague, open-hand gesture in front of his eyes, "...stuff?"

"You mean, do I have the Sight?" she asked as Chocolate

Box emerged amidst polite applause.

"Yeah."

She just smiled in reply and gave him a little pat.

In Velvet's trunk, there was a paper bag containing her attacker's wooden stake.

Since a blood-encrusted weapon isn't something you want to gawk at on a public street, even late at night, they decided to examine it somewhere private. After some discussion, Sylvia suggested her place. Baines was a little leery, since Sylvia's residence was also a Lancea temple, but she implied without directly saying it that her hidden senses might be clearer there.

It had once been a small, neighborhood Catholic church. Now converted into a private home, exterior accent lights rather than the sun lit the stained glass windows. Side wings had been walled off, making a bedroom and kitchen, while part of the back had been sectioned into two more sleeping quarters. But the open central space remained as a spacious living room.

"Mr. Baines, I don't believe you've ever attended a service of the Lancea Sanctum, have you?"

"Well, you know I'm... uh, I'm in the Invictus, like, official, y'know...?"

"I recognize the pressures of a political entanglement, Mr. Baines. Believe me. But we are creatures with eternity ahead of us. Do you want to spend that much time trapped in the coils of a self-devouring political monster? Or would you rather seek the truth about us, the Kindred, and about God above?"

For a moment, Baines actually looked abashed, but then he cracked his neck, met her eyes and said, "Oh, so there ain't a lick of politics in the Lancea?"

Sylvia stared back and then emitted a bark of surprisingly harsh laughter. "A touch, a palpable touch! Very well, Mr. Baines. This battle of wits is over... for now."

She led them past the tasteful modesty of the living room— deep sofas that looked at least 10 years old, an armchair with a worn arc where the recliner handle had rubbed the upholstery, a well-dusted coffee table that still had a few indelible scuffs and stains. They passed all that and went downstairs.

"I had the door to the outside concealed when the church was de-consecrated and converted," she explained as she turned a key in what appeared to be a thick door of aged wood. Humming a little tune, she opened a panel in the wall that was not readily apparent to the naked eye. Putting her mouth to a speaker she said something, clattering syllables in a language Baines didn't recognize. Velvet knew it was Greek and guessed it was the ancient North African dialect, but she got no meaning from it.

"If you would turn your backs?" Sylvia asked, her tone apologetic. When they did, they heard a few tapped keystrokes and then some other vague sounds of movement.

"All done," the old woman said. When they turned back she turned the knob and the door—now revealed to be steel-cored, with bolts like a bank vault's—opened. On the other side, when the door was closed, Baines would have needed a few squinty minutes to find it again.

"I told the contractor I wanted one of those panic rooms, but he questioned why I wanted it so big," Sylvia said as she led them deeper inside. "Such a nice man. I'm sure his wife misses him terribly. Then I had Ned, you know him? Dumptruck Ned? I had him work in a few things to keep the temple safe."

Baines just stared.

The basement had once been a meeting hall where Catholics shared casseroles and ate ham for Sunday brunch after weddings and baptisms. Children had squirmed there during catechism classes and teens had gone on sleepover retreats. Now, the space was transformed.

"It was all linoleum when I moved in. Horrible stuff. I had it tiled and thought about putting in a mosaic, but that would have taken forever and cost a fortune. The pews are from the church upstairs. I had to buy them separately. Can you believe that? But I kept the light fixtures. Those were upstairs, too, but it was easy to move them. Dirty, though. I don't think those Christians ever cleaned them."

Earth moved forward, slowly, toward the front of the room,

his eyes fixed on a display behind the altar.

"They wouldn't sell me the original altar, so I had this one made from New England granite. It's actually supposed to be a sort of tomb cover."

"Is that spear...?"

"Well it's not *the* spear, of course," Sylvia said with a laugh. "But it's a real antique. The blade is, anyway, the shaft we had to re-create."

"And the armor?"

"Authentic as well. From one of Caesar's campaigns in Gaul. Not cheap at all, I assure you."

Now Baines was standing at the front, his foot nearly touching the altar.

"And the bones?" he asked.

She smiled.

The armor of a Roman centurion stood upright, strapped and tied on a clear Lucite mannequin. Inside the Lucite, encased but visible, were aged brown bones. When Earth stood between it and the light, only the bones showed.

"When I bought him, there was no way a mortal researcher could know," she said. "The age was right and he was found on the battlefield, but he could easily have been a barbarian. But I touched him and I know. He was a true Centurion. He died bravely—see the chip on the front of the skull?"

Earth kept looking, finally saying, "Cool, yo."

Sylvia's mouth tightened briefly in annoyance, but Velvet said, "Here's the stake."

Sylvia held out her hand and laid the wooden weapon on the altar. It was ugly—an inch-thick dowel rod, crudely whittled sharp. A palm-sized metal disc from a barbell set had been threaded on the back to give it some heft. The weight was held in place by screws set through drilled holes. The whole thing was perhaps eight inches long.

Sylvia knelt, folded her hands on top of it, and lowered her head.

For a moment, they were all silent. Earth took an uneasy step and Velvet instinctively put a hand on his arm to keep him still.

Finally, Sylvia opened her eyes and shook her head,

apologetic. "I'm very sorry," she said. "If you don't mind I can pray and try again. Perhaps tomorrow will be more auspicious."

"Sure," Velvet said. "I have no use for the fucking thing."

"Um," Earth said. "I guess that's okay. After that though, I should, you know, dust it for prints an' everything." He turned to Velvet. "You want a ride back to your car?"

"Have a nice night, dears," Sylvia said as she showed them to the door. "Mr. Baines, we have services here every Thursday at 9:30. I'd really love it if you could come."

"Uh, I'll see," he said. "Honest."

"Happy hunting."

As they walked toward Baines' Escalade, its car alarm chirping to acknowledge him, Velvet said, "So, what's next?"

"I'll ask around. You know, talk to my peoples. Don't worry about it. I'm in the wind, y'know what I mean?"

After dropping Velvet off, Baines was already on the phone to his favorite escort service. "Yo, how 'bout Julia and Vernisha? Those bitches open fo' bidness tonight? Solid. Send 'em on down. Usual place. Half an hour. Straight up."

He really wanted to kill them, particularly Vernisha who was fat and black and, he felt, authentic (though he would never think to use the word). But people remembered seven-foot-tall men, and getting tangled in a homicide investigation would definitely cramp his style.

Chump vampires who look like accountants get to kill like mad fuckin' dogs, he thought. *I gotta settle with just drinking and banging them.*

Vernisha and Julia were always thrilled when Earth called. They discussed his lovemaking technique in detail but could never figure out why he could affect them so—and they'd had the chance to compare and contrast a lot of men. It wasn't that he was gentle, lord knew, or a generous lover—ha!—or even that his johnson was unusual. They couldn't figure it out.

A vampire's kiss can seal the marks of the teeth, and his bite brings pleasure, not pain. The two hookers had no idea.

Chapter Four

Jerome Trafford figured they were Satanists, and in the rare moments when he was too exhausted to be terrified, he felt very sorry for himself indeed.

Jerome had spent a large part of the last few years feeling sorry for himself. He'd had bad luck in his marriage and in his business. Hell, he'd even developed colitis. His wife was divorcing him and suing him over money and that, in turn, was quite probably going to reveal the fact that the retirement fund he managed for a local construction firm had been thoroughly looted and was now little more than an outline on paper with nothing left inside. That, in turn, would probably get him jail time, at best, assuming the mob pals of the unionized construction workers didn't kill him before he even came to trial.

Despite those unenviable factors, Jerome Trafford ardently wished he hadn't called Vic's Friend.

If he hadn't called Vic's Friend (Jerome didn't know the guy's name, no names were used), he'd be at home right now, probably sitting on the toilet gasping through another colon spasm while his wife shrieked outside the door about where all the money went and he was never any good in the sack anyhow, with the phone ringing off the hook from some investigator. At the time, that stuff had seemed insurmountable and he'd called Vic's Friend. But now, naked except for an ankle chain sunk into a dank and rough-carved limestone wall, he'd go back with no regrets.

Vic's Friend helped people disappear. For $10,000 he could help you vanish and never be heard from again. At the time it sounded irresistible and, shit, Vic's Friend had been incredibly charming, persuasive, frank, sympathetic. He'd been about the first person Jerome had talked to in *months* who wasn't pissed. He'd even agreed to give Jerome blue-book value for his two-year-old BMW. But he'd gone to the "safe house" and showered and eaten some pretty good carryout tapas, and then the next fucking thing he knew he'd woken up stripped and manacled.

Jerome had been expecting a private-sector version of the Witness Relocation Program. He'd believed it, he'd taken the hook, line, sinker. He'd practically jumped in the boat. Now Jerome was thinking it was more like Amway meets *Rosemary's Baby*.

He blinked. There was a flickering orange light, a line of it. He moved closer and stretched out but couldn't quite touch it.

The door opened. Two figures in long black robes entered. One held a torch aloft and the other carried a length of rope.

"We can do this the easy way or the hard way," the one with the rope said.

"Oh Jesus, man, don't kill me, I've got money. I swear if you let me go I won't tell the cops!"

The rope-bearer made an irritated noise and said, "*Stand still while I tie you up.*" And just like that, Jerome found himself stunned, motionless, as the rope wound around him—quite tight, enough so that his middle-aged plumpness bulged slightly above and below it.

He's done this before, Jerome thought inanely, observing the speed with which his captor immobilized his wrists behind his back and, by means of some deft looping, got a coil inside his mouth as a gag.

Jerome never even considered moving until he was firmly bound. As the robed man (woman? Hard to even tell in this light) unlocked his ankle, Jerome discovered that moving his hands down or to the side pulled slack out of the loop in his mouth. Struggling to free his hands just jerked his head back and started rope-burns on the corners of his mouth. It tasted bad, too. But his legs were completely free.

Before Jerome himself even realized it, he'd taken off running. He had no idea where he was going, but he was pretty sure they'd come from the left, so he got into the hall and bolted right. He took two steps, glimpsed something that looked like a bank vault, and then the torchbearer tripped him. Hands bound, unable to catch himself, he slammed into the wall, rough limestone scratched his skin, and then he crashed toward the floor... only to be caught before his naked knees could slam into it.

"Good rabbit," his robed captor said. "You've got the instincts, but not the physique. Of course, if you'd looked fast, we'd have hobbled your knees. C'mon now. Walk."

When Jerome balked, the robed man (he was sure it was a man now; he'd seen male hands holding him, black skin with a wedding band, but the hands were so cold) grabbed him by the ear and pulled him like a reluctant child.

They emerged into a long, low, rough chamber of echoing stone. It was lit by torches and braziers. Jerome could see an altar, some low rough monolith, and even though the light was dim, he still squinted after a day in darkness. He could see a figure between him and the stone, man-shaped and muscular. His eyes adapting, Jerome saw an inhumanly luminous face and hands tipped by glinting razor claws.

He let out a little shriek into his gag before realizing that the face was a mask, the hands armored gauntlets. It didn't help much when the robed pair marched him forward and hoisted him up on the cold stone like an impatient parent hauling a toddler into a car seat.

"*Lie still,*" the masked figure told him, and Jerome went limp. If the words of the black-handed man had stunned him, these felt like they'd just about killed him. Under the force of the words, he not only obeyed, he forgot how to disobey, how to imagine disobedience, how to do anything other than "lie there" and "be perfectly still."

The mask leaned closer, and if the first command had struck like a hammer, this next whispered into his mind like a drill. "*Think about your life.*" The next words were in the same low tone, the same voice, but were somehow lacking that fierce, unearthly power. "Think well, for it is about to end."

Against his gag, Jerome began to cry. He turned from the

mask, from those eyes that cut through him. He looked out and realized that this temple was full of monsters. They stood on two feet and gazed on him with two eyes. They had human shape, but he intuitively knew they were something else. As commanded, he thought about his life—something he'd never really done before.

I'm a greedy, selfish screw-up, Jerome thought. *That's my life.*

Under the force of the order, he was appalled to realize... that was it. He'd always pooh-poohed navel-gazing introspection, just like all his friends at the country club and his business-college pals, but still. He'd assumed that if he ever *did* choose to contemplate his life, it would be a complex, deep and lengthy process. Not one sentence that could easily fit on a needlepoint sampler.

I'm a greedy, selfish screw-up.

It was painful. He tried to dig a little deeper, just to get past the starkness of it.

I failed at greed because I'm a screw-up. I'm a screw-up because I'm selfish. I'm selfish because I'm greedy, and I'm greedy because I always knew I was two steps behind everyone else. So being a screw-up made me selfish.

That was it. He was out of introspection. The masked priest chose that moment to speak.

"Behold, you faithful, the frailty of man. Here he is, and to all appearances he is fruitful and prosperous." The cold back of a talon poked Jerome in the flab for emphasis. "Yet in an instant he is brought low, subdued, and lies, his nakedness unconcealed, before a crowd of the Kindred, any one of whom might dispatch him to his fate, even as he himself might dispatch a hot meal."

The metal mask leaned closer. Jerome could discern the fancy embroidery on the speaker's robe, the heavy gold adornments on the red stole.

"Yet we are wrong to disdain this man, this food, weak though he lies before us. Who among us has not been laid as low, or lower? But for the bleak grace of the blood within us, we would be as this one. Or worse."

He straightened again and looked out over his listeners.

"Yes, you in the forefront, you armed with strength and pride and the power to bend and break them. Were it not for the blood, were it not for God's preserving curse, you would be dust, as would I, and even the mightiest among us. You in the back, flame-startled and modern—oh, do not duck your head! There's no shame in it. We the elders were once as you are, new to the blood and trembling in our grasp of its power. Upon you, our damnation lies yet awkwardly. Without it, you would *live*. You would go upon your way, the youngest of you, ignorant of the wrath with which God scourges the just and unjust alike.

"It is to you, the young, the future of this covenant, that I address myself tonight. We, the old, are set in our ways. We elders are stagnant, plagued by inertia, prone to remain in the same circumscribed behaviors. We find it hard to change even if we want to, and we rarely have the desire.

"You, however, have a freedom we lack. Like unfired clay, you have not taken your final shape. You have been transformed by your Embrace, you need blood to live and you have the power and authority to take it, but each Kindred predator is as different as the hunters of the natural world, as different as a spider from a shark. The choices you make now, the attitudes you shape at the beginning, are what will harden into your eventual beliefs and behaviors for the remainder of your existence. You take your first steps and can choose your path, turn back easily, retrace a mile walked along a sinful road. We, the old, have walked our chosen course for a thousand miles and a hundred years. For good or ill, we cannot readily change.

"Thus, tonight I speak to you on the sin of mercy."

Hearing that, Jerome's sphincter clenched.

"Damned by God as a plague on this sinful world, mercy should be anathema to us. Every drop of the blood of damnation cries out against it, demands that we feed unto death and gorge onward to the next victim. Yet time and again, we stumble. We let slip the pretty woman who reminds us of a lost love. We surrender to the begging of a child. Worse still, some of us have shown remorse to those we slay and have brought them back as parodies of ourselves, as warped killers like us."

Oh Lord, no, Jerome thought. *Okay, yeah, I'm a worthless fuck-up, but don't make me that.* Jerome had never been particularly religious, and he'd never given much thought to what he'd consider a fate worse than death, but looking out at the monsters before him... hearing the regret and revulsion and *rage* in the speaker's voice... he hoped against hope that they were just going to kill him.

Please.

"In this, we dilute our purpose, spread our curse, widen the wounds of the world. And that is *not* our duty! We are the adversaries of men, but not of mankind. We are here to draw up the individual, good or bad, young or old, rich or poor, draw him up and force him into decision. We give him the freedom we lack, the last razor choice of faith or apostasy. To give him a hard challenge is a crucial form... of respect. Mercy, that insidious vice, leads us to cheat on his behalf, soften the blow, point him to the so-called 'right choice.' But we do not see as God sees! We must never shirk the responsibility of holding out the highest redemption of resistance, nor the lowest depths of degradation.

"Too many young Kindred I see treat mankind as if they are there solely for the gratification of our bloodlust. It's not only the unbelievers who take this odious stance. No, the sin lies within us as well. Are we superior to humanity? Undoubtedly so. But all our faculties and dark miracles are bent toward their ultimate judgment! Not for ourselves are we given speed, strength, majesty and command. These are not reward, for what reward is due to the iniquitous damned? No, the powers of the blood are tools with which we can tempt, threaten and ultimately destroy humans... so that they can resist and defy and ultimately show faith in the Lord!

"Oh, it is an easy lesson, mercilessness, to elders. To those who have slaked their thirst nightly for a hundred years, pity is almost an alien concept. The temptation to withhold judgment is sweet only to those who recall warmth and breath, to those who can think of their own necks bared and helpless. But just as mercy is a sin, so too is callousness. We must be strict, cruel even, in our zeal for stringent tests, but it is essential to be *fair*. We serve *them*. We serve them as tempters and terrors, but that is a high service, and a hard one. As the Testament of Christ teaches, the last shall be first and the first, last. We are set above men that we may separate the wheat from the chaff, divide the fit from the foul, but we must respect our duty to them far more than their utility to us.

"Feeding must never be meaningless. The world is chaotic, and random death can come to anyone living. We must take care to ensure that *we* are not random death.

"What is right action for one damned to darkness, soul-shorn, blighted and cursed to drink blood? What is right action from one dead to the Lord? Only this: That by the rightness of our role—by our service to the soul—we may be raised up and shriven on the last day.

"So again, I say to you the young: Do not waste your youth. You, from whom the warmth of life had not yet fled, pay heed. Do not listen to those last gasps of mortality that lead you to mercy, but neither must you fall heedlessly into the clutches of your curse. Now, while your blood is weak, feeding is a struggle, but in time it will seem effortless. Lack of effort must never become lack of meaning!

"Thus we return to this man, our prey," the speaker said, then stepped and bent so that his head was near Jerome's. "So easily molded and moved, he is like a doll in our hands. So easy to make him *weep*." At those words, and the talon caress that accompanied them, Jerome's tears and rope-gagged sobs redoubled as if on cue.

"In fact I believe if I press *here*..." Jerome gasped at the hard pressure of a metal knuckle in his abdomen. "I can make him soil himself like a baby."

Jerome bit his cheeks and blushed and fought hard, but it hurt *so much* and the shame was a new layer of awfulness that in the end his colitis-wracked body betrayed him again and he heard their laughter and jeers.

"And yet!" The priest held up his clawed hands, straightened and gestured and they were all silent. "And yet at his lowest... this specimen is still a man, still formed in the image of the almighty and still deserving of our respect."

You just made me shit myself! Jerome thought.

"The soul of man, even at the utmost, can still choose."

Jerome flinched back as the claws closed in on his face, but he felt no pain, only that icy chill as it slipped behind the rope, turned and, with a muffled pop, parted his bonds. He spat the cable out.

"Let me go," he said, his voice scratchy and guttural.

The masked figure laughed. "No, that's not an option. But I will do this." The claws picked and prickled but did not break Jerome's skin as the robed man parted the ropes around him.

"Stand, if you wish." The priest turned and nodded and someone else—the same man who'd tied him? No, this one had white hands, slender and feminine. She carried a pillow and on it...

...was a *sword*.

Jerome sat up on the altar, aware of the burning eyes in the dead faces, surrounded by the reek of his own feces. He hugged himself and hid his penis from their gaze and tried to chafe some vigor into his arms numbed by constriction. And the robed woman held the sword out to him.

"Take it," the masked priest said. "If that is what you wish."

Jerome just looked at it. In fact, he found it hard to look away. The sword was plain and unadorned, straight-bladed, shiny bright and scrupulously clean. The handle looked like it was made from some high-quality plastic, like the hilt of a kitchen knife or the grip of a handgun. It was, he slowly realized, what you'd get if you applied modern technology and materials to making an antique weapon, with a total focus on practical use.

"You have been ill used by us, and you have clearly realized that we are nothing natural," the priest said. "I freely tell you that we intend to drain your body for our sustenance and then dispose of it in a fashion you'd no doubt find humiliating. Your death is as certain as anything can be in this... unruly world." Chortles rippled through the crowd.

"Nevertheless... the sword. Yours to seize or deny, as you wish. You can fall on it like a Roman soldier, making an easier death than you'll get at our hands. You can make a last stand, if you wish, accepting your fate with the serenity of a martyr. Or you can refuse it and beg for mercy."

The priest reached up with one clawed hand and removed his mask. The face beneath was criss-crossed with scars, blotchy pallid like a corpse, and the prominent fangs put a slight mushy tone into the pronunciation of *f* and *p* and *s* sounds.

"You are a man," Bishop Solomon Birch said. "You have a soul. Choose wisely. It is your final decision."

———

While Solomon was conducting his ceremony, Earth Baines was in the basement of a tenement on the deep South Side, visiting a vampire named Russell Aaronson.

"Come on, Baines, you could bring me someone alive. Shit, a girl, a guy, I don't care. Bring me some smelly old bum, a runaway, someone who won't be missed. Fuck, I'm tired of this crap." Petulant, Russell shoved a Lunchmate cooler away with his foot.

"Quit your yapping," Baines said and kicked the cooler back. "You think I'm room service here? You're a wanted criminal and I'm protecting your ass. If Prince Max found out, you'd be in one of those bone-breaking machines like they used on that Kleinhauser guy, and I'd be right next to you, know what I mean? I got my white booty flappin' out in the wind for you so you'd best shut up and like it."

Aaronson sighed and curled his lip as he opened the cooler. Inside was a donation bag from a blood bank.

"At least it's human this time." He gnawed a hole in the top corner and upended it into his mouth.

Baines tapped his fingers impatiently while Aaronson guzzled. "Now, your end of the deal," Earth said as soon as the other vampire was finished.

Aaronson sighed, but he really didn't mind that much. Hiding out was a pain. It was boring. At least teaching Baines broke up the hours. *Even if the dumbass can't learn to hide worth shit*, he thought.

"All right, watch." Aaronson held up a book, one of the P.G. Wodehouse paperbacks that he'd begged Baines to get him. "Now you see it? Now you don't."

And the book vanished from his hand. Only it didn't, really. Aaronson still knew it was there, it had just become... something no one needed to see.

"There is no book," Aaronson said. "You have to halfway believe that, even though you know the book is there and it's in your hand. But you have to make it gone, like, gone in a layer of your mind. Then you push that layer out and wrap it around the other guy's brain. Try it."

"There is no book," Baines said. But the book was very clearly present.

"No, *believe* it. Believe there is no book."

"How can I believe there ain't no book when I'm holding the book in my fuckin' hand?"

Aaronson sighed. Maybe it wasn't worth it, having his hours broken up. *But it's sure as hell worth not getting caught,* he thought, so he tried again.

"Back when you were alive, did you ever think something was true but, like, you didn't *want* it to be true? So you lied to yourself, even though down inside you knew?"

"Huh?"

"Look." Aaronson twisted in his seat and turned away. "In high school, right? When I was breathing? There was this girl and, you know, I was a dumb shit. I fell for her and everything and I knew she didn't dig me. All right? I knew there was no way. But! I stayed away from her and didn't talk to her and didn't meet her eye because as long as I didn't *ask* her, there was no way she could tell me, right? I knew she didn't but, I made myself think that she might. That she still could. I told myself there was no rejection."

"Man, you were a chump."

"Okay, fuck it, you'll never learn, okay? And you'll never learn to think that you might not be a vampire, that you *can't* be vampire, and you'll never learn how you might not even be there, might not even *be*, and that's how you make yourself vanish from plain sight. But you'll never get it because *I'm* a loser, *I'm* the fucking chump! Fine."

For a moment, they were quiet, and when Russell looked up,

Earth's face was inscrutable.

"Sorry, Baines. It's just..."

"So it's shame? Is that it?"

Russell wobbled his head, side to side, uncertain. "Um, well, it doesn't *have* to be shame. But... I guess when I do it, it mainly is."

Baines looked down at the book, which he'd paged through while waiting in line at the store. Edwardian fops and grown men with little-boy names and butlers and tea. He'd felt like an idiot buying it. He'd thought about how he'd like to smack Russell for whining so much about it.

"Look away from it," Aaronson said quietly. Earth glanced up and saw the other vampire smiling.

"What?"

"It's fading."

"Straight up?" Earth looked down, squinted, cocked his head. "There is no book," he muttered.

"Ah, now you lost it again."

"Damn!"

———

Leaving Aaronson's, Earth got a phone call.

"Yo yo, Earth," he answered, pulling into traffic.

"Mr. Baines? I thought of something." It was Sylvia.

"Uh huh?"

"Velvet told me that she'd called a police officer friend of hers about that situation the other night. You remember?"

"Wait, she got a breather cop involved?"

"Not in any way that was indiscreet," Sylvia said.

"Shit, callin' a fuckin' warm *cop* about a motherfuckin' *witch-hunter*? That's about as in-fuckin'-discreet as it gets!" He gunned the engine and merged onto the highway. Tonight he was driving an old beater Chevy so patched with rust, Bondo and half-assed paintjobs that it was impossible to ascribe one color to it.

"Mr. Baines, I'm not accustomed to being addressed—"

"Listen, if a *cop knows* and he ain't under her thumb.... Wait, hold up, is he a red cop?"

There was quiet, except for the labor of the Ford's engine.

"I'm not sure. He may be."

"'May be?'"

"Even if he's not, I'm sure Violet has him well in hand—bribed, blackmailed. In any event, *he does not know*. I assure you, his stance toward the witch-hunter was purely adversarial. Velvet called him to chase her off… accuse her of prostitution, I believe. Just who is a policeman going to trust? A legitimate musician he's known for years? Or a drunken harlot declaiming about vampires?"

"That ain't a situation to take no chances with."

"Control your panic, Mr. Baines. I assure you that there's no leak on our end."

"Not yet, maybe."

"If you'd like to keep things quiet, maybe get the make, model and license plate of the hunter's car. The police officer has that information. *That* was what I called to suggest."

"Word?"

She sighed. "Will you be able to get the woman's address and name from that information, or must I do *that* for you, too?"

"Don't get all uppity on me. I respect you for your Lancea position and for being an elder and all that jazz, but, shit, I ain't your parishioner and I ain't your childe." He honked the horn as a Lexus cut him off.

"Are you suggesting that Velvet is?"

"Huh?" Earth was momentarily nonplussed by the sharply angry tone that had entered Sylvia's voice. He thought she'd been pissed before, but that had been a schoolmarmish annoyance. Now she sounded ready to flay him alive. From what he'd seen and heard of Lancea rituals, it wouldn't necessarily be her first time doing it.

"Do you think I created Velvet? Do you think that *I*, a priestess of Longinus, the Dark Messiah, violated his creed against the creation of new Kindred?"

"Whoa, no! No, I, hell, I didn't mean *that*. I mean, serious, I know y'all don't do that, even before the Prince's Tranquility and shit. No, you misunderstood me there. I just… just meant…"

He braked for a red light as he left the highway.

"Just meant what, Sheriff Baines?"

"Um, just that you should, you know, respect my position. As an officer of the court and, uh, part of the Invictus and… and all."

"I'd find it easier to respect the office if I respected the man, Mr. Baines."

Then he heard a click.

For a moment he just stared at his phone until the car behind him honked. Reflexively turning back a middle finger, he muttered to himself, "Bitch hung up on me!"

"C'mon Stingo. It's fo' the mission. It's fo' *your* mission!"

"Mayfield, it's *your* mission. Isn't it? It's the mission *you* requested. What am I supposed to think about someone who comes back to me every time he needs aid with his investigation?"

"Look man, I don't think it's out of line for me to ask you to track back a simple motherfucking license plate. I had to promise that Raines bitch I'd go to *church* to get it out of her. You got all kinds of hooks in the DMV don'tcha? It ain't nothing to you."

Chris shook his head sadly. "If I give you a runaway, you eat for a night, but if I teach you to troll bus stations you can eat forever," he said.

"Don't give me that ABC preschool crap! You think I don't know you playin' me? That's all right. I don't mind the game, but don't let's pretend I ain't doing work that should be *yours*. I don't know what play you're runnin' on the Lancea, but they think I'm a Sheriff and if they find out I'm just muscle, you think they'll be happy? I'm your tool, cool, whatever, but if you don't take care of a tool you gotta share it, know what I mean?"

"What *do* you mean, Earth?" Stingo said, with a cold glint in his eye.

"I mean Norris could do this for me, too, and he wouldn't give me all this high-box bullshit about teaching me to stand on my own two feet. He'd just do it and I'd *owe* him. You want me to owe Norris?"

Chris glared. Then he smiled. "You really *should* get your own contact for these matters. Let me introduce you to somebody who works for a bail bondsman. Remember Anita from Cicero? This was her ghoul. Now that Anita's gone missing, he's pretty hard up."

The name on the registration was Gladys Plover, which hadn't rung any bells when he called the Jade Room bartender, but Earth supposed that if his name was Gladys he'd change it, too.

He'd been surprised that Chris' ghoul associate had been able to do a search in the middle of the night, but she said the computers were always running, that she could patch in from home. So Earth drove his Ford, which had developed a worrying clatter from the back. He wondered if it was the transmission or just the stuff in the trunk. He'd helped himself to more of Watts' merchandise than he'd mentioned to Stingo, and the Ford now contained a tiny arsenal. Putting it out of his mind as a problem for later, Earth parked near the house, dialing the phone number to the house that he'd been given.

No answer. No lights. No one home.

He watched the place for a good hour, slouched down in the car, a black Kangol cap pulled low over his forehead. He'd dressed all in black: black Adidas sneakers and a black Bulls tracksuit with red piping. He carried a black gym bag, and had even left his jewelry at home in an effort to stealth himself up.

Plover was apparently the sole tenant of a three-story brownstone, which meant she was doing okay in the cash department. It was an all-right neighborhood. Lots of white folks in jeans and khaki shorts walking around with strollers and mocha lattes, enjoying the early night air. No thick pedestrian traffic, but there were people.

When he was certain no one was home, Earth got out of the car and went directly into a nearby alley. He emerged a few minutes later and started his car again. He idled around the block and into the alley behind Plover's brownstone, lighting a smoke and checking his watch until he started to hear shouts. The fire he'd lit in the alley dumpster had been noticed.

Another look left and right, and he was out of the car, easily jumping the fence. He looked at the back of Plover's house, slung the gym bag over his shoulder, and tried to make himself mad.

Nosy bitch comin' in to fuck with vampires, shit, can't mind her own business.

Having grown up pork-fed on a working farm, and having played football and lifted weights, Mayfield Baines was strong on his own. But he'd learned quickly that as an undead creature he could be stronger still. If he got pissed off.

Like all those teachers in high school frowning at the cheerleaders and it was their titties, right? If a girl wants to show off her titties, that's her right, isn't it?

He felt his muscles begin to twitch and burn. *Somebody needs to be taught a lesson.*

He'd put a box of firecrackers in the dumpster, too, and when he heard them go off he ran to the back of the house, jumped, and started scaling the bricks. It would have been easy to simply bust the door or crack a window, but Earth didn't know if she'd be coming out the front or the back. He also figured that a mortal who hunted vampires would be pretty twitchy about home security, so he didn't want to mess with any silent alarm nonsense. He was going for roof access.

His muscles were purring with unnatural power, strong enough that he could hang from a one-handed grip on a half-inch margin of brick. Even without good grips, he reached the roof quickly. At the top, he belly-crawled to the edge and looked out over the street. Everyone was looking at the fire, muttering about crazy teenagers. All good.

From the bag, Earth produced a drill and a crowbar. The roof was flat and there were no higher buildings for a block or two, so he had a good chance of going unobserved—as long as no one from a skyscraper was being nosy. But the cure for that would be to get in as soon as possible, right?

At the darkest corner of the roof, he drilled through the

tarry plastic covering until he hit wood. He drilled through that and started tearing with the crowbar, muttering swear words and keeping his angry on about how much work this bitch was making him do.

When he'd made a sufficient hole, he squirmed in, burrowed through pink fiberglass insulation, and then punched his way through the plaster ceiling.

He emerged in a bathroom and was glad he couldn't see his reflection.

Plaster, that pink shit, tar—I must look a fool, he thought. He dusted himself off and set himself to looking around.

Baines had determined that there was nothing of interest under her mattress or in her underwear drawer when he heard the front door open. He crept, as silently as he was able, to the top of the stairs as he heard sounds of movement below.

Was she alone? He supposed it didn't matter.

A shadow, vaguely feminine, fell on the bottom of the stairs and then stopped.

What's she waiting for? Baines wondered. *C'mon. Come upstairs.*

But she didn't seem to be coming. Had she spotted something? Heard something? Been warned by feminine intuition? Baines didn't know.

Fuck it, he thought. *It's on.* He started pounding down the steps and heard her feet clatter against hardwood in reply.

She was going for the front door and had a head start, but Baines hit the juice, beat her to the door and slammed his hand onto the top of it just as she was yanking the knob inward with her left hand. He loomed over her. Her head came up to his collarbone, and then she shot him.

She shot him point blank in the groin.

"Gawwd*damn!*" Baines hollered. The gunshot wasn't even that loud. She'd pressed the muzzle against his nylon-clad crotch and his flesh had muffled the report. The pain was dizzying, but Baines didn't let go of the door. He had cultivated an ability to pursue a physical goal even through hardship, and he didn't retreat. Instead, he let his anger out with a down-swept blow to her forearm. It made her gasp and the gun skittered across the floor.

"You'll pay for *dat*," he growled, but she was running for the back door now and Baines had to catch her, even with his legs badly hurt.

When he'd first seen other Kindred move at a blinding pace, he'd expected it to be like a slow-motion movie from the other side, but it wasn't at all. He didn't perceive anything clearer or better. It was just like he was racing down the hall at her on a motorcycle instead of having to run. Not enough to see a bullet in flight, but enough to catch her. He finished with a full-weight tackle at the backs of her thighs that earned him another gasp. He felt the crackle of bones shifting beneath him as her body whip-cracked face down into the hardwood floor.

She still had her arms free and she pulled a wooden stake out of her purse, but he crawled forward and disarmed her before she could bring it to bear. This time, when he hit her, her forearm broke.

"Okay, *Gladys*," he said. "You gon' get it slow."

"No," she gasped. "No, ahh..." She was trying to scream but couldn't seem to catch her breath.

Earth was still pissed, but he was on top of it just enough to haul her into the bathroom and dump her in the tub first.

"Listen up," he said. "You gonna answer some questions now, got it?"

"Oh please," she whispered. "Please don't..."

"*Who did you tell?*"

"Nobody, I swear it!"

He punched her in the face.

"Who did you tell about *vampires*, bitch? *Who knows?*"

"Nobody, I didn't tell anyone, nobody, nobody!"

"Awright. The trail ends here then." He stomped an ankle, eliciting another mewl of agony, the sound of a scream without breath.

He wasn't gone long. Her kitchen knives were in a block, right out on the counter.

"You sure you didn't tell *anyone?*"

She shook her head.

"'Cause if you did, I'd have to get their name outta ya." His fangs were out, barely visible in the darkened bathroom.

Eyes wide, she kept shaking her head, hair flying back and forth, snot and tears and blood flying.

"Please," she said through split and fattened lips. "I'll be good."

He barked with laughter. "That you will," he said. He sank his teeth into her thigh, the big vein high on the inside, and as she went limp he wondered if the pleasure of the bite overweighed the pain of her wounds, or if they all got combined somehow. But then he was lost in his own bliss, the joy of feeding. He got the knife up to her neck, but he didn't want to raise his head from his meal. Feeding was what he was meant for, so he slashed and stabbed blindly at her throat while she feebly tried to stop him. He'd positioned her head by the drain. It was all good. It looked like a reasonable bleed out and now he could enjoy it, he could finally relax, feed without fighting himself, feed fully to the death without fear or consequence, at last, *at last.*

When he was done, he licked the wound on her thigh and, magically, it closed. Nothing for the cops to see there. More blood was still trickling from her shredded neck but he felt fine, he was sated.

He looked down at himself and saw that blood had gotten mixed in with the tar and plaster and all the other stuff. Hell, there was a piece of toilet paper on his shoe from somewhere.

Now he had to get from the house to the car unobserved.

"There is no me," he thought, but he knew he'd have to do better than that.

Velvet sat in the park and played the violin. It was a very good violin, several levels above the typical instrument. She was a very good player, several increments better than the typical street musician.

She was dressed in a loose skirt and thick boots without heels and a blue tank top. She had her hair pulled back with a batik scarf. She had eyeliner on and was deliberately walking the costume line between "homeless" and "confident bohemian."

She played, people walked by, and a few tossed cash in her

case, but no one had stopped. Yet.

Velvet didn't care. At least, she told herself she didn't care.

She held the violin bow with her thumb in its notch, at a right angle to the wood, a very gentle grip, thumb and fingertip. She bowed down and her fingers straightened as a smooth note sailed out, then back up with a finger curl, concentrating on technique, and then she didn't need to think about technique, she was just in it, playing, thinking of nothing, suspended in time and music. As she played she could even ignore the hunger, ignore the luscious scent of lively blood that seemed to drift from every passing human, ignore the traffic noise that grated against her sounds and ruined them because she wasn't listening, she was feeling them flow from the instrument through her shoulder and then right down into her dead and still heart.

"Whoa."

…and then it was over.

Velvet didn't stop playing, and the man who'd said 'Whoa' didn't hear a difference. (Man? Boy, really. A teenager in baggy skate-punk pants and a stocking cap even in summer.) Perhaps even a music aficionado wouldn't have heard any difference, but it felt different. Now she was just going through the motions again, playing expertly, but cynically. She looked up at her admirer without changing expression and played through the rest of the piece. He stayed to listen and before even asking his name she knew she'd have a piece of him before sunrise.

The people at the shelter knew her as Sylvia Aigler and they thanked her regularly. Sylvia was a volunteer, and the shelter had a lot of volunteers. Sylvia was calm and pleasant, and many other volunteers were calm and pleasant (though not all). Sylvia had been coming for years. She knew the shelter and its rhythms and its routines inside and out. (Very few volunteers stuck around for years.) Best of all, Sylvia was reliable. The shelter director could count on one hand the volunteers who were pleasant, experienced *and* reliable, and of those Sylvia was the only one who'd also work the late-night shift.

She'd shown up halfway through dinner and had uncomplainingly washed dishes. She'd excused herself to 'powder her nose' and had returned 10 minutes later to help assemble sandwich lunches for the working poor. She'd listened to the sounds of the game coming from the TV in the common area. She'd heard groans as the White Sox blew it *again*. Throughout, she spread butter on sandwiches she couldn't eat, doled out cheese that would make her vomit, and smiled and made small talk with the churchgoers (Unitarians, tonight) who'd come in to volunteer, just like her. They had what she really wanted. They were full and throbbing with *her* food. But they weren't for her. That wasn't her purpose.

As she idly chatted, Sylvia thought about what she'd heard, about Solomon Birch's sermon. She couldn't find much fault in it, though she felt it was interesting how he'd stressed the immutability of elders.

We know that isn't true, don't we Bishop Birch? She thought. *You are a very different creature than you were a year ago. Changed, now that you've suckled at the Prince's vein.*

She thought of the frenzy at the end, when the man went down beneath a heaving pile of Kindred. She remembered the feeling of hands clawing and trying to pull her back, the feel of her own hands clutching and pulling hair, and she smiled.

When the Unitarians were finished, Sylvia went and sat at the admissions desk. As she sat she said rosaries, the beads whirling through her fingers with practiced ease, her lips soundlessly moving, praying for the souls of all those around her.

The admissions desk was boring after 11 at night. Dead. Only a fraction of the needy came in that late. It was what the director called a 'warm-body job,' though technically Sylvia didn't even qualify as that.

Around midnight, she saw Sam Warchosski come down the steps. He seemed to be walking unevenly.

"Samuel?" she asked. "Is everything all right?"

He looked over at her with a haunted expression and she knew.

"Uh, yeah. Everything's, you know, fine."

"Okay."

"I just couldn't sleep," he said. "So I thought I'd, you know, come down and, um, walk around. A little bit."

"I'm sorry you're having trouble resting." He'd found it. She knew. She blinked and peered *through* him, looking deep with the Sight. She saw green and violet swirling and chewing on each other in his soul, churning brown and miserable. He'd found it but hadn't yet used it.

"I'm just going to… um…" He gestured toward the men's bathroom.

"Is there something wrong with the restroom upstairs?"

"Oh it's always fucking dirty and smells like shit," he said. Then he paused. "I'm sorry Miz Aigler."

"It's all right. I know that insomnia can make people cranky."

He half smiled and shook his head lightly. "Cranky. Yeah."

He went into the bathroom. Sylvia gave him a couple minutes, then listened. No one. She stood and pushed the door open.

Sam's head whipped around and she could see the baggie in his hand, a residue of white powder still lining it.

He'd dumped it in the toilet.

"It's, it's not mine!" he said, eyes wide. "I just found it! I ain' lying! I just found it in, in my stuff!"

"Shh, yes, I know Samuel. I believe you."

"You… you do?"

She nodded and he relaxed.

"I'm clean, Miz Aigler. You know I been going to the meetings and I…" He blinked and she saw the tears. They thrilled her. "I don't do this shit no more." But looking down at the powder in the toilet bowl, she could tell how much he wanted it. She didn't need to see his aura or smell his sweat of desperation. His need was obvious in his posture.

She stepped closer and put her hand on his arm, and blinked back tears as she smiled up at him.

"Oh Samuel, I'm so proud of you. So proud. You passed the test."

"Huh?"

"It's a special man who can fight his addictions. It's a special man who can beat down his devil."

He looked away and started to show discomfort. His need for his drug had been so strong that the incongruity of the situation, the toilet, this woman, her words—it was sinking in only now. He took a half-step away from her, as far as he could get in the small bathroom, but she maintained a light grip on his forearm.

"But Samuel, will you win the fight next time?"

"N-Next time?"

"Surely you know you'll be tempted again. That you'll have another opportunity."

"Uh..."

"To be human is to be free, and you have used your freedom well. But next time, would you choose as wisely? Can you be *sure* you wouldn't weaken?"

He slumped, staring at the white dust still floating in the stainless-steel bowl. "No," he whispered.

She nodded. She gave his hand a tight squeeze and raised it to her mouth.

"It's better this way," she whispered. He didn't even feel her teeth break the skin. All he felt was relief, the delicious lassitude. It was like his first cherry run. It was what he'd gone back to the drug for over and over, that sense that nothing burdened him, the annihilation of the world.

He knew it was death, the sweet ease of it, but it couldn't be wrong. He'd stayed clean, he was clean, he'd resisted, and he sank to his knees without even realizing how weak he'd become. He was vaguely aware that Ms. Aigler was doing something to his arm, to the one she wasn't holding, but it didn't matter, because everything was all right, he'd done the right thing.

"For what I am about to receive, oh Lord, make me truly thankful," Sylvia whispered around the bloodied wound. Then, "It's better to die in a state of grace, Samuel." Crimson tears of joy leaked from the corners of her eyes. With one hand she held the wrist to her mouth while the other thumbed the blade out of a box cutter. Through his dying bliss, Sam Warchosski didn't even register it when she sliced his other wrist, three times lengthwise, over the toilet. Then it was an even bleed, half into the bowl and along its sides, half into her mouth, warming and preserving her.

When it was done, she wiped her mouth carefully and pocketed the handkerchief. She said another quick prayer, though she felt right that Samuel had died well, had died a brave man and not a coward, not a suicide, *not an addict*. Looking at him sprawled over the filthy and bloodstained toilet, she saw a man who had recovered his dignity.

She checked herself, pressed the knife into his hand, pulled the door open and emitted a well-practiced, earsplitting shriek.

———

"I appreciate you meeting me on a Sunday night," Solomon said, trimming the sails on his boat as it slid into the moonlit waters of Lake Michigan.

"It's no problem," the man said. The man had a name, Solomon could've remembered it with a slight effort, but it was an effort he chose not to make.

"It is the day of rest, after all," Solomon said, his voice low and rich. "The Sabbath. Technically, we should eschew labor."

"Is this really work?" the man said, gesturing at the magnificent skyline, the luminous Ferris Wheel slowly turning in the sky over Navy Pier.

"Well, you didn't hire me as a *friendship* consultant." Solomon chuckled and the man laughed back.

"Seriously, though." Solomon turned and met the man's eyes. "*You will give the contract to the Brigmans. You will remember a lengthy discussion with me, in which I narrowed the choices down to Brigman Transport, the Bartholomew brothers and Eola City Shipping. You will recall cogent arguments about the pros and cons of each corporation, and you will remember me slightly favoring the Bartholomew brothers because of their reasonably low bid. In the end, however, you hire the Brigmans because you are personally impressed by their integrity and by the consistent high-quality service their firm provides. I take your disagreement with good grace and assure you that it's also a fine choice, and then we discuss politics and sports for the rest of the trip. That is what you will remember. You will not remember me controlling your will. You will forget that your memories were altered. And you will sit, silently, until I drop you off at the dock."*

The man sat, silently, until Solomon dropped him off at the dock, and the next day he gave a $2.2 million building contract to Brigman Transport, Inc. Solomon sailed in the dark silence and contemplated his situation, pausing sometimes to pray silently.

Longinus, guide my actions. Help me retain your mask and your claws, that I may shudder the living and guide the dead in grace.

He thought about draining the man and making him forget the loss, but he felt honor-bound to have some sort of spiritual dimension to his feeding, and it seemed imprudent to terrorize or tempt a man who would be doing business with the Brigman family. The family was quite important to Solomon.

After dropping the man off, Birch took a cab to the Brigman home and entered through the back door with his own key.

Margery was sitting at the kitchen table, doing calculus homework. She looked up when the door opened, and sat up straight when she saw Solomon.

"Margery," he said.

She swallowed and took a deep breath. "Solomon," she said. He laughed.

"Suddenly so formal?" He reached out a hand and ruffled her hair, as he had when she was a newborn and a toddler.

She flinched back.

"Now, what was that?" he asked, his smile fading.

She didn't answer.

"Margery?" He took a step closer, and now his hip was inches from her face. She leaned away.

"What do you want?" she asked, her voice low and neutral.

"Why, Margery, can't I cheerfully greet the daughter of an old friend without being met with... suspicion? Mistrust? You wound me."

"If you want it, ask for it," she said. "But could we please stop pretending we're friends?"

"Stop pretending...? Margery, I *am* your friend. I have been your family's friend for..."

"This charade demeans us both," she said, interrupting him. "I heard you say that once. To one of *them*. To one of the *others*... like you."

His jaw tightened. "I'm shocked that someone of your fine breeding and temperament is a bigot, and against someone you've lived with since your infancy."

She raised her eyes to his, though she knew what he could do. It was a gesture of half bravado, half surrender. "If you're going to suck my blood," she said, "could you do it and let me get back to my homework? I really don't have time to make you feel *better* about it."

"I have ensured your family's fortune for generations. I have fought off the death of your beloved great-grandmother. I—"

"You suck our blood! *You suck our blood!* Giving us money we didn't ask for doesn't make that somehow okay!"

"Were it not for me, your parents would never have met!" Solomon raised his voice and acted angry, but it was a mask for his inner exhilaration. *She resists!* He thought. *The Brigman strength emerges, but has it finally grown into a moral dimension? Will she be the first to overcome my threats and blandishments?* Out loud, he bellowed, "If not for my 'interference,' you would not exist!"

"And that's supposed to what? Make me your pet? Make me something you can come and... and *defile* whenever you feel like it? It if it wasn't for you, my grandparents wouldn't both have AIDS!"

"Don't you dare lay that on me. It hurts me more than you that my enemies would strike me in such an... an underhanded and..."

"Your enemies! Strike *you*. You're the reason they're infected!"

"And I'm the reason they will not die. The power of my blood can keep even that great plague in check."

"Yeah, just like it keeps great-grandmother Elena alive and desperate and makes her your fucking *slave*."

"I will not be sworn at, Margery. That language is inappropriate."

"You're a blood-sucking killer and you're offended by my *language*? Oh my God, you're such…"

His hand whipped out, lazily, with only a fraction of his full speed and strength. He aimed for the back of her head, the occipital lobe, knuckles loose. It wouldn't leave a lump. Even if she bruised, her hair would conceal it. The blow didn't even hurt that much. It was just jarring, stunning.

It shut her up.

"Thou shalt not take the name of the Lord thy God in vain," he said quietly.

"God," she said. "You're an offense to God."

"Oh yes. That's my duty. I am the emblem of this fallen world's corruption. I am a monument to man's choice of evil over good." He leaned in. "I am God's whip, and a loving God must hate his implement of punishment… but a just God must still wield it."

"You're a monster."

"Indeed. All of us are. So why don't you do anything about it, hm?" His eyes twinkled. "Why not run to the papers? The police? Not your father, of course, but maybe a nice Catholic priest?"

"Maybe I will."

"And maybe you'll be locked up in an asylum for the rest of your life. Even if you betrayed me that deeply, Margery, I would protect your priceless life. If you did make some futile, impotent gesture those *enemies* of whom you so dismissively speak would leap at the chance to grind you into hamburger. But I would protect you from them, even in the eleventh hour."

"You don't defend me. You, you *defile* me! And then you justify the blood with the 'good' you've done. I've done nothing," she hissed. "Nothing to deserve this."

"Deserve what? A life of luxury? Excellent schooling and fine tutors? A genetic bounty sculpted *by me* over generations, to gift you with beauty and intellect, ability and strength? You are not quite the apex of humanity, Margery, but you are a step up from your father Ian, just as he was a step up from David, who was a step up from Elena. I have given you everything, even your very life, and I have never taken your blood against your will."

"Never against my will? You threatened to let Grandma Elena *die!*"

"And she yet lives because of your decision. Can you tell me you regret it?" Once again he closed the distance between them. "But that was just once. The first time. The time that showed you the delights of sin. Even now, there is part of your will that longs for it... even as your great-grandmother promised." His mouth, the lips split by scars in two places, was now inches from the rapid pulse fluttering in her neck. He could hear her breath becoming hoarse...

...but she pulled back.

"You can make me do it," she said. "You can even make me want it, but you can't make me believe in it." Clumsily, she stood, gathering her books, papers and pencils. She backed away from him, fleeing toward her bedroom but watching to see if he would stop her, perhaps partly hoping he would.

He didn't.

"You can't make it right," she whispered and slipped away from him.

"When shall we three meet again, in thunder, lightning or in rain?"

"Give it a rest, Annie."

"How about *both* of you shut up? Dagmar's never on time and the only thing worse than waiting is waiting and listening to the two of you bicker."

"Man, Tom, what crawled up your ass and died?"

"I think it was his sense of humor," Anne said.

The three of them were in Bachelor's Grove graveyard, a historic place with tall and variegated monuments. The highway was only a quarter-mile away, over a hill, but this late at night there was little to disturb the silence.

Anne, Tom and Phoebe had met at the grave of Professor Candace Murphy. She'd lived, died and taught Latin at a local college in the '50s and '60s, and very few people even suspected that she'd been one of Chicago's most influential and powerful occultists. While living, she'd compelled ghosts and spirits to do her bidding, had foreseen the future and had even been known to control the weather when circumstances were auspicious. When she'd died, she'd given very specific instructions about her funeral, which were largely worthless after Dagmar Brock broke into her apprentice's house, killed the apprentice, and devoured the contents of Candice Murphy's ritually prepared canopic jars.

Dagmar insisted that since that time, he'd received weird visions and gained insight into the practices of those who pursued sorcery while still alive. Only Phoebe was old enough to know Dagmar had puked for hours after his funeral feast.

Dagmar, along with the others, belonged to a group of vampires called the Circle of the Crone, and he had called them together at Murphy's grave. When Dagmar called, all three of them made sure to show up.

"So what's this about? Anyone know?" Anne broke the silence first. She was the youngest of the three, both in terms of her physical appearance, and by her time spent undead. She'd been just 17 when changed over, and had only been a vampire for eight years. Tom was her sire, the vampire who had changed her. To all appearances, he was in his mid-50s. He'd been dead since 1972. Phoebe seemed to be in her late 20s. She'd been dead since 1961.

"I think Dagmar's got a new pretty young thing." If Phoebe sounded bitter, neither of the other two was surprised. Once upon a time, she'd been Dagmar's pretty young thing. Once, back in 1961.

"Oh no," Tom said. "This better not be what I think it is."

"What do you think it is, Tom?" Phoebe's tone was neutral. Butter wouldn't melt in her mouth. Literally.

"I think he wants to ignore the Prince's decree, bring his new paramour into the family, and have his loyal coterie of followers—that means us, Anne—cover it up so he doesn't get in trouble."

"Half right," Dagmar said, stepping out from behind a bulky tombstone. Dead people are hard to startle, but they all knew for a fact that he hadn't been there a moment before.

"Dagmar, you've taught me a lot and I respect you..."

"Thank you, Tom."

"But I can't..."

"Tom, why don't you shut up while you're ahead?"

Tom bit his lip but was silent.

"What did you mean by half right?" Anne, as the junior member, was permitted to ask the questions that her seniors would not.

"I mean that Monica deserves, so fully, the perfection of her nature through the Embrace."

Phoebe couldn't suppress a snort. Dagmar ignored it.

"She has already killed," Dagmar insisted. "As a mortal girl! She has already killed for *me*," he said, voice heavy with self-satisfaction.

"Then why bother?" Phoebe asked. "Why not just give her enough to keep her pretty—she is *pretty*, I assume? I thought so. Why not just feed her your blood and preserve her and let her do your bidding by daylight?"

"She is a goddess!" Dagmar exclaimed, eyes bright. "To reduce her to slavery and addiction to my blood would be a travesty. A goddess, Phoebe. Even as you were."

"As I *was*?" Phoebe hissed, glaring at him. He shrugged, meeting her gaze evenly.

"Listen," Tom said. "I'm as hesitant to hide a goddess as I am to hide a newly hatched neonate," Tom said. "I am not going to get into a situation where I baby-sit her, teach her how to put her trash away, *hide* her, and spend tedious nights showing her how to take a punch while *you* skim the cream and show up when you feel like it to act like the Playboy of the Western World."

Dagmar turned his head from Phoebe, and raised his eyebrows at Tom. "Sorry? I must have tuned you out. What exactly were you saying after, 'You've taught me a lot. I respect you?'"

"Dagmar, you can't go against the Prince... can you?"

"Who says I have to?"

"The Prince's Tranquility is law," Phoebe replied. "I agree, the ban on Embraces is bullshit, but—"

"What about the other half? The ban on Kindred killing Kindred?"

She shrugged. "I remember how it used to be," she said. "Do you really want it to be like that again?"

"What if I told you that I could bring my darling Monica over legitimately? That I could openly share my love, power and immortality with her, introducing her to the Prince and the court with head held high? Then would you be willing to *aid* me in raising her up? Tom? Would you teach her what you know?"

He shrugged. "That's a pretty wildly hypothetical situation."

"Phoebe? Could I rely on you to give her shelter?"

"Oh, I'd be *delighted* to give your new *lover* someplace to stay."

"I'll take you at your word. Anne?"

"What?"

"You'd no longer be the youngest. Surely that means something to you."

Anne blinked, then narrowed her eyes. "I wouldn't have to...?"

"Yeah," Tom said, turning to Dagmar and putting his hands on his hips. "You've always said that shit work's the neonate's duty. You willing to put your 'goddess' through that?"

"Ishtar had to shed her veils," Dagmar said, "to navigate the realms of death. Humiliation is as much a part of the goddess story as exultation." He didn't look at Phoebe as he said it, so she didn't fight the shiver that coursed through her.

Anne looked at Tom. "Oh please? Please let him? I'm so ready to be done with... that."

Tom looked between his offspring and his elder. He shrugged. "If you can get the Prince to be okay with it... But shit, how are you going to do *that*?"

"The Prince himself has been rather soft on the Embrace ban."

"Oh, so he's above the law. I'm shocked, shocked to find that his own rules don't apply to him. Come on!"

"And you know there is a legal provision for a... vacation from the Tranquility."

"What, you mean that Prince's Indulgence thing? He just

threw that into the laws as a sop to the Circle. He'd never *invoke* it. The Lancea Sanctum would throw a shit fit and he's thick as thieves with them and their psycho fundie leader. Do you really think he'd cross his old pal Bishop Birch?"

"I was there when he beat his 'old pal' with a burning brand. I was there months later when the Prince forced a vinculum on him. The Prince's friendship to Birch has left the Bishop more scarred and enslaved than any strategy of Birch's enemies."

"He had no choice," Phoebe said. "Anyone but Birch, he'd have flayed them into the big sleep."

Dagmar smiled.

"The Prince is not as strong as it may appear to *you*. In his brief tenure he has already fought off one ouster, *led by Birch*. The Bishop, I think, was willing to destroy the village to save the village." He smiled and looked up at the stars, his eyes distant. "He really did want to save his good friend's *soul*. But his good friend is damned, and now the Lancea is weak, and I think it will soon be weaker. I think," he said, smile widening, "that the Prince will disavow the Lancea to keep his throne. I think that if the pressure is sufficient, he will let us be monsters as long as he can remain the chief monster."

Chapter Five

Aurora woke up to a buzzing noise. At first, confused, she thought it might be in her head.

That's just what I need, she thought, and then she recognized it. Someone out on the street was pressing her doorbell.

She stumbled out of bed and un-gummed her eyes.

No one I know would be here this early, she thought, and that notion snapped her alert. She ran to the window and peered through the blinds.

No cop cars, but that didn't mean anything. Heart pounding, she slipped on shoes and pulled out her pistol.

It buzzed again.

I could just ignore it, she thought. *If it's a cop, he'll go away, try later. Right? If it's not a cop… if it's someone they sent…*

She had no idea how she could find out safely. If she'd been discovered and identified, she knew she had to run. No matter that it had been hard enough to find *this* place, that she could barely make the rent, let alone walk away from her deposit, to say nothing about having to make *another* deposit immediately.

Shit. She pushed the intercom button.

"Who's there?"

"Aurora Barclay?"

That was the name on her buzzer. So he didn't know who she *really* was. That was something.

"Yes?"

"I've got a package for you."

"You can leave it in the foyer." Any relief she'd momentarily felt evaporated when logic reminded her that she hadn't seen a

FedEx or UPS truck outside, either.

"If that's what you want. We'll be in touch."

What the fuck? She hesitated before hitting the switch, but in the end she did it.

If they've found me, they've found me, and a locked door won't stop them.

She pressed the buzzer and went back to the window, staring down over the entrance. She saw a man leave. From eight stories up it was impossible to see details, but he wasn't wearing brown UPS shorts, that was for damn sure. He was balding and wore a suit and drove away in a dark-green sedan.

Aurora sat down at the apartment's tiny breakfast nook and took a deep breath. Then, feeling like something was missing, she lit a cigarette and took a deep drag.

Better.

She knew she should go check this package immediately, but she was still afraid. She turned on the coffeemaker and ate two Hostess donuts while it gurgled, then had a cup with two sugars and still couldn't bring herself to go after... whatever it was.

C'mon, she told herself. *You fight* vampires. *You can't be scared of a box!*

But she stared at a little mark on the kitchen linoleum and was scared. She was scared that the package would be a bomb, or an envelope of pictures of everyone she'd ever loved, or a cooler holding some melting ice and a severed head.

As she ate, she picked at the butterfly bandages on her left arm. The cut was five inches long, thin and shallow. She'd been lucky. She'd had a bracelet on under her leather jacket. The knife had grazed off that and lost half its force. The band had an ugly scratch in it now, and it was just a cheap hammered piece of shit from Mexico, a memento that a pothead ex-boyfriend had given her that didn't even *work,* since she could kind of picture his face but not recall his name. She ran her thumb over the ragged edge where the metal had curled up, and she took some comfort from it. She wore it all the time now. Her lucky bracelet.

Aurora showered and changed her bandages and winced as

she put more antibiotic ointment on her wound. It was healing nicely. She hoped it wouldn't even scar.

She'd been *very* lucky. She'd examined the dropped knife and it was unusually heavy, and sharper than the razor she shaved with. She'd tested it against one of her kneepads and one good jab had not only gone through the plastic, it had sunk a quarter-inch into the floor beneath. That was the mark on the linoleum. She found herself staring at it often.

That was one sharp goddamn knife.

Ultimately, she didn't have the courage to go downstairs until she'd put on makeup.

The package in the foyer wasn't the brown cardboard box she'd expected. It was a metal briefcase.

At least a head wouldn't fit in it, *she thought.*

Back up in her apartment, she took a deep breath. *Bombs away,* she thought, and clicked open the latches.

It was lined with foam, cut to hold the contents immobile.

Two guns, both .45s with short barrels, with strange lensed devices on the front of the trigger guards. *Are those laser sights?* There was something she'd seen in dozens of movies but never in real life: A silencer. Looking closer, she could see how it screwed onto the pistols. There was ammo, too, bullets with little dabs of paint on the tips. She thought that meant they were special somehow, like armor piercing or hollow tips or something, but while Aurora knew how to shoot, she was no sharpshooter. There was a tiny, sleek new cell phone. At least she knew how to use *that.*

What really caught her eye was a pair of wooden stakes. She picked one up and it was ridiculously weighty. It was the same balance as the one she'd made—heavy in the back, so that the tip wouldn't waver while you slammed it in. This was much nicer, though. It was some kind of hard, dense wood that had been drilled in the back for a lead core. As she lifted it she thought it might actually be laminated.

Is that to make it… penetrate better? Clearly this stake was the result of some intense thought. Maybe even experience.

Hope flooded her as she saw paper under the stake slot.

Lifting out the weapons and the foam revealed a thin second layer. There were eight stacks of cash—freshly minted bills. *Hundreds.* Eight stacks of $100 bills, 10 to a stack, someone had just *given* her *8,000 dollars.* So much for rent!

There was also a buff envelope, unsealed. She opened it.

Congratulations. Welcome to the counterinsurgency. Carry the phone with you at all times. Keep it charged at all times. Do not ever make outgoing calls without our explicit instructions.

Do not approach the biter you saw on Thursday. She's got your scent now, and she's out of your league. Further instructions are forthcoming. We'll be in touch.

Burn this note after you read it.

For a few minutes, Aurora just stared.

We, she thought. *I'm not the only one.*

Tears of joy, of crazy relief, flooded her eyes.

'*Biter,*' she thought, caressing the note, the weapons. *Someone else knows.*

Someone else is fighting them.

———

As soon as he got home from school, Steve was on the phone.

The Velvet Four hadn't been playing the Jade Room when he'd gone, she hadn't been there, and the bartender hadn't known much. But persistence had gotten Steve a brief talk with the manager, who had shrugged and given him a phone number for the Four's booking agent. On Saturday, he'd called first thing.

Only, like a dope, he told truth.

Well, not "the truth and the whole truth." He hadn't said, "I think one of the band members is a vampire and I'd really, really like to see her again." He'd said that he was a fan, dug the band, blah blah blah. The agent had politely given him the band's schedule and pointed him toward a website. If Steve had been patient, he would have contented himself with seeing them play at Perry's on Wednesday.

Instead, he'd started asking personal questions. He'd heard a distinct chill enter the agent's tone when he asked about maybe getting a phone number to talk directly to the band. The agent hung up after he asked about Velvet specifically.

Steve suspected something in his voice had creeped her out. He didn't like the thought of that.

Why am I doing this? He asked himself. He didn't have any kind of solid answer. Instead, he had two equal and opposite answers. He wanted to find Velvet because a fucking *vampire* is something you want to watch closely so you can stay as far away from her as possible. *Especially after she's gotten a taste for you,* he found himself thinking, late at night, lying in bed with the lights off and the windows locked, despite stifling heat and indifferent air conditioning.

But at the same time he wanted to find Velvet because… because…

Because you want it again.

That was the crazy thing and was it like drugs? This must be what drugs were like, being a drug addict, or maybe this was a death wish. When he was being completely honest with himself he had to admit there was something very wrong, pathological even, about his thing with women and, yeah, he dressed it up as romanticism and, yeah, he really *did* want a soul mate, but come on. He wound up going a lot further than a healthy ego would in pursuit of ladies way, *way* below soul-mate caliber. There was a sick hunger there, and Velvet had somehow filled into that hole like a key into a lock. He didn't want to die. He wanted to live on, feel that *feeling* again and again, that violent closeness, that entwining that obliterated everything.

He had to believe she wanted to find him, too. That it was the same for her as for him. Lying in bed with eyes wide open at night, he desperately *hoped* that she had a taste for him now.

The agent picked up the phone and Steve attempted to disguise his voice.

"Hi, this is Jake Steubbens and I was wondering if—"

"Mr. Quartermain, I have caller ID. I have a gun in my desk, and more relevantly I have a lawyer. If you persist in stalking my client, I'm going to sign an affidavit about your *highly* suspicious behavior and submit it to the police. Do I make myself clear?"

Steve opened his mouth, then closed it again.

"I guess I'll just hang up now," he said, and did.

Then he scratched his chin and started calling the places where the Velvet Four were scheduled to perform.

Aurora finally got up her nerve to call Steve and check on him, but the line was busy.

Stingo had pulled strings and the body had gone to a corrupt morgue. For $50, the attendant would go take a leak for half an hour while his 'clientele' got a chance to peep at the dead bodies. The attendant was adamant about *no touching* and, with a glare that was half-scared, half-aggressive, told Velvet and Earth that they had to 'clean up any messes' they made.

He thought he was taking bribes from necrophiliacs and other seekers of morbid thrills. He had no idea.

"This her?" Earth said, when he'd opened the drawer and yanked back the sheet.

Velvet looked down and said nothing.

"Well?"

"It's hard to tell," she said.

"Whaddaya mean, hard to tell? She was driving the car. She had a fuckin' wood stake in her purse. She didn't seem all that surprised about vampires. You think there's more'n one lady who's all up in the Van Helsing scene?"

"Her hair was different."

"Wig," Earth said. "Homeys put on wigs to do drive-bys all the time, shit. Or hair dye. Or maybe it looks different under fluorescents than in that crusty old jazz dive." He had his hand in his pocket, jingling his keys. He hadn't fed yet and wanted to be done with this.

"Her arm isn't hurt."

"You're sure you cut her?"

"Blood was spilled. I'm sure."

That gave him pause, made him frown.

"Huh," he said.

"Yeah. And, I mean, she'd be a lot easier to identify if she had a *face* left, you know?"

"Hey, do I tell you how to do *your* job?"

"It could be her, I guess. But the arm..."

"Well, you know. Someone gets a taste of vampire blood in her, she can heal like we do. Just shut it on up, y'know?"

"You think she was a ghoul?"

He rolled his neck and shrugged. "It would explain a hell of a lot, wouldn' it? How she knew about us. Why she attacked. Probably wanted to get you down and tank up on *you*."

For a moment, Velvet just stared. She *wanted* this to be the woman, wanted it to be over.

"It could be her," she said at last. "I just don't know."

———

Twenty minutes later, Earth was rolling. The stereo was cranked to bone-shuddering volume.

She's young and drunk

With some funk in her trunk

Just the type to bunk with a punk like me

It's no crime, just time to pass the VD

Girl I know you lose your mind

'Cause my penis is large

But in a week's time

Watch for greenish discharge...

As the MC rapped about a dose of penicillin, Earth pulled into an illegal parking spot and powered down the passenger's side window.

"Yo, ladies!" he bellowed at a pair of girls in hip-hugging skirts and tank tops. "Y'all wanna hop in the Escalade? C'mon, now."

They giggled but kept walking.

"Don't be shy, girls. You're walkin' away from the Penis Genius here! Get on in!"

They turned the corner and he pulled out. *Perhaps I overplayed my hand*, he thought, but he hadn't been too serious. He'd just felt like playing a little fool for them. The night was young and he had plenty of potential.

While the exterior was immaculate, inside the SUV was a mess. CDs, rap magazines and Chicago newspapers were piled messily on the passenger side, while bouncing on the floor was a box of garbage bags, a big Swiss Army knife, and a pair of bolt cutters. If he'd bent down, Earth would have spotted the handle of a Glock pistol under the seat, the mate to one of the several spare clips rattling around in the glove box beside a band-aid box full of X tabs and amyl nitrate capsules, a tire gauge, a small flashlight with dead batteries and a motley collection of pens. All that junk was padded by maps, napkins, and scraps of paper with scrawled directions.

He glanced down at the cell phone rattling around the drink holder, banging against the GPS locator, and he raised an eyebrow as he realized it was ringing. He picked it up and flicked it open.

"Yo, Earth," he said. Then he frowned, braked at a light, and punched the pause button on the stereo.

"Hello? Is this thing on?" The voice was unfamiliar.

"Had the stereo going. Who dis?"

"Is this Mayfield Baines?"

"Who dis?"

"I need to speak to you."

"You are speaking to me."

"Not like this. In person. Face to face."

"Oh, uh, okay, except—who the *fuck* is this?"

"Do you really expect me to give my name to an Invictus officer on an insecure cell connection?"

"I think it's pretty clear that I do. I don't like people playing with my phone. G'bye."

Earth broke the connection, shaking his head.

Solomon nodded at the guard standing in the temple hallway, approving of the way the young Kindred straightened at his approach.

"Bishop Birch," she said.

He smiled an easy greeting. "All quiet?"

"No real disturbances," she said, but her eyes slid down the hall to a barred, steel door.

"Has he been acting up?" Solomon asked.

"Just screaming," she said. "Nothing too unusual. Are you going to...?" She trailed off as she realized she might be prying.

"I'm going in," he said, nodding.

The bars on the door weighed over 400 pounds. Solomon could have lifted them himself, but it would have required invoking the power of the blood, and that was not something he did frivolously. Instead he set down the small cooler he'd brought and got the guard to help him. He could tell she was somewhat nervous, and that irritated and gratified him at the same time.

What will her comrades think when she tells them? He wondered. *What will they think of Bishop Birch and the mad elder Cass?*

Cass was not a member of the Lancea Sanctum. He was a rogue, a crazy and dangerous narcissist who had launched an attack-by-proxy against the Temple almost two years ago. Sanctified had perished in the assault, and Solomon had hunted Cass down, rooting him out of his lair near Malta, Illinois, and delivering him to the Prince with a stake in his chest. It had been a celebrated triumph for Solomon, though the loss of his congregates still hindered his covenant.

Back then, Solomon and Prince Maxwell had still been close. The Prince had given Cass into Solomon's custody, with a stern command to keep him safely imprisoned. The other covenants, and even some grumblers within the church, had called for the Final Death of the mad elder, but Solomon insisted that Kindred blood should not be shed by Kindred. Since he led the Lancea, and it was the injured party, he had final say.

Few people were permitted to visit Cass, and those who did rarely felt that Solomon had done the elder a kindness by sparing him from destruction.

Bishop Birch pressed his face into a retinal-recognition scanner, then typed 12 digits into a keypad. A light went from red to green and the door swung open slowly.

He walked in and grinned at his prize.

Cass was suspended in a device of the Bishop's design, known as "Solomon's Swastika." It was a series of struts, tubes and straps, holding a prisoner's arms and legs spread-eagled. Unlike a traditional rack, the limbs were confined, enclosed at angles at which no natural arrangement of bones could fit.

Vampires do not heal with time, but with blood. Thus, one of the Kindred (when well fed and determined) can get through standard prison bars—if he has the will to break all his own ribs. Similarly, a shattered arm or leg can be healed in moments by one who has stolen sufficient life from mortals.

Cass was not given sufficient blood by any decent Kindred standard, but even if he got it he would not be able to heal his arms, his legs and his burned-out eyes. They were broken with no space to straighten, and they kept him in great pain. In any event, he probably would have healed his eyes first—not only to see, but because, like Solomon, he had the power of seizing will through his gaze.

All those features were standard on Solomon's Swastika, but this particular device had been modified with eight applewood stakes, surrounding his chest like a crown of thorns, locked in place against powerful counterweights. If Cass ever moved out of the device they would close like fingers with splintering force.

Solomon considered it a sign of his respect for Cass that he would build so elaborate a prison.

Incongruously, there was a cheap digital radio in a corner, playing staticky AM talk radio.

"How are you enjoying the modern world?" Solomon asked as the door closed behind him.

"I've learned that even our malignance and evil has been surpassed by some mortal sect calling themselves 'Democrats.'"

The elder's voice was scratchy and dry.

"I've brought you something." Solomon carefully disconnected the triggers on the tubes and tilted them upward. They moved in unison, linked by a series of gears the Bishop had lathed personally.

"I know it isn't warm blood, because you have no mortal with you," Cass said. "And I know it isn't the binding taste of your own Vitae, because your religion forbids the exercise of that power on your fellow Kindred. So I am curious. What wonder of the technological world have you brought to lord over me this night?"

"No modern wonder, but an ancient one, oh ye of little faith. Open your mouth."

With one eyebrow raised, Cass did. Solomon opened his cooler and brought out something red and frozen.

"What is it? Something to eat?" Cass asked.

"A dog's heart. Open wide."

"You never tire of humiliating me, do you?"

"Open your mouth, Cass. Come now."

With a sigh, Cass once more parted his lips. Solomon placed the organ between them and spoke words in a long-dead language. Cass' eyes widened as the tissue seemed to melt, pouring down his throat not as the lifeless stuff of stored blood, nor the soulless bare sustenance of animal blood, but as the hot, rich, incredibly potent thrill of human blood infused with Kindred power. He sucked greedily and blinked.

"Some trick of your Theban rites, then?"

"A lesser trick. It's called Vitae Reliquary."

"Why reward me?"

"I believe you can be saved."

Cass laughed, long and harshly.

"Oh, not tonight. Not this year," Solomon said. "Not this decade even. But in 50 years, when your treachery against the Temple is only a memory? Then I might see fit to release you. Perhaps permit you to feed more... normally."

"Even let me restore my eyes?" Cass' lids were closed over the blackened sockets where Solomon had dripped molten solder. He was already developing the blind man's habit of turning an ear, not his face, toward the person addressing him.

"Let's not lose our senses," Solomon replied. "I *know* the power of your gaze."

"Hmph. Is that what brings you here tonight? A bribe for me and your first inching step toward my conversion?"

"That, and your delightful company. I remember from days long past, before your slumber. I thought we might enjoy the old-time pleasures of conversation."

"You are a real piece of work, Birch."

"What modern phrasing you use!"

"Last time someone changed the channel, it had a program called 'Loveline' in which people discussed their sexual deviances, illnesses and inadequacies, in-between performances of the most hideous music history has seen fit to devise. I learned the phrase there."

Solomon walked over to the radio and fiddled with it until it was tuned to WBEZ.

"You can enjoy National Public Radio for a while," he said. "It's the antidote to right-wing propaganda." His finger stabbed down to turn it off. "But that can wait until I leave." He stood and turned back to his prisoner. "I am under vinculum."

Cass cackled. "Hah! Compared to that, my humiliations are minor! At least, according to your stern creed of religious purity. Who did it, Maxwell?"

Cass couldn't see it, but Solomon twitched. "Who told you?"

"A lucky guess," Cass said, his voice suddenly silky. "Who else could? And now you find your tenure as Bishop beleaguered, for the Sanctified would find it strange to endure the leadership of one who is, himself, a slave."

"My bondage is not complete," Solomon began, but Cass interrupted him.

"The Birch I knew—the one who was no Bishop, admittedly— would have spat pure contempt on such waffling evasions. You are condemned by your own doctrine. That's a tough row to hoe."

"Maxwell is no less a traitor," Solomon muttered. "He has broken his own law and retains praxis."

"Maxwell can rule by force, I should guess—force or fear

or, hmm, perhaps by snaring troublemakers with the emotional chains of the vinculum? Eh? You must rule by faith and must therefore seem to be its champion. Not easy to do when you have surely dismissed others who were found to be untrustworthy."

"What do you think I should do, Cass?" Solomon said it with an amused tone, but his lips were curled back in a sneer and his teeth were beginning to project.

"Should? Meaning, the morally correct action? Meaning, the action in keeping with the precepts to which you have, I somehow suspect, loudly and publicly declared yourself dedicated? That's obvious. You should step down."

There was a brief silence. When Solomon smiled, his teeth were normal again.

"But I don't want to," he said.

"And now we come to the core. You don't *want* to. From what I gather you've wrapped yourself in a cozy blanket of fanatics and ideologues, with anyone moderate—meaning, anyone who might overlook a vinculum—cast into the outer darkness to wail, gnash teeth, and discuss paralyzing subtleties of religious doctrine." Cass snorted through his nose. "I prefer *my* punishment."

"That's easy to say when you have no choice of a different one," Solomon said. "But consider this. If I—the fundamentalist, as you rightly surmise—am cast down, who do you think will take my place? Possibly someone else as fervid as myself to scrupulously avoid the murder of one Kindred by another, yes. Or possibly one of those wafflers you rightly despise, who might well decide that the entire covenant is safer with *you* converted into fine, harmless ash."

There was a pause.

"Ah," said Cass.

"Yes. Ah."

"Am I really the only person you can come to for counsel?"

"Not the only one, but I'm confident you won't go blabbing my concerns to all and sundry."

"Having no choice, I should be trustworthy. In theory."

"You know what the difference is between theory and practice, Cass?"

"In theory, there is no difference. And in theory, I have the choice between sticking with you, the lion of the faith who will, in 50 or 100 years release me—once I've converted. That, or gambling on another Bishop who might respond to my history more sanely by covering me in kerosene and burning me to death."

"I imagine they'd use gasoline these days, but that's basically the situation."

"How do you know I won't simply tell you what you want to hear?"

"First off, I think you'll be tempted by the intellectual stimulation of advising me, even beyond your own self-interest. I think being an aide-de-camp, even to someone you despise, will be more *fun* than lying here night after night listening to random stations on the radio. Furthermore..." Solomon reached into an inside jacket pocket and produced the thumb-sized shell of a discarded cicada carapace. He muttered again in that lost language and smiled as the husk crumbled.

"Tell me a lie, Cass," he said.

Cass tilted his head and said, "I believe Solomon Birch truly possesses unvarnished and selfless faith."

Cass spoke, then began spluttering as live beetles crawled across his lips and teeth. He spat, despite his dry mouth, and they crawled down his wattled neck and over the straps on his chest.

"It is called the Liar's Plague," Solomon said.

"Another of your Theban tricks?"

"I prefer to call them tools of the faith," Solomon said, drawing closer and leaning comfortably on the Swastika. "Now we have much to discuss."

———

Steve was at the Trumpet. The Velvet Four were not scheduled to perform there for a week and a half, but he had to get out, had to take some concrete step.

"I can't believe you dragged me along on this," Tyler said. "What do you want me here for anyhow?"

"Your wife asked me to get you out of the house."

"Why? Is that mailman coming around again?" Tyler said it with mock-fierceness.

"No, she wanted to prepare a special surprise for you with Saran Wrap and one of those Thai sex swings." Steve was scanning the crowd. He sighed.

"Is this about hickey girl?"

"Please don't call her 'hickey girl.'"

"Then please tell me her name." Ty pushed his drink back on the bar a little and furrowed his brow at his friend. "Look, can I be honest? You've got me a little concerned. You've gone all..."

"What?"

"All *something*, I don't know what. You're acting like a motherfucking music teacher." The math teacher felt the need to pause before swearing, as if he was double-checking.

"I'm not sure what her real name is. She introduced me to her... she introduced herself by her stage name."

"Oh good Lord. Now, this is the woman who was there the night the *other* woman was there, right? Excuse me if I'm having a hard time keeping track, but, you know, without details everything gets kind of fuzzy."

"Yes, that's the... the night."

"And it was the *other* woman who was kind of flaky? The woman who gave you her *stage name* as the normal one?"

"She's a jazz musician!"

"Oh, well, in that case. No jazz musician's *ever* been mental. Is she here?"

"No."

"Is she playing tonight?"

"No!"

"Then why are we here?"

Steve sighed. "I don't know."

Hesitantly, Tyler put a hand on Steve's arm. "This isn't about... something else, is it? I mean..."

"What?"

"I don't know, a... a family problem? Something like that?"

"No! Jesus."

"Why so touchy?" He looked really uncomfortable, but went on. "I knew this guy in college. He was in my fraternity."

"Ty..."

"No, *listen*. He seemed okay and then he started getting kind of... I don't know, kind of weird. Distracted and not focusing and spending a lot of time in bars. Does that sound like anyone we know?"

"I'm not..." Steve squirmed on his barstool. "What happened to your frat brother?"

"He tried to kill himself. We found him in the bathroom. He'd slit his wrists and later he told us he'd been taking cocaine."

"Jesus! You *found* him?"

"I didn't find him, but I saw him. Another guy, our treasurer, he found him and started screaming and freaking out and I ran to see what was the matter and that's when I saw him."

"Wow."

"Yeah. Wow. So, Steve. Is there something you want to tell me?"

Steve widened his eyes, then gave a sharp laugh.

"You think I'm...? Tyler, that's *ridiculous*."

"Okay."

"It's insane!"

"Okay."

"I'm not..."

"*Okay*, Steve." Tyler sat back and took another sip. "It's just that you're acting exactly like he did."

A half-hour later, Tyler had finished his beer and Steve was ready to leave anyhow. Tyler offered him a ride home, but Steve said he'd take the train, which he did.

He took the train to the next bar on the Velvet Four's schedule, The Green Tree.

Aurora had copied down the Velvet Four's club dates, but hadn't gone so far as to check the locations. She was, in fact, working her night-shift job when her brand-new cell phone rang.

Heart beating fast, she answered.

"Where are you?"

"I'm at work," she whispered.

"Order up!" the cook called, and she instinctively looked over.

"What time do you get off?"

Shaking her head at the weirdness of it, she told him. She thought it was the same voice, the same man who'd delivered the package.

"When you finish work, go to the park three blocks from your apartment. Go to the corner farthest from your home, the southwest corner. There's a garbage can there. Inside the garbage can will be a FedEx box sealed with duct tape. It will contain further instructions. Then go home."

"Am I... doing anything... tonight?"

"Never do anything by night." The phone disconnected.

Velvet tuned her violin and looked at Danielle, who was doing the same. "I have a problem," Velvet said quietly.

The other musician looked up at her, face neutral. They'd been playing together a long time—since they were both alive. "Oh?"

"I got jumped the other night. Fearless vampire hunter."

"Really? Are you sure he was... one of them? Not just some psycho?"

"She. She was carrying a wooden stake."

"Wow. What happened?"

Velvet frowned, turned a knob. "I cut her, then she set my shirt on fire and I ran away."

Danielle said nothing. Then, "Don't let it affect your performance."

"I won't."

Velvet and Danielle played in the same group—not the Velvet Four jazz combo, but a classical ensemble with a much smaller and more select audience. Known as the Thanatos Quartet, they played for engagements that were primarily (or exclusively) vampiric. Danielle and Velvet were the only surviving members of the original four.

"Earth Baines is investigating," Velvet said as she set her instrument aside. "I think he killed the wrong woman."

"You think?"

"It was hard to tell after he was… done."

"What an animal."

Velvet shrugged and almost said, 'Like you never did,' but refrained. Danielle was very private about her feeding. For all Velvet knew, Danielle hadn't ever murdered.

"Do you think she'll come back?" Danielle asked.

"Probably not. If she does, I'm ready."

"Then what's the problem?"

"She made me sad."

Danielle put her violin down. It was nicer than Velvet's, a Guarneri. She pushed aside her blonde hair and looked into Velvet's eyes.

"Sad?"

"It was like… she was so determined. So angry. Maybe I've been sheltered, I… I never saw anyone fight me and look so… so… I don't know."

"What about that guy in the '70s, the one in the museum basement?"

"That was different. He was angry, sure, but he was out of his head. It was easy to… I mean, he was *mad*. So it was him or me and I… I mean, I'd attacked him and he was defending himself. He was doing what was natural and I was doing what was natural and it… it was hard and unpleasant, but it made sense."

"This new hunter doesn't make sense?"

"She was *brave*, Danielle. That's what it is. The basement guy wasn't brave, he was just cornered. And other times I've killed, when I've had to, they… I mean, this woman hunted *me*. She knew what I was and probably knew what I could do to her— would have done if she hadn't…" Velvet shrugged and looked away. "What would make someone do that?"

"You're asking the wrong person. I thought you were a member of the Lancea Sanctum. I thought they had all the answers about mortals and Kindred and why things are the way they are."

At that moment, there was a buzz from the front door. The Thanatos Quartet practiced at Danielle's studio, so she rose to see who'd arrived.

"I joined the Lancea for Sylvia, really," Velvet said. "I never thought it might... be important."

———

The house looked perfectly normal. It was not a creepy, rundown warren of vice set in the depths of the inner city. It was not a lonely haunted mansion on a hill. It was not a faceless, characterless box, chillingly anonymous to those who knew what lurked within.

It wasn't even a particularly *nice* house.

It was a small blocky number with a sickly lawn and Easter decorations that someone had forgotten to take down. It had a modest front deck with a nice flower box on it, and peeling paint. It was under the flight paths at O'Hare, which kept the prices low, and Aurora had been told there was a vampire sleeping inside.

She looked at the paper from the FedEx box and double-checked the address. This was the place.

She looked at her watch. It was time. Her 'controller' (that was how she thought of him; it was a phrase from some spy movie or some TV show) had told her that the neighbors wouldn't be home and, furthermore, that three planes would probably go right overhead in short succession starting around 11:17, more than covering a silenced pistol.

I could probably scream my lungs out and no one would hear, she thought, and was uneasy that screams might be part of the plan. She looked at the house, then drove around and parked in back.

The backdoor was sturdy and there were bars on all the windows, but the backyard had a wooden picket fence, about six feet tall. In her mind, she knew it was unlikely that anyone would spot her by accident. Somehow, though, the fence did not make her feel safer.

At her controller's suggestion, she'd brought a chisel, a crowbar and a heavy hammer. As the first jet screamed across the sky she began chiseling into the wood by the door latch. The door itself was metal, but its deadbolt was set into ordinary wood.

I wonder if a blowtorch would work better, she thought as she hammered as hard and fast as she could - thud, thud, thud. With each blow the wood jarred and splintered. Then the plane was past and she switched to the prybar, gouging, sweating and grunting to work its black steel behind the brass of the deadbolt socket.

By the time the second plane went over, she'd made a hole in the doorframe about the size of her two fists. She rattled the door back and forth. It opened inward, and she wedged it with the crowbar at its greatest width so that she could eel her fingers in and undo the locks.

Expecting entry, she pushed inward. The door moved a few inches and stopped.

What the hell? She pulled in and out, and heard a metallic sound. She recognized what it meant from an old apartment. A metal rod diagonal to the door and braced against the floor. It was designed to stop kick-ins and battering rams.

Fuck! He didn't tell me about this. Probably didn't know. *What else did he miss? There could be a silent alarm going off right now!* She almost threw her junk in her bag and fled, but didn't. She suspected the mysterious cell phone would never ring again if she bagged on this job. Besides, what if she got caught? Her record was mostly clean, she could probably plea-bargain a B&E rap into community service since there weren't any drugs involved.

Bullshit, *she thought.* There's a *gun* involved. Not to mention the fucking undead in there who probably wouldn't let me come to trial once I was a nice sitting duck in jail. That, in turn, could out this whole 'counterinsurgency' operation, whoever and whatever they are. They've really put a hell of a lot of trust in me.

She reached in and her fingertips brushed the bar, just glanced off it. She shoved harder, feeling the jagged wood scratch her armpit and shoulder through her shirt, but she couldn't grip it. She picked up the crowbar and used that, trying to catch the blocker in the crotch of the pry-tip, but the angle was so awkward that it slipped from her hammer-numbed hand and clattered loudly to the floor.

Dammit! I hope he was at least right about them being sound sleepers. That had been one of the lines in her instructions: that no amount of noise was likely to wake the dead. That was what it had said, 'Wake the dead.'

She squatted, but the hole she'd made didn't go to the floor and she couldn't bend her arm around the angle. She almost laughed. To come this far, to do this much and be foiled by a five-foot inanimate rod.

She stepped back and took a deep breath just as the third plane screamed overhead.

I should be killing him by now, she thought. *It. I should be killing it.*

She thought about the bar she'd known. When the door was closed, you could push the bar forward a couple inches and it would slide out of the stopper on the floor. She frowned, then bent down and unlaced her shoes.

Weight, she thought. *I need a weight to make the string wrap around the bar.* She took off her lucky bracelet.

On the third try, it wrapped, and after a few minutes of grunting and pulling, the bar slipped free from its mount.

Aurora gathered her tools back into her backpack, put it on, stepped inside and drew her gun.

She was in a kitchen and it was normal, expect for being spotlessly tidy. No dishes in the sink, nothing in the drying rack. She stepped forward and realized that there was an odor... dust. She ran a finger across the sink and there was a very tiny smudge.

In Aurora's experience, kitchens only looked this neat right after being cleaned, so it should smell like cleanser. She finally got the creeps. That was good. The heebie-jeebies made her alert. Having the hair on her arms stand up distracted her from thinking about the cops, about jail, about humiliation. It kept her mind on the immediate danger of a *vampire.*

Where would he be? It.

If this was a horror movie, it would be the basement. She opened a door, found a pantry with boxes of unopened, expired dry goods—stage setting, she figured. There was a doorway into a dining room with papers and bills and magazines scattered comfortably on the table. She tried one more door off the kitchen and found stairs going down.

At the bottom, another dead-bolted door, but this one was wood and it didn't take much to punch a hole through so that she could reach in and unlock it.

It was a small basement with no windows—a cellar, really. There was a light switch, but Aurora reached back into her bag for a small electric lantern instead.

Who knows? Maybe the switch is rigged.

It was cool, even in the summer. The lamp's dim and even light showed cheap wood paneling on the walls. The floor was carpeted, but she could feel there was no pad under it. It was just glued onto the concrete. There was a closet and a drop ceiling, but what really caught her eye was the bed in the corner and the man lying on it.

He had normal clothes, hair, features, proportions... but he was somehow repellent. She crept closer and stared. His chest didn't rise or fall. He was lying on his back, tennis shoes on, dressed in jeans and a T-shirt, eyes closed, ankles together and hands folded over his heart. He didn't look asleep. He looked very much dead. In fact, he looked more dead than the people Aurora had seen at funerals, because with this corpse, no one had bothered with embalming fluid or makeup. He wasn't rotting or moldering, just dead. He looked like he'd been dead maybe a day, she guessed. She wasn't all that familiar with dead people, but a day sounded right.

She took a few steps toward him and then stopped.

In a horror movie, I'd go after him and someone would jump out of the closet. She turned and got her back to the wall so that she could face both the door and the dead man, and then set her lamp down. Gun ready, safety off but her finger outside the trigger guard, she reached out with her left hand and opened the closet door.

Clothes hung inside. Under them, there was a sump pump.

She breathed a sigh of relief and closed the door again.

Time for it, I guess.

She slipped her finger inside the trigger guard, pointed it at his head, and stopped.

C'mon, she thought. *Drop the hammer on him.*

But she couldn't. The thought of his face shredding under the bullet's impact. She'd never thought of herself as squeamish before, but she'd never contemplated shooting a sleeping man in the face before.

He's not sleeping, she told himself. *It. It's dead. It isn't asleep, it's dead.*

Nevertheless, she set the pistol down on the floor by her bag and pulled out the wooden stake.

This will be better, she thought, raising the mallet. *More traditional.*

With the pointed tip, she moved his hands out of the way. She didn't want to touch his flesh with her hands. She held her breath, braced for him to move and lunge. But he didn't.

The tip was centered on his sternum and she struck, hard.

"*Aaaaaowwww!*" The man's eyes opened and his face creased with shock and surprise, and something like indignation.

"Eeeee!" Aurora shrieked in reply, thinking, *I shoulda used the gun.* She swung the hammer down again while the vampire feebly tried to bat it aside. He couldn't block it, but his waving hands, not the stake in his chest, took the blow with a sharp crack.

"What the *fuck?*" He seemed disoriented as he sat up and shoved her back, but he was still plenty strong. Aurora stumbled away and threw the hammer at him, missing. Then she scrambled for her gun as he swung his legs off the bed and came at her.

She got the gun, but tripped over her backpack. She accidentally kicked the bag into the lamp, which bounced and flickered and rolled, her shadow leaping and racing across him as she pivoted. He was almost on her and smelled like dust as she pulled the trigger.

He stumbled and fell to one knee. "Shit," he wheezed and

pulled out the stake. Blood came out of the hole, but lazily, like seepage from a pricked canteen. There was no rhythmic pumping like from a living heart.

Aurora took three quick steps back and hit the closet door as he staggered to his feet. The expression on his face wasn't anger. It was fear, and bafflement and sadness.

He looked at her and dropped the stake.

"Hey," he pleaded. "C'mon."

Aurora paused.

Any human being would have earned her mercy at that point. Any man, bleeding and begging. She couldn't have fired.

But this thing wasn't living, and she paused, only to aim before firing.

He fell back and she fired again, and then something entirely unexpected happened.

"Yeah, it went... yeah," Aurora said, hours later. She was back at work, mechanically schlepping burgers and omelets. Her hands had finally stopped shaking when the phone rang. She'd ducked into the ladies' room to answer it.

"Yeah, it's done," she told the voice on the other end. "Only... there was something weird. He rotted away. I mean, in just *minutes*, like a special effect, like... like butter melting on a hot stove, you know?"

She listened for a moment, and her face became still.

"What do you mean 'They all do'?"

Her eyes widened.

"But I... what about a stake in the heart?"

Under her rouge, Aurora paled as her controller explained that a stake would immobilize a vampire, but only until someone pulled it out or it fell out.

"You mean... oh shit."

She could hear his voice, insistent as she lowered the phone and closed it. Then she left the bathroom and turned toward the back door.

"Hey, Aurora! Hey! Where the hell do you think you're

going?" Her coworker yelled.

"Joliet," she whispered.

"Aurora! Order up!"

She stopped and stood up straight.

If he's there, he's there, she thought. *I can't afford to lose this job.*

She turned slowly and went back to work.

Her hands were shaking again.

―――――

Bernard's Southside Grill was not the sort of place one expected to find vampires. It was lively, down-home, blue collar—a place where railway workers and cops went to get big greasy burgers and Americanized burritos at a cheap price, in an ambiance that was all NASCAR calendars, football posters and freebie banners from beer companies. Underneath that, and a layer of accepted grime, Bernard's Southside was linoleum, wallboard and blackened metal.

Three vampires met in the back corner, block-muscled men in coveralls and boots, or jeans and flannel, all three wearing ball caps. They had genuine dirt under their fingernails and they had their guard up. They were passing for human in one way or another. No one gave them a second look. No other customer noticed that their meals had been mangled and stirred but not eaten. No observer would guess that their deep tans were carefully applied chemicals, the kind office workers use to make their colleagues think they can afford to visit the Bahamas.

They were vampires, Carthians, which meant they thought the mystic mumbling of the Lancea Sanctum was bullcrap and that the forelock-tugging and tyrannical authoritarianism of the current regime was oppressive—in a word, dumb. In life, the three of them had been blue-collar union reps. In death, they still stuck together.

"Mike," Pete said. "You hear?"

"Hear what?"

"People talking about an Indulgence."

Mike stroked his chin. He'd been killed into the Carthians

in 1937 and knew his stuff. "Why would Prince Max give us a vacation from his favorite law?"

Pete shrugged. "Joe said the Circle wants it."

Mike turned to Joe, who'd only been dead since 1991. "The Circle?"

"I know someone," he said.

"That Anne chick?"

"Uh... yeah. You know. You said it's important to get to know people."

"Yeah but... one of *them*? Why do you hang around with her so much anyhow?"

Joe replied with a look that was macho-coy. "You know those spooky chicks. She's a wildcat in the sack."

"Yeah, well, wildcat or not... when was the last time the Circle got organized enough to do *anything*?"

"Bella's been pushy," Pete said.

"Bella's outside the loop," Mike replied.

"If Rowen's not careful, Bella's going to *be* the loop," Pete answered.

"Probably someone will propose it," Joe said. "And the rest of the Circle won't be organized enough to say yes or no. Or they'll just go along with it because they hated the Tranquility anyhow."

"That's a valid point, but you still haven't answered my question. Why would Max go along?"

"To make the Circle happy? To show he's not in the pocket of the Lancea?" Joe said.

"You're assuming he *ain't* in the pocket of the Lancea."

"Come on, the beatdown he gave Solomon for fuckin' with his little chick? I think that's a pretty deep crack."

"Joe's got a point," Pete said. "I mean, Birch was the one who pushed for the Tranquility in the first place. What's he going to do now? He won't be back in Elysium for months, and even when he's back, is he going to throw another tantrum? If Maxwell wants it, Birch has no choice but to want it, too. Right?"

"His political capital is pretty lean," Mike admitted. "So maybe this isn't so farfetched. You think the Ordo will be for or against?"

"Against, if they even give a shit. The question is, is it good for the movement?"

"If Maxwell thinks it's good for the movement, he'll oppose it."

"But he won't want to *look* like he's just blocking us to be a dick. 'I'm a uniter, not a divider,' y'know?"

They all snickered.

"I got no beef with it," Mike said at last. "It doesn't cost us much to appear a little indifferent to it, a little negative. Let the Circle make its noise and if it happens, we should be ready to... hmm..."

"To do whatever we do," Pete supplied.

"Sure."

"Now, this Indulgence deal—it's not just Embrace, right? If he calls one, then it's okay to run around and..." Joe looked right and left, leaned in and lowered his voice. "It's okay to take out other vampires. Right?"

"That's the law on the books," Pete said.

"What gives?"

"Keep the balance."

"But it'll be like a one-night war!" Joe said.

"Better that than gettin' it on all year round. It's also one night of creation."

"Even if all you're creating is more creeps like us," Pete said. "But yeah. Everyone serious is going to hunker down. Everyone angry is going to try to settle a score. Everyone lonely is going hunt their one and only." He shrugged. "I think some middle-aged Kindred will get caught with their pants down and get wacked, and there'll be a fresh crop of newbies looking for guidance. It's good for the Carthians. Who else are they going to turn to? The Lancea's fucked up; they got leadership worries. The Circle's all goofy New Age bullshit. We're the only ones who even resemble the democracy they know. I think we'll do all right."

"So we support it, by appearing to reject it," Mike said.

"Sure. There are some loudmouths on our side who'll be loudmouths for and against it. They'll muddy the issue. The Carthians will look disorganized and what else is new?"

"But if it comes down…?"

"If it comes down, we gotta be ready to catch it."

———

"It's an outrage!"

"Absolutely," Solomon replied.

"I mean, the Invictus has just gone too far this time! It's appalling!" The speaker was squat and pasty, and in death his features had lengthened unnaturally. His nose, his chin, the tips of his ears—all had become pointed and thin, like the long-nailed fingers with which he gestured angrily.

"Certainly, I'm appalled," Solomon said, his tone conciliatory. "Vadim, would you like something to drink?"

"I'm fine."

"Really, it's no trouble. I'll just… Hortense?" He leaned out the doorway of his study and raised his voice. "Hortense, if you could ask Margery to…?"

"No, Bishop, I'm *fine*. I don't need a drink. What I need is an explanation for why one of the Prince's heavies tore apart one of my people for *no fucking reason*."

"Now, you're sure this outrage was committed by this… Baines?"

"I know from Smitty that Baines and Stingo were hunting somebody. I got someone to look in the past at the scene and a seven-foot blonde guy was gnawing on the inside of her thigh. I know he went to the cooler where her body is and checked it out. So yeah, I'm pretty motherfucking sure."

Solomon stroked his chin. "This is a serious matter. Are you sure Baines knew she was your ghoul?"

Vadim looked away and shrugged. "I didn't take out an ad in the paper or anything. Whose business is it? It's nobody's business."

"Well, at least it's nothing personal."

"The Invictus killed my ghoul and I should be glad it's nothing *personal*? Jesus Christ!"

"Vadim, do not blaspheme in my home."

The other vampire took a deep breath.

"I'm sorry, Bishop. I apologize. It's just… she was my best agent. Hardly anyone knew about her. She could move around without… well, you know how it is. I was *close* to her, you know? She…" He sighed and sat down. "Now she's gone."

"A grave injustice has been committed, Vadim, and I give you my assurance that you will have redress."

Vadim glanced up at him, and the low light of the 40-watt bulbs put a glint of cunning in his eye. "This is why I support you and will always support you."

"Your confidence is appreciated in these trying times. As a surety, why don't I have some friends of ours look into that automotive business of yours? I'm sure the police investigation is just a misunderstanding."

"You're sure, huh?" Vadim cracked a smile. It wasn't pretty.

"I'm sure that's how it will be seen. Does that salve your anger?"

"Absolutely. You, I take it, will negotiate some kind of settlement with the Invictus?"

"Consider it my problem now. My condolences on the loss of your servant, but all that is mortal…"

"…is dust, I know." Vadim stood and straightened himself. "As always, Bishop, your counsel is wise and just."

"You're sure I can't offer you that drink?"

"No, I'll be on my way."

When Hortense arrived to show Vadim out, Solomon asked after Margery in a low voice and was told the girl was nowhere to be found.

"We'll see about that," Solomon muttered, opening his laptop computer.

A half-hour later, Margery sat up suddenly when Solomon loomed over the top of her library carrel.

"What are you doing here?" she asked. "How did you find me?" He just smiled.

He watched as she involuntarily raised her arms across her body. It was a close and muggy night, but she suddenly had goosebumps.

"There is nowhere you can go that I can't find you," he said, neglecting to mention the tracking device sewn into her backpack. "I thought you were studying at home this evening."

"I... I came here to... to look up..."

"This is a college library. Can a high-school student even check out books here?"

"I was looking in... in the..." Margery flushed and looked up at him, glaring. "Why shouldn't I study here? Why shouldn't I go anywhere I like? Why should I be stuck under house arrest? How does it hurt you if I'm *just normal*?"

Solomon chuckled. "Margery, you could never be normal. Come, let's get some ice cream."

"No! Do you really think that your, your friendly uncle routine can *cut* it anymore? Do you think I'm just going to..."

"Shh, Margery. *Come with me and have some ice cream.*" This time his words were backed by occult power, and she wordlessly stood to obey.

After the first bite, she broke the spell and started frowning again, but this time she looked away.

"I thought I might have need of you tonight," Solomon said.

"I can't stop you," she muttered. "Here. Why not right here, right now? Come on, in front of everyone, why don't you?" She reached for the top button of her shirt, but ceased when Solomon made no move to stop her.

"Margery, I can't help being what I am. I can only attempt to make what peace with it that I can."

"Oh yeah, you're the victim."

"I give and give, and you resist and resist. We've fallen into quite a pattern."

"You *take*," she hissed. "You want my blood."

"But it's not about that, is it Margery? Hundreds of people, every day, donate blood to hospitals and think very little of it. They don't feel the shame you do. You do, don't you? Don't deny it, I see your blushes and misery. I don't think it's *that*." He leaned in, his predatory eyes instinctively prowling the busy ice-cream parlor where they sat in a corner booth. "I think you're revolted by the *pleasure*."

She looked away. "I want to be done with this."

"You are a Brigman, Margery. You will never be done with this. You have been given a higher destiny, one which weaker mortals could not bear. But you are not a weaker mortal. You are the finest that humanity has to offer."

"The finest *you* could build, you mean. Just how do you come off as humanity?"

"I tire of this pedantic niggling. Are you going to eat that?"

Petulantly, she crumpled a napkin and put it on the sundae.

"Fine." He stood. Dragging her feet, Margery followed.

In the car, he waited until a red light turned green to say, "You dislike being fed upon, which I can… understand, if not respect. Very well. I can, perhaps, offer you a compromise."

"What?"

"You think I'm a selfish monster who desires nothing so much as to maul your tender flesh," he said, pretending not to notice her reaction when he said 'flesh.' "But if you are unwilling, I think I have a proposal whereby you'd be able to defer my needs for some time."

"An 'option?' A 'proposal?' What do you mean?"

"You're maturing daily and I certainly wouldn't want to risk your strength for the nine months it would take to bring the next phase of my project to term."

At a red light, he coolly turned his head to her. Her mouth was gaping open.

"You want to get me pregnant?" she said. Her tone was curious, almost detached. It was like she was trying to muster up astonishment and repugnance, but was just too overwhelmed to be surprised any more.

"I've acquired some excellent material…"

"So it's time for the next phase of Operation Brigman. Just like that. I get no say?"

"If you feel unready, well, I respect that judgment. But given your distaste for the other duties of your family line, I thought this might be more to your liking."

"What will people say?"

"We'll tell your school friends that you're going abroad for a year or something like that. There needn't be any *scandal*, if that's what concerns you."

"Scandal?" She shook her head and gazed out the window as streetlights flicked by. "Unbelievable," she said. A tear trickled down her cheek. "Why don't you just have my father do it? Keep those 'Brigman genes' all in the family?"

"Now Margery, don't be vulgar. Or ignorant. You know as well as I do that incest produces aberrations. You wouldn't want a baby afflicted with hirsutism or supernumerary digits would you?" He looked over with a grin, as if hoping she'd share the joke. She kept staring out the window.

"No," he said. "As it happens, you'll be bearing a Fontaine baby. The Fontaines are as genetically gifted as the Brigmans, if not more so. Of course, the father can't acknowledge the child, as he is quite literally 'Father Fontaine.'" Solomon smirked at his own joke. "He's back down south now. He doesn't even remember his contribution to the betterment of humanity. To think that a plastic tube, frozen at a sperm bank, could hold such a promising future."

Margery kept staring out the window.

It was a complete coincidence that Aurora, Steve and Velvet all arrived at Perry's at the same time.

Velvet was there because the Four was playing, and she wanted to be early to make sure everything went smoothly. Steve was there to see Velvet, and he got there early to be sure he didn't miss her. Aurora was there for the same exact reason.

In one of those rare convergences, each of them got what he or she wanted.

Velvet tuned her instrument, nodded to the other three musicians, checked the sound, and saw Steve walk through the door. She smiled a little, excused herself, and went out to meet him.

Steve saw her coming and stopped, stock-still in the middle of a moderate crowd, and that made Velvet's smile widen.

Aurora came through a different door, so she saw Steve first and then Velvet's back. Instinctively, her hand went to her purse, but there was no way. There were too many people and, besides, she wasn't sure how Steve would react.

"I didn't think I'd see you again," Steve said as Velvet

stopped three feet from him.

"Funny, I was going to say the same thing." Then she saw a change in his face and spun just in time to stop Aurora in her tracks.

The redhead gave a little wave. The brunette replied with a little sneer.

"If this is an ambush, it's the worst one I've ever seen," Velvet said.

"Ambush? Hell no, don't be crazy. Tonight I'm just out for some jazz. After all, if I need to find you I've got your performance schedule, right? Or maybe I could just stake out Steve here and wait for you to come slinking around his window some night."

"Look, ladies, why don't we—"

"Why are you here, Steve?" Velvet interrupted him.

"Um, I'm... it's... do you two want to sit down?"

"Sure," Velvet said, batting her eyes. "As long as I get the wall to my back."

"Oh honey, anything I'd do to you I can do to your face," Aurora said, and in that spirit of suspicion they moved into a booth.

"Look," Steve said as they sat, "I think we all need to... um..."

"You're a vampire, aren't you?" Aurora asked. She kept her voice low and pleasant, kept the smile on her face.

"If you didn't think so, jumping me was pretty crazy. Why even ask? You've got those big mirror shades. Didn't you check my reflection? Don't you *know*?"

"I want to hear you say it. I want *him* to hear you say it."

"Fine." Velvet tossed her hair back and tilted her head. "I'm a vampire. What the hell are *you*?"

Aurora spread her hands, shrugged her shoulders.

"Ladies, please," Steve said. "Let's take it down a notch, huh?" They both turned to him, equally incredulous, and spoke simultaneously.

"Take it *down* a notch?"

"Steve, you can't be serious." Velvet quirked an eyebrow. "When we were talking, I got the impression you'd been searching for a way to... intensify."

"He doesn't need your kind of intensity," Aurora said.

"Why don't you let him decide?" She turned back to Steve. "I'm a blood-drinker, Steve. Isn't that exciting?"

He flushed bright red.

"Leave him alone," Aurora said. "I don't know what you did to him, but..."

"Did? You mean did I brainwash him? Hypnotize him with my voodoo powers? Maybe put the Evil Eye on him?" Velvet snorted. "I didn't have to do any of that. Did I Steve?"

"I don't know," he muttered, staring down at the table.

"All I did was give him a taste of what's real," Velvet said. "You, Red—I gave you a glimpse, too. But you'd already seen, hadn't you? What are you, really? Why can't you walk away from me? You know it'd be the smart move, if—*if*—I'm really the killer, the monster you think I am."

"Maybe if I don't stand up for him, there'll be no one left to stand up when you come for me."

"Nice line, Reverend Neimueller. But you don't know me. Aren't you the one judging me, judging all my kind, based on what little you've seen? One of us—one of my race, my clan—someone did something to you. I don't need the evil eye to see that. Stole your boyfriend maybe? Broke your heart? Something worse?"

"Much worse."

"You found out we're real—more real than your old life. You've seen a flicker in the dark and you think you've seen the whole thing." Velvet shook her head. "You have no idea. You're the Klansman who judges all blacks by the one who beat him out for a spot on the football team. You're the Nazi who wants to kill the Jews because he read *The Protocols of the Elders of Zion*, only in your case what was it? Brian Lumley? Or did you just rent *Lost Boys* one time too many?"

"Jews and blacks don't kill to survive. They don't have to *steal blood*. Or are you claiming you don't? Or maybe you just do it because you like to?"

"Ask Steve how horrible it was."

"I don't know much, but I know enough. I know what you are, what you need, what it makes you do. I know your *victims*.

That's more than enough. That's too much to pretend I don't see." Aurora was leaning forward on the table, her teeth pulled back, her hands clenched on the lip of her purse.

"Aurora, come on," Steve said. "Take it easy. That's enough."

"Aurora, huh?" Velvet smirked. "Pretty name."

"It means 'the dawn.' Dawn kills your kind, doesn't it?"

Velvet's smile widened. "How literal... You've both peeked behind the curtain a little. One of you wants to burn the theater down and the other..." She turned to Steve and he looked embarrassed, but as he met her gaze he became unfocussed, as if everything else in the room had become invisible, inaudible. "The other wants a seat for the show. Maybe even hopes to get up onstage."

"The difference is, I've seen the final act," Aurora said.

Velvet shook her head. "Steve's a grownup. He can decide if he wants more. I don't have to slink around his window." Her lip rose in a half-smile. "You ever read G.K. Chesterton? There's a line in there about how, 'I have tied him with a thread that is so thin it can't be seen, so long he can fly anywhere in the world without breaking it, and so strong that I can bring him back with but a single tug.' Of course, the speaker in that story was talking about *faith*. What I used on Steve was no trick. He can walk away and I'll leave him alone, I give you my word. But what I gave him was *truth*."

"What good is your word?" Aurora asked, but Velvet had already stood and started striding back toward the stage. Aurora turned to Steve, who was staring after the musician.

"You can't trust her."

"Look, I..." He tore his eyes away and tried to be comforting. "I can take care of myself."

"I have to get out of here, now. She's going to have someone on me soon, if they're not already coming. Come with me."

"I..."

Aurora looked at him and his eyes had drifted back to the vampire. After a moment, he met her gaze again, after Velvet had vanished behind the stage door.

The sorrow and pity he saw made him duck his head.

"Listen," Aurora said, and then stopped. "No," she said. "I

can't tell you. But I can show you. She's shown you her side. Come see mine. This Saturday. Keep your schedule open." She stood, looking around. "She's right. I don't know everything. But let me show you what I do know. What got me in."

With that, she hustled to the exit.

Beatrice Cartwright rolled her eyes and said, "No."

The man before her was handsome. He'd been a Rhodes Scholar, he wore an expensive suit. Once, in high school, he'd made the winning three-point shot of a basketball game with two seconds left on the clock. That night, three different girls had fellated him.

"There must be some way," he said. He was on his knees, sniveling. Begging didn't come naturally to him.

"You've become quite boring," Beatrice said.

"No, Dora, you've got to…" Beatrice had told him her name was Dora. "There's got to be something I can do. All I've done for you, doesn't that mean anything?"

"It means you've done all you can. It means you're done. We're done. Go back to your wife. She's prettier than me, isn't she? Isn't that true?"

"No, I don't care about *that*," he said.

"She loves you. I don't. Does that matter?"

"No."

Her cell phone rang and she reached into her purse.

"Dora, you can't…"

She silenced him with one upheld finger and spoke into the phone. "Hello? Yes… I'm almost done here." She listened for a moment. "Why don't you meet me in the parking lot?" She named the hotel and paused once more. "Yes. Okay. Bye." She closed the phone and turned back to her prey. He looked like each word on the phone had been a hammer-blow to his guts.

"Almost done?" he said, his voice bitter, and there was a trace of his old command, the old pride, the easy arrogance that had drawn Beatrice from the first, that had made her entice and challenge and, ultimately, break him.

"Yes," she said. She put the cell phone back into her purse. When her hand emerged there was a small black Beretta pistol in it. "This is for you."

He made no move to take it. "What on earth would I want with that?"

"Are you unhappy?"

He said nothing.

"Are you unhappy?" she repeated. "Have I made you unhappy? Made you miserable? I've made you commit adultery. You've embezzled on my behalf. You've lied. You've become a thief."

"Dora, I can make all that up, easy, and my wife doesn't know, she's never known."

"Come to me," she said, her voice suddenly soft. She opened her arms and he flowed into them eagerly. She dropped the pistol on the hotel-room bed and held him, kissed him. He was ardent, he was passionate. He crushed her body to his and then...

...then he became impatient. "Bite me," he whispered. "Please. Come on. Come on, Dora, take it. Take it away."

Her lips brushed his ear as she said, "No."

"Dammit!" He shoved her away hard enough that she struck the wall. Hard enough that there was a thud and a picture tilted. Hair mussed, Beatrice's gaze was neutral.

"Never again," she said, allowing her voice to be smug.

"I'm begging you!"

"The gun," she said. "You could use it on me. You could kill me. You could ease the burdens of the world by slaying a damned thing. You could make this world more pure, in a tiny but concrete way."

He just stared.

"I could never hurt you."

"Then perhaps you'll think of another use." She turned to the door, and when he grabbed her shoulder all it took to get him to let go was a cool glance.

In the parking lot, Xerxes Adrianopolous was leaning against a street lamp. He was wearing a natty brown suit.

"Did you hear thunder?" he asked as Beatrice strode up to

him. He looked up at the clear sky.

"It was a gunshot," she said, unlocking her BMW.

Beatrice picked a place at random on a map of Chicago. They discussed casual matters in the car, in case it had been bugged. When they reached the corner her idly stabbing finger had poked, it was desolate, empty under sepia streetlights, a closed coffee shop with a laundromat next to it and a check-cashing storefront above.

The vampires got out, looked down the streets and started talking.

"Have you heard about the Indulgence?" Xerxes asked.

Beatrice's eyes got even colder and she shook her head. "Who's proposing such a thing?"

Xerxes shrugged. "The Circle, the Carthians... the usual shit-stirrers. Does it matter?"

"It matters if we can stop this before it gains momentum. Who's pushing it?"

"I first heard about it in connection to a Carthian named Emily Elizabeth. A neonate, not tough to crack. I took a picture of her cousin, discussed Lancea philosophy as it relates to the corruption and ensnarement of the mortal soul, and suggested that a 15-year-old girl would have little defense against our methods. She blustered and threatened, and in the end wept and bargained. The Carthian had heard about it from someone in the Ordo Dracul, someone lowly like herself, and she was foolish enough to tell a similarly young and vulnerable member of our own covenant."

"Who came running to you."

"Wisely, yes." He smiled. "It's a dismal shame what they did to Solomon. He brought us so much obedience."

"One day he will recover and be stronger and greater for learning the truth about his slippery 'friend' the Prince. Until that time, we must protect him from himself."

"And protect ourselves from him, of course."

"Yes." She frowned. "Can we protect everyone from the

nightmare of an Indulgence, though? That's the question."

A squad car rolled down the street and stopped. For a moment, everyone was as still as a painting—the two dead, the car and the man inside. Then his engine purred and he rolled on, windows up, saying nothing.

Xerxes showed teeth in what would have been a smile on a living man. "Smart cop," he said. Beatrice grunted.

"Do you think we can prevent this thing from being proposed?"

He sighed.

"It's hard," he said. "It's out of the box now. If the barely cold neonates are chattering about it in the Circle, the Movement and the Order, you can be sure their masters and superiors are discussing it too."

"And with greater insight," she said. "Greater purpose."

"It sounds like the Invictus opposes it."

"Of course. They're holding the whip hand. Why would they want to change anything?"

"Can you think of a reasonable argument to turn the Acolytes and the Carthians against it?"

"We could argue that they shouldn't squander, uh, political capital on such a risky and uncertain gambit."

Xerxes shook his head. "The Circle thinks a mass Embrace, permitted by the Prince and the court, will gain them clout. They probably think we won't do any creating..."

"And we won't," she said sharply, glaring.

The glance he returned was cool. "I know what *you* believe about that," he said.

"What the *Bishop* believes."

"But will he be Bishop forever? Will he be Bishop next year?" Xerxes stroked his chin. "This will be distasteful to contemplate but... are you familiar with the concept of a 'wedge issue?'"

"Don't patronize me."

"The Indulgence is aptly named. Any number of our congregates would love an excuse to settle some final score against Kindred rivals, and I think a few would, if permitted, Embrace as well."

"Such a thing is unthinkable!" she said. "It's disgusting."

"Unthinkable to Solomon. Disgusting to you. But if you wish to unseat him—even for his own good—you might do well to appeal to the element that disagrees with his more stringent policies."

"Are you suggesting that I make an alliance with... with who, Sylvia Raines? With her posse of milk-livered hypocrites?"

"If I've learned anything from mortals, it's that you can never beat a politician by becoming exactly like him. I think you'll like it better if you hold your nose, ally with Raines and pretend to be a hypocrite than if Solomon falls and she rises into his place."

"She could never replace Bishop Birch."

"Don't underestimate her! She's not a powerful speaker like him, and she's not nearly as prominent at court, but she is the most powerful Theban sorceress in Chicago. Anyone of any skill at our most secret rites has studied with her." He tilted his head. "Even me," he said.

"You're not saying you agree with her policies."

"I agree with the Bishop."

Beatrice narrowed her eyes. "And if she was Bishop you would agree with her?"

Xerxes shrugged and looked at his watch. "I don't think we can talk the Circle out of pressing for an Indulgence. I don't think we can put the genie back in the bottle. It's an *issue* now. It's going to be proposed. If we can get the Carthians to pull out their support, it might fail, but pissing off the Acolytes is going to be a very tough sell—especially if it comes on top of 'please forego murdering every Invictus yahoo who's pissed you off since Maxwell took the throne.'"

"What about the Order?"

"Their strength is not in numbers and it doesn't lie in politics. Why would they get their hands dirty one way or the other? More likely they'll lay back and look for a way to capitalize on either decision." He straightened himself and looked her in the eye. "Speaking of which..."

She sighed. "If it goes through, what do we do?"

"Speaking as one of the Sanctified, it is always wrong when Kindred shed each other's blood. Speaking as a political officer within an embattled organization... well, I'd cry few tears if someone murdered that schemer Bella Dravnzie. Or any of those strange and fey Kindred who spend all their time sleeping under the Chicago River. If such a thing *were* to happen, of course, who would suspect the Lancea Sanctum? Who would think our officers would betray our own beliefs?"

"I think you drastically underestimate the cynicism of the average Kindred," Beatrice replied. "I think they have no trouble imagining our hypocrisies. Furthermore, every night we are ruled by a Bishop under vinculum, their suspicion of us deepens. And rightly so."

"If that's the case, you might want to think about how we can ply this issue to place someone more reliable and responsible in the mask and claws."

"We are then to endorse sin on behalf of our own righteous power? If we do so, in what way are we righteous?"

"I'll leave the weighing of such matters to you, the priestess. I'm just a cop or, if you prefer, a spy. I'm concerned with results."

With that, Xerxes opened the passenger door of her car and got in. Moments later, a bat of singular size and sinister aspect flew out of the open driver's side window and up into the night.

Earth Baines took the stairs two at a time, thinking that maybe tonight he'd ask Julia to take it up the ass. No, just tell her. Demand it.

Bitch is halfway in love with me, he thought. *She's all doped up on the blood loss. She'll do anything I tell her to.*

He knocked on the hotel-room door, heard the click as someone inside turned the lock, and pushed inward.

"Yo, trick," he said, and then stopped short as he realized the figure before him lacked Julia's voluptuous curves and cascade of dark, fragrant hair. Instead, this figure was bald, scarred, and definitely male.

Oh snap, he thought, and then Solomon Birch's eyes hit him like a runaway train as the Bishop of Chicago said, "*Freeze.*"

Baines heard the sound of the closing door but stood

stock-still as Solomon stood before him again, putting those killer .44 caliber eyeballs in Baines' view once more.

"*Sit on the bed until I'm done with you.*"

Fuck that bitch-ass buggity bullshit, Baines thought, but his feet toddled him over regardless. He not only sat, he folded his hands politely in his lap.

The leader of the Lancea Sanctum looked at him with his head tilted to the side.

"My congregate Vadim suggested that I stake you and dry-rub your body with fine sulfur dust. I wouldn't know—yet—but he insists that if you spark Kindred who have been so treated, the surface of their skin rapidly burns crispy black. Not fatal in any sense." Solomon smiled and tilted his head the other way. "*Answer my questions honestly, without getting off the bed or taking any violent action.* Do you even know who Vadim is?"

"No, man. Yo, what the fuck?"

"I really shouldn't let you ask questions, but you remind me—very, very slightly—of myself when I was young. Dumb and newly Embraced. However, I'm going to ignore any question that's vague and ignorant. Or that's prefaced with 'Yo.'"

"Who's this Vadim cat? What'd I do to him?"

"Vadim is sneaky, angry and very pious. You killed his ghoul."

"Naw, man, I don't know no ghoul of his. Shit, I don't even know *him*!"

"Gladys Plover."

This time, Earth said it out loud. "Oh snap."

Solomon blinked. "I don't know what that means," he said briskly, "But if it expresses dismay, you're on the right track. Gladys was his favorite ghoul and you dispatched her with what seems to have been undue drama."

"Yo, man, I was just doin' my job. That Gladys chick was outta control! She tried to kack Velvet. Y'know, Violet Metzenger? She's a bad ghoul! Your Vadim, shit, I did 'im a favor!" Earth took a deep breath, tilted his head to the side and cracked his neck. "Hell, I'm willing to let it slide that she was going apeshit on Kindred, now that, y'know, she's dealt with. S'all good, part of the job, a day's work. Just let him know he owes me one, awright?"

Solomon laughed out loud.

"I enjoy your chutzpah," he said. Seeing Baines' blank incomprehension, he clarified. "Your big brassy balls...You're up to your nose in shit, but you're still looking for the pony. That's an admirable quality." He put a finger on his cheek. "When, exactly, did this alleged attack occur?"

Baines told him. Solomon shook his head. "Poor lost lamb, she should have come to me. How did you arrive at the conclusion that Ms. Plover was the culprit?"

"Velvet called the cops on her. Cops wrote down a license plate. Shit, I go to her house an' she's got a wooden stake. I did the math, yo."

"Perhaps you weren't as half-cocked as it initially appeared. Though eliminating a suspected witch-hunter without a thorough interrogation."

"Man, I interrogated the *shit* outta her!"

"Oh, really? You, what, battered and assaulted her and asked her a few questions? Then, when she told you what you wanted to hear, you killed her?"

Earth resisted, but the compulsion to answer honestly was too strong for him. "Uh... well, I guess..."

"Primitive methods like that never work. Oh my heavens, you're not even a Sheriff, are you?"

Again, the compulsion. "I ain't officially been put up for it..."

"You're a Hound and they set you on this scent because someone... Norris? Stingo? I suppose it doesn't matter. Someone thought, 'It's the Lancea, we can do a half-assed job,' and they sent *you*."

"Hey now!"

"They sent you, figuring that we were unwilling to kill other Kindred, no matter how useless..."

"I ain't useless!"

"Oh, I'm sure you're the cat's pajamas when it comes to... what's the phrase they use these days? When it comes to 'Laying the smack down' upon some hapless wayward servant. But for the finer work of Kindred investigation?" Solomon shook his head. "You've made a terrible enemy in Vadim."

Earth shrugged. "Let him bring it."

"Oh, he won't jump you from an alley shouting 'booga booga' and swinging a tire iron. Maybe he'll just find your feeding vessels, as easily as I found Julia, and he'll infect them." For a moment, Solomon's eyes got positively vicious and Earth found something inside him fighting an urge to cringe and whine like a rope-whipped dog. Then it passed and Solomon was back in the moment. "Maybe he'll start by junking your car, or by burning down that haven you keep down in Soxville. Or just maybe, he'll follow you around for a couple months, or a couple *years*, until he knows all your hiding holes, all your secrets, all he needs about your afterlife to utterly ruin everything."

Earth felt that scalp-prickle common to everyone who has secrets, but it was nothing compared to the scare he got when an ugly, elongated face darted in inches from his own and a thick nasty voice said, "You'll never even see it coming."

"JAYZUS!" Earth bounded away on reflex, flailing his arms to keep the apparition back. There hadn't been anyone but Solomon in the room, he'd have sworn it.

But no, this asshole's one of those ugly fuckers, like Aaronson. He's got the spooky-boojums to hide in plain sight.

"Mr. Baines, meet Vadim Siorkov."

"I bet it wouldn't take me six months, either," Vadim said.

"Look man, I'm sorry. The thing was a misunderstanding."

"It's fine, Vadim. Why don't you let the 'Sheriff' and me continue our chat?"

The ugly dead man looked between the pair and gave a wet chortle.

"The good Bishop has bought you out," Vadim said. Then he turned to Solomon. "You say the word and I'll pounce on him."

"I'm sure Mr. Baines is far too reasonable for that." Solomon smiled benignly as Vadim wiggled his lengthy fingers in an over-cute wave. And then he was suddenly gone.

Earth jerked his head to the right and left, now thoroughly unnerved. "What was that about?"

"Vadim and I decided that you owe him. I felt that you two would be untenable as a working pair—personality conflicts—and I assumed the burden of your debt to him by smoothing over some small but irksome matters that need not concern you. This means that your debt to him defers to me."

"Wha?"

Solomon sighed. "Very well, I'll explain again in small words and I'll speak very slowly." He leaned in. "You're... my... bitch."

———

Velvet and the rest of the Thanatos Quartet were practicing in Danielle's home when the door buzzed. With an impatient sigh, Danielle rose and went to the speaker grille. When she came back, she gestured to Peter and Mark. "We're going," she said.

"What is it?" Velvet asked, standing with the others.

"The Bishop is visiting and wishes to speak with you."

"I'm sure you can..." But they were already heading for the door. They all paid their respects as Solomon Birch entered, smiling, nodding his head. Tonight he was dressed in slacks, loafers, and a conservative navy sports coat over a lavender polo shirt.

Earth Baines shuffled in behind him, wearing a Marshall Faulk jersey over baggy FUBU jeans and immaculately white puffy sneakers. As usual, his neck was heavily blingified.

Velvet slowly put down her instrument. "What can I do for you gentlemen?"

"I understand you were attacked," the Bishop said. "I was concerned."

Velvet was pretty sure he'd never even spoken directly to her before.

"And Mr. Baines...?" she asked.

Earth shrugged and gave her a hood-eyed stare. "Me and the Bish are teamin' up, yo. Gettin' to the bottom things."

Solomon laughed. It sounded like a large dog barking. "Yes," he said, eyes twinkling. "I'm Crockett and he's Tubbs. Now, tell me everything."

"You've heard about the first attack, right? Well, a couple nights ago I saw her again," Velvet said.

"What?" Solomon said, turning on Baines with his eyes

wide and round, a perfect burlesque of surprise. "I understood
you'd killed her attacker."

Baines just sighed and looked at the floor, fists clenched.

"Did she say anything to you?"

"Not too much. She said she wasn't going to back down, that
she'd 'seen too much.'"

"Then, I imagine, she backed down?"

"She left, yes." Velvet smoothed a strand of hair behind her
ear. "I think I've got her measure now. I don't really consider
her a threat. She got the drop on me once, but that won't happen
again."

"She knows about us, yo. She's a Masquerade failure."

"My inarticulate friend raises a cogent point. Even if she
herself is little threat, she might *tell*. She might wander out one
sunshiny *day* and inform someone whom you would not see
coming, someone who would finish you and then possibly go
on to educate the masses about the rest of us."

At that point, Velvet almost opened her mouth and told
them everything. Almost told them Aurora's name (well—first
name), almost gave them the full description imprinted on her
mind after the staredown in the bar, almost told them about
Steve and his uncertain connection to the vampire hunter... but
something stopped her.

Perhaps it was some stirring of predatory instinct. Perhaps
a deep bloody level inside her had tagged Aurora as *her* prey,
and like a dog growling over a bone was unwilling to let go.
Maybe it was a simple, pragmatic caution: Solomon Birch wasn't
known for anything resembling a 'proportionate response,' and
Earth Baines clearly wasn't the smartest hat on the rack. A very
practical part of her worried that the two of them could get
along like gasoline and fire.

Then too, there was Steve. Steve was... sweet, and *living*, and
clearly had a thing for her that she could snack off like a buffet
for a long time, years if she was careful. He could be something
good in her long undead span, but to Baines and Birch, vampire
detectives, he'd just be a disposable source they could wring out
for clues and then discard when he stopped yielding.

Maybe it was pride, making her stubborn and unwilling to

admit she wasn't up to the challenge. Maybe it was the weary Kindred certainty that both Baines and the Bishop would try to claim she owed them one if they found and killed Aurora.

Just possibly, it was something deeper still. Something from her mortal days, something almost romantic, some longing for things, people or events that *meant* something. Some instinctive need that had led her to the elegant structures of music, that made her want to be a part of the Aurora story up to the end, even if the end was tragic. Aurora was a pest and a menace and an irritating puzzle, but Velvet had been dead a long time without anything nearly so interesting coming along. To hand the whole situation off to the menacing Bishop Birch and the ham-fisted Sheriff Baines wouldn't just feel like cowardice, it would go... unfinished. It would all become pointless. Absurd.

All those competing drives and viewpoints sprang into Velvet's mind in an instant. But they weren't really competing, they were in agreement, which was why she coolly shrugged, looked at the pair—one big and one enormous—and said, "I don't know what more I can tell you. She's alive, she's out there, and she hasn't brought the whole thing crashing down yet."

Solomon looked at her for a long moment. Earth looked from her to the Bishop and then back.

"If anything else develops," Birch said at last, "let me know immediately."

"Shouldn't I tell the Sheriff here?"

Solomon shrugged. "It all comes out to the same thing, since we're working together now. You're a friend of Sylvia's, aren't you?"

Velvet felt a cold trickle of fear down her back. One didn't need to be a Lancea backroom insider to know about the friction between Solomon and Sylvia. Nonetheless, she said she was.

"Give her my regards. Ask her to keep me in her prayers," Solomon said.

She probably prays that your house gets hit by a meteor, Velvet thought, but she said, "I'll do that."

When they were gone, even though she didn't need to breathe, she gave a great sigh of relief.

"...and then he said I was his *bitch*," Earth said. "Now he's riding me like this is porno and he's Ron Jeremy."

"Wow," Aaronson said. "It must really suck to be at the mercy of some enormous prick who treats you like his slave just because he can."

"True dat," Earth said, either deliberately ignoring his captive's sarcasm or being too distracted to parse it out. He shook his head and said, "The Bish is *on* me, man. He's on me like badonka on J. Lo."

"Yeah..." Aaronson said, not even bothering to try and understand. "Well, okay. You ready for the next lesson?"

"First, I gotta ask you something." Earth focused his attention and gave Aaronson a shrewd look. "You know all this no-see-um mojo? How come you didn't use it when I got the drop on you?"

The captive shifted, looking away. Perhaps he was embarrassed. "I didn't have time to put it up," he said.

"Umm, look man, I just met this guy Vadim who's got his Obfuscatin' going *on*. I didn't *see him*, even in a little hotel room, until he was up in my grille. You know what I'm sayin'?"

"Vadim Siorkov? Ooh, he's not anyone to mess around with."

"Yeah, I *clued* up on that. What I'm sayin' is, he just fuckin' de-materialized in front of me, like a ninja without the little smoke bomb, just *gone*. And I got a pretty clear recollection of collaring you without you doing anything nearly that slick."

Aaronson turned his head side to side. "It's not as easy as you think," he whined.

"If you could really do that, really just go poof, how come you haven't just done it when I come to see you, then run through the door while I'm rubbing my eyes?"

The prisoner said nothing.

"You can't do it, can you?" Baines grabbed him by the shoulders and shook him. "*Can you?*"

"Okay, hey, watch the material! You're right, fine, I... yeah, I can't. I hid from the other Sheriffs and Hounds because I can hide pretty good without *needing* the power." He shrugged. "I'm a sneaky guy. But, yeah, I never learned that far. I just faked it and, you know, wore dark clothes and stood still a lot. There's still some stuff I can teach you, though!"

"Uh huh," Baines said. "Well, you sure know how to hide your *lies* well enough, but I think I've learned about all I'm gonna from you. I can't have you around here. Can't risk Solomon finding you and getting another hook in my butt."

Aaronson's face lit up. "Hey man, the road's long but it's all good. I'll be in Gary before sunup, and I swear it the next night I'll be as far as Indianapolis. I'll be out of your hair like forever, man. You'll never hear from me again."

"Look, Aaronson…"

"Or since you did so right by me, since you saved me from this hunt I'll… here, I'll fix you up, sweeten the deal. I got this block of primo hash hidden away…"

"Man."

"Unstepped stuff, Baines. C'mon, man, it's…" But Aaronson had read the decision in Baines' posture, stopped begging and lunged.

The captive was desperate, but Baines was braced for a charge and was bigger and stronger. His fist swept out. Backhand. Aaronson had his arms up to protect his head, but the blow was still strong enough to stagger him, to ruin his momentum. He tried again, this time with eyes wild and fangs gaping. He shrieked and spat and clutched and bit, but before he could sink his teeth in, Baines had picked him up in a fireman's carry and flung him into the corner. Aaronson scrambled to his feet, but Baines flooded himself with blood, burning like gasoline to propel him. He was just a blur that swirled around the door and slammed it shut. Aaronson crashed into it, clawing and hammering. On the other side, Baines heard only muffled thumps.

"Sorry-ass punk," he muttered. He thought one more time about dragging Aaronson before the Prince and getting some kind of reward, but he couldn't think a way around getting ratted out. He was pretty sure Aaronson would sink into the big sleep within 48 hours—probably the next night. Then

Baines could come back and bury him alive or stake him or, hell, just leave the door locked and let Aaronson be someone else's problem. Baines didn't think anyone was going to come poking around. The room was in the basement of a slum with an absentee landlord. The locks were thick and the place had a bad reputation, based mostly on the presence of Earth himself.

I'll come get him when the heat dies down, Earth told himself, not letting himself think about Aaronson being trapped, slumbering in the nightmares of death until Baines got around to freeing him.

Chapter Six

Steve chewed his fingernails until he heard a car horn. He looked out the window—a window he'd peeked from only a few minutes earlier—and saw Aurora behind the wheel of a blue Ford Taurus. Swallowing hard, he picked up his gym bag.

"Is this a new car?"

"I borrowed it from a friend," she said, giving him a look. She didn't pull out.

"What?"

"How'd it go at Perry's after I left?"

Steve almost took the cue from her voice and ducked his head with shame, but didn't. He was used to confrontational insinuation. He was a teacher.

"You missed a good set. Better than the first time we heard them, I think."

Aurora shook her head as she pulled out into traffic. "You're unbelievable, you know that?"

"What?"

"You remind me of this kid I met once. One time I was out with... I was walking around this little downtown area and this kid comes up all hysterical and crying, right? He'd lost his mom."

"And I remind you of him? Thanks a lot."

"Forget it."

"What."

"No, forget it."

But Aurora couldn't forget it. The kid had been at his mom's office and had wandered out of the building and gotten locked out, and because he wasn't allowed to cross the street by himself he hadn't been able to go to a phone or find anyone. He could have walked into any restaurant or shop, but there was no place open on that side. It was a lazy Sunday afternoon with no one around until Aurora and Valerie saw him and helped him, called the cops and sat him down until they arrived. No big thing for a grown-up, but the kid had been utterly terrified. Until the night she rescued Steve, Aurora hadn't seen anyone else that was that utterly terrified.

Except Valerie, but Aurora didn't like to think about that.

"Steve, she is a *vampire*. Do you even get that? She's a vampire! *She* is a vampire. I don't know how else I can get it through to you that…"

"She deserves to be killed without mercy?"

"I'm pretty sure she's already been killed without mercy." She shook her head. "You'll just have to see."

"See what?"

Her head kept shaking.

As they reached the city's edge, the gas stations started to thin out and the prices began to drop. She pulled over before they got on I55 and said, "You gotta go? I'm going to go."

"I'll get some snacks. What're you drinking?"

When they started off again, Aurora seemed to thaw a bit. She had a Diet Coke with Lime. He'd grabbed an overpriced Starbuck's mocha bottle and there was a bag of Combos on the armrest between them. A few miles passed and their fingertips would occasionally touch as they reached into it.

"Okay, I gotta ask you something," Steve said. "I've been wondering this since that first night."

"Shoot."

"Would you really have done it?"

"Done what?" She glanced over at him and he raised his eyebrow with a half-smirk. She laughed. In fact, she laughed hard enough that Combo crumbs rebounded off the steering wheel's airbag plate.

"You're thinking about *that*?"

"Well, yeah. Must be the warmth of the car, the, uh, vibration of the road."

"Jesus Christ. You have a name for your penis?"

"Excuse me?"

"I hope you do, 'cause it's always good to be on a first-name basis with the boss." She stole another sideways glance from the highway. "I guess I would have, yeah. You seem clean. I might have done it, *if* I thought it was the only way to keep you away from her."

"Oh, so it would've been for my own protection?"

"Yep."

"So manipulative!"

"It's a poontangled web we weave."

Then it was his turn to laugh and snort.

"I'm sorry," Aurora continued. "Would that rob it of all the pleasure?"

"I think it might actually add a fun, kinky edge to it. Oh, hey look, there's a Motel 8 at the next exit!"

"Sorry, pal. You lost your chance when you believed I was a ho."

"I never..." She shot him a warning glance and he shut his mouth. "Okay, maybe for a few minutes." There was a pause. Then the pause stretched out.

"I'm sorry for that," he said after about a mile.

"Hey, who can blame you?" In the post-laugher lull, Aurora's voice sounded tired. "I'm still waiting for you to thank me, you know."

"Yeah?"

"Yeah. You know. For saving your life? That thing?"

"You really think she'd have killed me?"

"I didn't want to find out."

He nodded. "Okay, thanks."

"You're welcome."

"But I think you're wrong about her."

"I'm not."

Another mile. Traffic was getting heavy.

"How did you find out about her?"

"I'd been working the clubs. Remember those mirror shades? I used those, looked for messed-up reflections."

"They really don't cast reflections?"

"They... they kinda do, but they're blurry. *Wrong.* If you

know what you're looking for you can spot it. If you don't think about it, it's just... you know. How much do people really pay attention to mirrors?" She frowned. "That asshole in the sport-ute sure doesn't." She honked and flicked him off.

"It's a truck, I think."

"Cadillac makes a *truck*? That thing looks about as legit as a cowboy with a feather boa and pearl earrings."

"And the payments on it are probably more than our rents combined." Steve shifted, reached in the Combos bag and then crumpled it when he found it empty. "Was she the first one you spotted, that way?"

"Yeah. There were a lot more where I just couldn't be sure. You know? Smoke, everyone's moving around, dim light..."

"How many do you think there are?"

"Worldwide or in Chicago?"

"In Chicago?"

She chewed her lip.

"I've been reading the papers, looking for stuff on mysterious deaths and stuff... I don't know. There could be a lot. Maybe as many as 20 or 25."

"Wow."

Steve was quiet and Aurora wondered if he was finally grasping how serious all this was, until he asked another question and revealed what was really on his mind.

"How did you find out about them?"

Aurora took a deep breath. She'd been expecting this, eventually.

"I had a daughter," she said.

Steve swallowed. "Had?" She could barely hear him over the rumble of tires on blacktop.

"Still have her, I guess. I mean they didn't..." She gave a cold, mirthless chuckle. "They haven't killed her yet, is what I was going to say. They don't really need to. I don't have custody anymore."

"I'm sorry," Steve said, but she didn't pause for his words. She kept right on going.

"She... her name is Valerie and she ran away. A while back she took off." Aurora almost brought up Ian Browden, almost told Steve that Ian had been hitting her daughter when Aurora wasn't around, almost mentioned her sister Andrea who'd always said you could put Aurora in a room full of men and she'd beeline for the biggest jerk. "She ran off. I don't know what happened to her. The police found her in Chicago." She took a deep breath. "There was this guy, this... this sex offender. He was on the registry and she'd *gone* to him."

"Christ," Steve whispered, and he hoped it would make her stop, but she didn't.

"His name was Pete Staggers and he disappeared the night Valerie showed up." Aurora swallowed, keeping her eyes resolutely on the road. "I think he was one of them."

There was a pause, and Steve knew she was waiting for him to ask 'What happened?' He didn't want to say it, he didn't want to know.

"What happened?"

"It's... it's not clear. She showed up at a gas station, crying and screaming. She described Pete Staggers to the cops, said she'd gotten away from him. They looked her over. She'd been choked, there were these big bruises on her neck? But she hadn't been raped."

Steve was leaning against the door and felt ashamed, not even for anything he'd done, but just ashamed to be alive.

"How old was she?"

"She was 16 when it happened."

Like a reflex, Steve almost told her she didn't look old enough to have a teenage daughter. He stopped himself just in time and then he had a reason to be ashamed of himself, ashamed that he was still, on some level, trying to get in her pants even as she was telling him about her daughter's tragedy.

"The cops said Staggers' house looked like... like a butcher shop, blood all over the basement. And Valerie's bus got in almost five hours before she showed up at the gas station. She said she went right to his... right to the house, but there are all those missing hours. They brought her back and she started therapy and she... that's when they took her away from me. They said it was just temporary, just a foster home..."

Now Aurora was crying and Steve said, "Do you want to pull over?"

She nodded, put on her blinkers and pulled off by another gas station. She parked in a far corner while the sun beat through the windows. With the engine off, she started to cry.

"I didn't fight it," she said. "I... there was this other stuff, from when I was younger, but I wanted to, y'know, show them I was cooperating. And she was so... Valerie was so messed up I didn't know what to do. I gave up. I gave her up."

Steve fumbled in a pocket for a handkerchief.

"They... the therapist kept... and Valerie started having nightmares. I'd see her? Like, on weekends? At first these supervised things and she was okay. She wanted to come home and I told her I'd gotten rid of Ian and..."

Steve took a breath to ask who Ian was, but Aurora's words kept tumbling out. He didn't have an opening.

"And then we were out alone at, like, the mall. We could go to public places and she started telling me about her nightmares. She started telling me about *them*."

"Them?"

"A monster in a parka... and a man in a scarf, a man whose mouth was all needles. There was a woman, too, and... and that was almost the worst, because the men scared her but the woman... Valerie sounded like she *loved* her. She said she trusted her, that the woman had made everything all right."

For a moment, they were quiet in the car, humid from Aurora's tears.

"She said the woman's eyes... swallowed her, but she liked it. Steve, she liked being swallowed. *Does that sound familiar?*"

Steve flinched. Aurora had reared her head up and her red eyes glared at him, her hands clutching his handkerchief like a ligature, white-knuckled.

"You think Velvet did something to your daughter?"

"Her," Aurora said coldly. "Or *something* just like her."

Steve met her eyes and opened his mouth, then closed it again. As suddenly as it had come, Aurora's anger seemed to drain. She looked back at the wheel and took a deep breath. She blew her nose again.

"Where is Valerie now?"

"She's in a lockdown ward. She was having... they called them 'episodes.' That's a word for you. She was throwing things, screaming, crying, freaking out, clawing her own face, banging her head, saying there were too many memories. The foster parents couldn't handle her and the state put her away. They put her on Prozac, Xanax, some of those other middle-manager drugs. When those didn't work they tried Thorazine."

"Aurora, I'm..."

"Now she's a zombie."

"I'm sorry. I'm really, really sorry."

"Oh, but there's more." Once more those red eyes were on him, now in a blank face, eyes like red rips in white paper. "One night, I went to visit her at the hospital. I got off work late. My manager made me stay and I gunned the engine all the way there. I got pulled over and had to talk my way out of a ticket and got there after visiting hours had ended. If you don't have a child of your own, this might be hard to understand, this next part. But I'd been looking forward to seeing her all day. Even drugged out and... and you can't imagine how much that *hurts*, seeing your baby girl like that... not seeing her was even worse. It was like a hole..."

Aurora's face crumpled and she looked away, wiping her eyes again, but she took a deep and unsteady breath before continuing.

"So they told me I had to come back later and I... I just wouldn't take no for an answer. There was this security guard on duty and I *convinced* him to let me see my daughter." She took a deep breath and she looked out the window away from Steve.

Something in her tone, some loathing deep enough for herself and for everyone else gave Steve a pretty good idea of how she'd persuaded him.

"When I was... I... I went down the hall to her... to where they kept her and I heard a voice coming from inside. It was dark in there, except for those red Exit signs and a few dim fluorescents. I wasn't supposed to be there so I tiptoed. I crept up and I heard this voice, this man's voice saying, 'There's no such thing as vampires. You know that Valerie. You will forget everything about vampires. There are no vampires, Valerie. They don't exist.' And then I heard him say, 'Give me your neck.'"

Even with the sun beating down on the roof of the Taurus, Steve shivered.

"I ran in. I didn't know what I was going to do, but I ran in and saw him. I saw him *feeding* on her." Aurora turned her face back to Steve and this time she was really looking at *him*, not looking through him into a sad past. She reached over and took his hand. "It was just like when Velvet was feeding on you."

He squeezed her fingers. "What did you do?"

"I screamed and I… I think I tried to hit him… but then there was just this blur and he was gone. He just vanished and I hugged Valerie and she had these two marks on her neck." She reached up and touched Steve on the throat. "Yours are almost gone," she whispered.

He drew back, covering the tiny scabs with his hand.

"There was a big commotion, of course. The security guard. I got out, told him I'd rat on him for letting me in, told him we both wanted to keep it quiet and he agreed."

She buckled her seatbelt and started the car.

"I called in sick the next day and I wound up losing that job, but I found him."

"Where was he?"

"I'll show you."

They didn't talk much until they were skirting Joliet. They spoke, but it was about trivial things. Their jobs. What was on the radio. Stopping for lunch—they went to a drive-thru, neither was hungry but they both felt an unspoken need to keep their strength up. They were driving through a rusted-out neighborhood on the border between a disused industrial area and the rustic acres of factory farms. Workers had once lived there. Now, Steve guessed, the people who lived there didn't work. The houses were small bungalows with peeling paint, here and there a bigger, older house, a diner or a closed-down grocery store.

"He was here?"

"I followed and watched him," Aurora said. "At first I couldn't believe what I'd seen and I thought *I* was cracking up."

"That's understandable."

She turned to glare at him and he raised his hands.

"Um, what I *meant* was, you know... it's a crazy *situation*, it's a crazy *thing*, not that you've been acting. I mean, you're just, like adapting to, to what you experience and to someone on the outside."

"Okay, I get it."

"It made sense when I was thinking it."

"We're here."

She'd pulled in behind a boarded-up gas station.

"He had another place," she said, "but I burned him out of it. That was after I'd started carrying a mirror. After I'd seen him feed a couple times."

"You didn't try to...?"

"Stop him? Of *course* I tried to stop him. I called the fucking *cops* on him. And then I got to see him put his brain-freeze shit on them and feed off *them*, too. He wound up making them arrest *me*."

"Holy crap."

She shrugged. "A night in the lockup, big deal. The next day they let me go and said they were giving me a 'warning.' Said there was no grounds for a complaint, but I could tell they were embarrassed. He'd told them some bullshit—like that I was a whore, maybe?—and the next day it just up and evaporated. But by then he figured I wasn't a problem. Or maybe he was planning to come and get me, too, only I flushed him out. I made him run during the day and I tracked him to his backup bolt-hole." She jerked her thumb.

"And that's here." Steve found that his mouth was suddenly dry.

"That was here. I got him when he was sunburned and crispy and out of it and I put the stake in him. And I *thought* that was the end of it." She got out, shouldered her bag and slammed her door. Steve wanted to stay put, but he found himself following.

"It didn't… what? Why wouldn't that…?"

She shrugged. "Now I find out they turn to dust when they're really done. A stake just hits the 'pause' button."

The back door was padlocked, but the lock wasn't all the way in. A tug from Aurora's hand and it came open.

Inside, lit by the cracks of light that sheared through the gaps between the window boards, they found a decaying counter and a litter of cigarette butts, beer cans, chip bags and condoms.

"Fuckin' teenagers," Aurora muttered. "They have no idea." She bent down and started messing with the floor. She looked up at Steve. "Lil' help here?"

He bent and soon discovered a panel, disguised with dirty linoleum, that they heaved up with some grunting. Beneath it was a broken-edged gap in the concrete foundation, leading to a raw-earth hole shored up with four-by-four wooden boards.

Aurora reached in a pocket and pulled out glow sticks. She snapped and shook them, then dropped a few down. Their sickly green light revealed that the tunnel went only a few feet under the ground and then turned, running parallel to the surface.

"We'll have to crawl," Aurora said. "Now you see why I told you to bring a change of clothes." She started down as Steve turned on his flashlight. He shone it down on her and realized that she was crouching at the bottom and screwing a silencer onto the barrel of a pistol.

"You think we'll need that?"

"If I don't, it means he got out and we're screwed," she said, then started crawling.

Steve took an almost atavistic moment to look at her ass as she went down the passage—as if his instinctive lust was a touchstone to draw him back to reality—and then he followed.

In the dank of the enclosure, even he couldn't find anything appealing about the situation, despite his proximity to Aurora's backside. From the green backlighting of her hair, he guessed she had a glow stick in her mouth and one in her left hand. She spat out the first after crawling about 20 feet, and he could see a right-hand turn.

"This is it," she said. "This used to be the big underground gas tank. Don't worry about fumes. I'm pretty sure Drac in here is just as scared of fire as we are."

She turned and crawled and he followed into a steel tank. It was six feet in diameter and she'd rotated until she was crouching again, her back against one curving wall, pointing her gun at a dead man.

"Still here," she whispered. She didn't dare glance back at Steve, but she said, "Get a good look. Here's what they *really* are."

Steve crawled into the cramped chamber and scrambled to his feet. He could see a figure, all skin and bones, clad in a dirty doctor's jacket. It looked more like a bundle of sticks bound in white cloth than anything alive. He moved closer almost against his will. It was curled in the fetal position and he could see its hands, its face… they looked like dried autumn leaves. There, in the middle of it, was a stake. Steve had never seen a dead body before, had never been so close.

He reached out and pulled the stake free.

"What are you doing?" Aurora howled, but she was drowned out by a cry, a mewling whine, a shriek that was loud and eerie. Yet Steve sensed a human element to it.

The dead man's eyes and mouth sprang open at the same time. Withered hands grabbed Steve. Its breath was like forest mold as it lunged at him.

Steve shoved it back. He stumbled and slid and it came after him, but he got his legs up and kicked it away again. He was shocked at how easy it was. He'd expected inhuman strength, unstoppable undead might but this thing, it was weak, it was like breaking up a fight between children on a playground.

"Get back!" Aurora shrieked. *"Gimme a clear shot!"*

Something in her voice got through to it, and it paused. For just a moment, there was a glint of human cunning in those animal eyes, and its lips twitched as it grunted, "R-Ricochet?"

Steve scrambled back and it twitched after him, but restrained itself, fighting its instinct as Aurora realized that, yeah, firing a bullet in a tiny metal chamber might be a bad idea.

Just as she hesitated, just as she started to find this thing the least bit pathetic, it charged Steve again.

"No!" Aurora ducked her head and fired, and even with the silencer on, the sound was loud in the enclosed capsule. The smell of gunpowder was overwhelming. The vampire howled again as its thirst changed to terror of the pistol's flash. It wrenched past them and charged mindlessly up the tunnel. Aurora turned but her feet slipped from under her. She tumbled into Steve and by the time she got free, the creature was rapidly squirming its way down the dirt corridor.

"You dumbfuck," she said to Steve before turning and crawling after it. He heard another muffled gunshot and more screams as he dug his hands and knees into the soil.

He almost butted Aurora as he tried to see around her in the hole's cramped and chaotic confines. The creature had stopped at the tunnel's end, crouching where it turned upward toward the entrance. It was lit from beneath by the first green glow stick. It was moaning, twisting its head side to side and clutching itself... and then, with visible effort, it regained its composure. Its posture changed from the straining crouch of a cornered animal to the huddle of a pleading human.

"I can't go up in the light. Just... put the stake back in. I don't care. I wasn't hurting anyone down here. Please. *Please.*"

In the muffled enclosure, Steve heard a metal click. He figured it was Aurora pulling the hammer back on her gun.

"Who sent you?" Steve asked. "How did you find out about her daughter?"

"Who?"

"*Valerie,*" Aurora spat. "Who told you?"

"No one... uh, I didn't, it's... I can't..."

"Tell me or I'll drag you into the sun."

"Okay, but gimme your word! You swear?"

"I swear."

"If I tell you, you let me go?"

"If I tell you," Aurora replied, "you go back in the hole with the stake."

Looking at the gun, glancing up at the dim shafts of light, the desperate creature apparently decided the offer was better than the alternative. Still, it tried for assurances.

"Swear to God? Swear to the Almighty that you'll just stake me again and go on your way?"

"I swear it before God the Father and Jesus Christ," Aurora said.

"Okay." It clicked its teeth and crept a little bit closer. "The Bishop sent me."

"Who's the Bishop?"

"The *Bishop*, Solomon Birch! Solomon Birch sent me, all right? He got wind that this dumb bitch had fucked up some little girl's head, did a half-ass job maybe, and sent me to keep track of the girl. Yeah, shit, her name was Valerie, she's the one. He sent me to take care of her. Not to kill her! He thought... I don't know what he thought. Maybe he was planning to keep her for blackmail, you know, evidence."

"Who was the first one?" Aurora asked. "Who messed up her head? Who did it?"

"I swear I don't know. I swear it on the Lance!"

"This Bishop Solomon guy, where can I find him?"

"I can't tell you that!"

"You sure?" She moved her hand, and the red laser dot moved from his chest across his eye, making him flinch and wince.

"I can't tell you!"

"Then I guess you're useless," she said, and pulled the trigger.

"Jesus Christ!" Steve yelled, and then he saw what she meant about them turning to dust.

They crawled up out of the tunnel and were both filthy. Sandy soil coated their backs and the knees of their jeans. Their hands were dirty to the wrists.

For a moment they just looked at one another. Then they opened their satchels and wordlessly started to change. Steve turned his back and felt no urge whatsoever to peek.

"Here," she said, and her voice was inhuman, disconnected. "I brought some Wet Naps." Those were the only words either spoke until they were back on the highway.

"I can't believe you just shot him," Steve said at last. He was looking out the window, not at her, so he didn't even see it coming when she reached across the seat and slapped him.

"Ow!" He turned and raised his hands, but she was holding the steering wheel again, turning from traffic only briefly to glare at him.

"You *shithead*! Do you have any idea what you nearly did? You could have killed us both and now you're bitching? I should have just left you there, let that freak drain you dry before you could fuck up anything else for me!"

"Hold on now!"

"I can't *believe* you pulled out the goddamn stake! What the hell were you thinking?"

"I don't know," he said. He shrugged, working his way back into the corner where the seat met the door. "I guess it didn't seem real. I couldn't believe it. I had to find out for sure."

"Oh for... Do you believe *now*? Or are you, like, going to have to touch every flame we pass to make sure fire is hot?"

"I believe," he said. "I guess I'm still shocked that you just... I mean..."

"I shot him and I'd do it again. Hell, how could I have let him stay there? Sooner or later someone would have bought that old piece of crap and dug him up. Then he'd have been doing it again. I did the world a favor."

"You don't sound too sure."

"I *am* sure. Maybe *you're* not sure. Maybe you're not sure whether these things are monsters or people. If you don't know the difference even now—even *now*—I don't think I can help you any more."

"Did you help me today?"

"I showed you the truth. I showed you what they really are."

"Isn't that what Velvet said, too?"

"And you still believe her?"

He turned to her at last and tilted his head. "Maybe you're both right. Maybe they're both part of a larger truth."

"No, Steve, they're *not*. All the truth we need to know is that they're vampires and we're human and they drink our blood. They kill us and fry our brains and God only knows how many of them there are, walking among us and snacking whenever they fucking feel like it. *That's* the truth. It's us or them. *That's* the truth."

"We've both been around for a long time and they haven't finished us off yet. Velvet fed off me and I survived. Does it really help for you to go to war?"

"Steve, you can't treat them like people!"

"If I hadn't treated that... that poor wretched creature in the hole that way, if I hadn't treated him like he was human, you wouldn't have your clue about 'Bishop Solomon,' now would you?"

"He was probably lying," she muttered.

"Whatever," Steve replied.

The Shedd Aquarium was stately in the moonlight. It had closed to the public a few hours earlier, but the vampires had been there since sundown. And since even before that, if Velvet could believe some of the crazier rumors about the Ordo Dracul and their mastery of daylight. As she approached the graceful structure, she spotted Chris Stingo sitting on a bench, innocuous, just another businessman listening to his iPod. Only she was pretty sure it wasn't an iPod.

He turned bored eyes to her as she neared.

"The perimeter secure?" she asked.

"You can proceed without fear," he said, not bothering to look at her. Was it contempt, or was he just reluctant to stop his scan of the area, watching for anyone who might see something inexplicable, someone who might uncover the secret?

"Is Baines working security?"

"I gave the giant a night off."

"Really? As a reward for his excellent work protecting me?"

Stingo finally spared her a momentary glance, but only because it was the most efficient way he could wordlessly communicate his question: *Are you still here?*

"I saw her again," Velvet said. "I saw her a few nights ago."

"You must've seen someone who looked like her."

"She came up to me and identified herself," Velvet said, and she stepped straight in front of him to look in his face. With the easy reflex of undead years, Stingo avoided eye contact. It wasn't an emotional thing. He was used to dealing with people who could steal thoughts that way.

"You don't really care, do you?" Velvet asked. "Maybe you're *hoping* she kills me. One less frothing Lancea believer to deal with, is that it?"

"I assure you," Chris Stingo said, his tone bored to death, "if you perish I shall weep blood tears and suffer, biting my pillow as if I was being buttfucked. Is that what you want to hear?"

"Your dedication is an inspiration to us all. If I play poorly, I'll tell the Prince I was distracted by your sarcastic assurances."

"Wait," Stingo said, as she turned to go. "Baines is still on it, and he's been… talked to about his hasty actions. Believe me, he regrets them more than you. But this time he's got your Bishop breathing down his neck. Now, does *that* make you feel better?"

"Infinitely," Velvet said, without turning, though in fact she felt worse that Solomon's meddling apparently had Stingo's blessing.

She went into the aquarium and put her worries aside. It was something she'd needed to learn as a mortal performer, and it was a skill that served her well in death. She was preparing to play for Elysium.

Once every month, on the first Sunday, the Kindred of Chicago gathered to plot and scheme and socialize, to meet openly in an atmosphere where a ban on violence was ruthlessly enforced by those most skilled at it. As the years had passed, it had become tradition that this meeting was where vampires could let their masks of humanity drop, where they could be themselves in the company of their fellows, no matter how repulsive or unworldly or bizarrely beautiful they might be.

This early, the crowd gathering inside was an odd mix of three groups. Some, like Velvet and Stingo, were functionaries, vampires tasked with ensuring the pomp and safety of the meeting.

Another group was what Velvet had lately come to think of as "the political grinds." Kindred whose involvement with the factional infighting of their peculiar and deadly subculture was deeply personal. Belonging to that group did not equate power or influence. Those with real juice didn't have to seek out politics. Politics found them wherever they went. But Velvet had made a point of being polite to the grinds ever since she'd noticed that grinds tended to develop a lot of pull as they matured.

The third group was the diametric opposite of the involved politicos. Like orphans, they had nowhere else to go. They were outsiders so clueless that they knew only the most obvious facts of their dim half-world. They knew that the Kindred met on the month's first Sunday at the Shedd, so they went there and waited, as (Velvet imagined) they spent much of their time waiting, idle, ignorant, just trying to respond to circumstances that they were powerless to shape.

She pitied them, the castoffs and dregs. She'd never had to survive like that. Since her first night undead, she'd had a purpose. She'd been Embraced to be a musician, all those years ago, and the Thanatos Quartet still gave her a place in Kindred society.

"Hey Flip," she said to a friendly face. Flip was, like her, a member of the Lancea Sanctum, though (like her) not particularly devoted. He was halfway between being a functionary and a grind—he did some work decorating because he liked it and because it gave him periodic access to Kindred of authority. (Elder vampires hotly sought the privilege of decorating for Elysium. It was a good chance to show off their wealth or to make an ideological point.) At this particular moment, he was pushing a cart piled high with red-and-white cloth.

"Velvet. You in tune?"

"As always. Cartwright is really pulling out all the stops, isn't she?"

"Wait'll you see the centerpiece," Flip said. "You'll skip a beat." He edged closer. "You hear she's talking about... you know, chopping down the ol' Birch tree?"

"I may have heard some gossip to that effect. You don't believe it, do you?"

He shrugged. "Are you comfortable with Birch in charge? Do you think being under the blood oath to the Prince is going to make him any more..." He trailed off, leaving the word 'stable' unsaid.

"I can't imagine Cartwright going head to head with him, though. I mean, she's always been so I don't know, so much of an echo chamber. Anything he said, she said it back louder."

"Once Solomon couldn't walk the walk. Maybe she figured she'd better stop just talking the talk. I dunno. She's dropped some heavy cash on tonight, that's for sure. Speaking of which..."

"Yeah, I gotta get set up, too," Velvet said. As Flip pushed his cart away, she wondered. If Solomon Birch's reign over the Lancea Sanctum was threatened, why would he bother with one measly mortal?

Outside, sitting on the steps of the Field Museum, Earth Baines fidgeted as Solomon ran his final, remote tests.

"Man, is this, like... okay?"

"It seems to be working," Solomon said. He was lounging on a leather divan in the Brigmans' cozy den, miles away from Baines and the Field. The two were talking on cell phones, but Solomon was also listening to a speaker plugged into an Apple G5 computer.

"No," Baines said, trying not to look down at the side of his pants, where Solomon had efficiently sewn a transmitter into the seam by his right hip. "Is it allowed to broadcast what people say at court?"

"I believe it's a gray area in the rules. Really, is this any different from you attending and giving a full report? No one would have a problem with that."

Bullshit, Baines thought. *Everyone would have a problem with that. It's just that no one would be able to do a thing about it, law-wise. They'd just beat the crap out of me or put a curse on me or some other damn thing.*

"This is merely more efficient," Solomon's deep, unctuous voice purred in Baines' ear. "Less wasteful of your time, it delivers the goods to me immediately, and I daresay more accurately. No offense."

"Oh, none taken," Baines said, silently adding *motherfucker*. "I gotta say though—if this is your 'gray area'—how come I always seen Norris' creepy spybusters hauling in big black boxes full of jamming equipment?"

"That's for the underlings," Solomon said dismissively. "I have the right to do what I'm doing. If I didn't, would I know the wavelength the security personnel are using tonight?"

"Wait, you're broadcasting this on the same, like, the signal that fuckin'... I mean, the signal Stingo and Norris use?"

"Relax," Solomon said. "It's being sent in encrypted bursts during dead-air times. Anyone listening will hear a second of static. Even if they realize it's a covert transmission, there's no way to decipher it without the key on my computer."

"What about, like, tracing and... and all that?"

"With the finest equipment available on the private market, they could probably track the signal enough to be certain that it was, in fact, coming out of the Shedd," Solomon said. "Possibly the delicate equipment pioneered by NSA could give them a location within a 100-foot radius, but I don't *think* Norris has that kind of gear. In any event, 200 feet is a pretty big space inside an enclosed building. Relax. You're fine."

"And if I do get caught, it's a gray area."

"That's the spirit, yo." As the Bishop disconnected, Baines felt like he could actually see the quote marks on the last word.

"Fuck you, Bish, yo," Earth muttered to himself as he stood and went toward the building.

"All I'm saying is that Kindred society is already brutal and aggravating enough. Present company excluded, of course. Why would anyone want to go and make more of it?"

Out of the murmur of voices, Velvet could hear one or two rising up, louder or sharper than the rest.

"This thing would just be an excuse for a bloodbath, and if you think it's going to open up the structure for advancement, you might as well rub your neck with barbecue sauce the night it goes down."

It was still early yet. The doors would close right before the Prince made his grand entrance, and Velvet judged that attendance was at about the halfway the point it would eventually reach. Those already present were mostly young, inexperienced or politically toothless Kindred trying to make up lost territory anywhere and any time they could.

"It's *not* just like before. Before it was every day. Before it was expected. Before, there wasn't years of pressure building up. If the Prince does declare this, it's going to be a hard and desperate time. I'm not saying the old way was better by any means—how we have it *now* is better. But if you go from now to then, it won't be like then. Instead of a dozen murders and sirings spread out over the course of a year, you'll get two dozen of each on that first 'now or never' night. Think about that for a moment. Think of how chaotic and dangerous things are for us *now*, and then factor in a sudden crush of ignorant newcomers, arriving just as their elders are reeling from a bout of savage violence."

That was Beatrice Cartwright, probably the oldest and easily the most influential of the Kindred who'd arrived so far. Privately, Velvet thought showing up early was a bad move on Beatrice's part.

Why pay for an extravagant soiree and then squander your chance for a grand entrance?

The Kindred met for court in the amphitheater of the Oceanarium—ranked rows of stone benches under an echoing ceiling, facing a pool of water in which ocean mammals were put through their paces by day. Tonight, the benches were draped in red and white, with blazing lamps shaped like Roman spears at each end. The lights were placed outside, ringing the seats, so that the aisle down the middle was the least illuminated.

Cartwright was wearing an elaborate tiara over a sumptuous white robe that dragged the floor and (Velvet suspected) hid platform shoes. Between the headwear and the footwear,

Beatrice towered above most of the others present. The white robe seemed dazzling, right down to the hem and train. There it faded and turned a dark, rusty brown that could only suggest, to its present audience, that it had been dragged through fresh blood that had saturated up into the fabric.

Velvet knew the stain wasn't blood. They all knew. If it had been blood, human or animal, they'd have *known* it. They'd have felt it, like they felt the crust of dried blood under the fingernails of the Invictus diplomat in his sharp three-piece suit. Like they scented the tiny drops that had aspirated into the wild blonde hair of a woman who had chosen to enter the hall stark naked and wattled with rolls of waxy white flesh. They'd sense it as they sensed it on each other's breath, as they focused in on dried residues at the corners of mouths, between shiny, white teeth.

Velvet was also in a white robe, as per the directions of her employer. She, and the other members of the Thanatos Quartet, had shaved their heads and submitted to having their faces painted like skulls, their hands decorated to resemble bones. Their four chairs featured elaborate swan-feather wings attached to the backs. Cartwright had discussed some sort of halo contraptions as well, before Flip had gently dissuaded her. Between the skulls and the wings and the robes, he said, the 'angel of death' concept should be clear without belaboring it.

"There isn't going to be a fucking *Indulgence*," Christoforo said as he tuned his cello. He scratched at his white-painted head, annoyed. He had long black hair, and it would be restored by the next nightfall—a side effect of being an unchanging and unliving being. Still, the absence of his mane distracted him. "Christ, the people on the bottom are anxious enough without adding a whole new layer beneath them. The people on the top, the last thing they want are more noses in the trough."

"Don't discount the appeal of vengeance," Danielle said lightly. "We've seen violence erupt even here, under the aegis of Elysium."

"Dani, you're the only person I know who uses the phrase 'under the aegis' in casual conversation," Christoforo muttered, checking the tension of his bow.

"I had a classical education," she said, "and don't change the subject. It's not just the hotheads who'd relish the chance to take off the kid gloves. Look around… Look at Louis Crowder over there. He's a veteran of the Pacific Theater in the Second World War, but because of covenant politics he's stuck kowtowing to Ingrid Favreau, who wasn't even *born* when he was Embraced. Under the Prince's Tranquility, she has no fear and can treat him like her pit bull. If Maxwell grants Indulgence, even if Crowder *doesn't* kill her, she's going to have to respect him out of fear that it could happen again—and that a second time he won't miss his chance. There are dozens of similar examples. Cordelia stole that 'sacred scroll' Dunphee was always boasting about. Everyone knows it, but Dunphee has no proof and no political juice, so he just has to suck it up. You think she'd survive an Indulgence? Even that, that fellow… what's his name… always hanging about with Persephone?"

"Bruce Miner?" Christoforo said.

"That's him. Remember when Solomon Birch killed his dog? He'd probably love a chance to even that score."

"Are you crazy? Solomon would knock him into torpor without batting an eye," Velvet said.

"That may be. I didn't say the Kindred who nurse grudges are *smart*. I'm just saying they'd welcome an Indulgence, that it would remove an impediment to their vengeance fantasies. No matter how unrealistic those dreams of reprisal are."

"There you go again, 'dreams of reprisal.'"

"It's called eloquence. You might want to try it some time."

"Eloquent or not, I am right and you are wrong. Anyone so set on revenge that he'd take a swing at Bishop Birch wouldn't let something as slight as the Prince's Law stop him. Same for everyone else. If they really wanted to kill, they'd kill and cover it up. How many Kindred disappear a year, blamed on suicide, sunburn or just slipping away?"

"What about the Embrace?" Velvet surprised herself with her own question.

"What about it?"

"Don't you think people want a chance to… to…"

"To what? Make themselves some competition?"

"Never mind."

Robert, the fourth member of the Quartet, had resolutely ignored all conversation in order to prepare. "It's time," he said.

As they'd discussed the Indulgence, the hall had gradually filled. Elder Scratch was resplendent in a rot-stained magenta tuxedo, complete with top hat and cane. Kitty and Cat wore complimentary dresses—Cat in black with white dots, Kitty in white with black—and they giggled and hung upon one another as they subtly insulted the oblivious Earth Baines. Xerxes Adrianopolous wore a black robe embroidered from hood to hem with red Greek letters. Velvet had seen him wear it to the Temple. It was covered with lines from the *Testament of Longinus*. Sylvia Raines was understated in a cobweb-gray skirt and a black blouse, its white pearl buttons done all the way up her neck. Persephone Moore, the Prince's impulsively created offspring, wore pearls as well, a choker over a sleeveless black dress and silk opera gloves.

The Kindred had arrived.

Velvet and her three musical companions counted in and began to play. At their first wailing note, Flip pulled a cord and the cloth concealing Cartwright's centerpiece fell to the floor.

Flip had showed it to Velvet as he was setting up, so she wasn't startled. It was a crucifix, life-sized. The cross was wood, but the man on it was wax, sculpted with the exquisite craftsmanship of a Toussard figure. On the floor beside it, striking with a wood and metal spear, was a wax Longinus, the Centurion, the founder of the Lancea Sanctum.

Velvet had been ready for the statue's grisly realism, but Flip hadn't warned her that it was not merely wax. Both figures were, in fact, gigantic candles.

A spotlight, fixed high in the ceiling above the water, rained light down on Beatrice Cartwright as she processed up the dim middle aisle, a bright taper held aloft. She touched the flame to the wounds of the messiah—his feet, his hands, the crown of thorns. Each held a wick and caught, lighting the shape of the Savior of Man with fire, the bright and treacherous reminder of sunlight, of all vampires' great bane.

Beatrice walked around him at a stately pace and lit the scourge marks on his back, the taper-strings worked into the exposed ribs. Red wax dripped down and the light showed a sculpted heart inside, the medieval Sacred Heart, now burning with real fire, its smoke escaping through the figure's open mouth like a cry to heaven.

The last wound she lit was the blow from Longinus' spear. That done, she touched her taper to a final wick, within the Centurion's mouth, where the Blood of the Savior had fallen, a piece of a death that had darkened the sun and made the Roman legionnaire into a slave to hunger for thousands of years.

"Let the court begin," she said, and then the spotlight swept down the aisle, away from her, rushing down to the water where a figure rose, dark, naked and commanding. He emerged with water glistening off perfect ebony skin, off a body that was the glory of life and death.

He stood, immobile, the focus of every eye, as the Thanatos Quartet's first tune crescendoed and was silent.

"Yes," the Prince of Chicago said, stepping onto the stones as functionaries brought him his robe, his chair and his sword of office. "Let the court begin."

———

After the opening ceremony, the court itself was nearly anticlimactic. Trey Fischer discussed a few minor violations of the Masquerade, the grand conspiracy to maintain the fiction that vampires were merely creatures of legend. He explained how he'd cleaned up after a few sloppy feeds—and made it clear that he'd noticed patterns, that if the same Kindred kept being lazy, he'd go to the source.

Beatrice Cartwright stood and gave an impassioned (and to Velvet's ear, highly scripted) invitation to all Kindred to attend the Temple on Founder's Day, the upcoming holiday for the Lancea Sanctum. The effect was somewhat spoiled by a sarcastic chuckle from the rows holding the Circle of the Crone, a guffaw that echoed from the small delegation of Carthians sitting in front of them.

The burning Christ's feet melted into red and flesh-toned blobs, while the fingers sagged and dropped to the floor. The chest burned open and the heart flared as more oxygen flowed through. Its heat widened the throat as the head tipped back, the screaming mouth open inhumanly wide. The head ran and distorted as hanks of human hair caught from the crown, falling away from Kindred who instinctively flinched from the flames. The Centurion, too, had become something from a Francis Bacon painting, the burning drop having melted his jaw, his throat, and now its smoke had blackened his remaining upper lip as runnels of red cascaded down the front of his armor like a turkey's crimson wattle.

At last, a low-ranking Crone Acolyte stood and tossed her hair and said, "With all due humility, my Prince, I beg an Indulgence from you."

It made sense to Velvet. Have someone young and unimportant ask the big question, so that if the Prince laughed down the very notion, if the other covenants banded together to fight it, the Circle would not be heavily invested in the suggestion. It was like a poker player buying in with a small ante and hoping for good cards. Depending on the reaction, the Circle could pull its suggestion and lose little. Even the stalking-horse neonate who spoke was at little risk: Any humiliation at court would be paid for by gratitude from her companions.

For a moment, all eyes were on her, and then they shifted to the Prince as he tilted his head and said, "Why would I want to do a dumb-ass thing like that?"

His timing was perfect and the room erupted in laughter. Waves of it rolled back and forth and Velvet could see even Earth Baines holding his side as he brayed.

Then a voice cut through the mirth like thunder through birdsong. "Because the propagation of our kind is in our nature, and to deny it is perverse."

The laughter faded fast as heads swiveled. That voice made it hard to believe anyone could ever laugh again.

It was a voice seldom heard, at court or elsewhere. Not a loud voice, but somehow resonant, as if heard not only by a thin membrane in the ear, but as if it echoed through one's entire skeleton, as if it used one's lungs as a sounding board.

It was Rowen's voice.

Rowen was the leader of Chicago's Circle of the Crone, and as one the Kindred present turned to her.

"Asserting arguments from 'nature' seems a little queer for creatures whose reflections don't even act right," the elder Scratch said. "Even if you want to use a less charged word—like, I don't know 'normal'?—I don't think the creation of new vampires counts."

There were murmurs at his use of the word 'vampire,' at his gaucheness. "You ever done it?" he continued. "I hear it's hard. I hear it's like giving birth and burying your parent and divorcing your wife all rolled into one."

"Yet giving birth is essential. Taking leave of your parents is essential. Sometimes, breaking away from a cherished emotion is essential, if that sentimentality weakens you. A sentimental fear of newness has stagnated this city. A lazy longing for comfort has made you think that things can't change, made you hope they won't change. But even for the undead and undying, change is inescapable. Your patron, Prince Dracula, learned that lesson well from us. You would be wise to heed his precepts."

"The dire effort of siring is no measure of its *worth*," Sylvia said, rising to her feet, but Beatrice Cartwright drowned her out, crying, "The effort of the Embrace is the effort of defying God! Our curse is to be alone, and seeking to inflict it on the innocent—that is the lazy act, the unnatural act, the *immoral* act!"

"You'll forgive, I hope, my philistine perspective," the Prince said, smiling lightly. "Perhaps I'm crass, but the philosophy of the Embrace concerns me less than its practical ramifications. Is a sudden influx of young bloods desirable? Especially as it is likely to be attended by an outpouring of old blood?"

"If the Embrace is the agonizing chore that Scratch and Priestess Cartwright suggest, what makes you think there will be any such influx?" The speaker was Bella Dravnzie, another member of the Circle of the Crone—though one frequently at odds with Rowen, her elder.

"If they're both in it, it's a big circle indeed," Danielle muttered to Velvet.

"I'm against it." Mike the Carthian dressed for Elysium the

same way he dressed to go hunting, the same way he dressed for everything—blue jeans, a flannel over a T-shirt, work boots with steel toes, and an AFL-CIO mesh-back cap. "I think our goal ought to be to fix the problems with our current situation, not change the situation so much that we can't hardly recognize it."

"Who's to say that the... changes... brought on by an Indulgence won't be just what we need to fix those problems?" This was Dunphee, his fangs prominent in the flickering light of the burning Messiah while he glared at Cordelia with naked malice.

"I believe *I* am to say," the Prince said, and smiled smugly at the Carthians.

"New Kindred are fun," Kitty said unexpectedly, standing up and twisting a lock of hair around her finger. "Let the young, dumb, violent types kill themselves trying to drag down an elder. We'll all be better off after they're out of the way."

"Have we so little regard for the importance of the task that weighs upon us?" asked Sylvia. "We, whose very existence is an aberration of the natural order... are we so very casual about altering the balance of that order?"

"I think it's pretty clear we *are*," Cat said, rolling her eyes. Sylvia glared and went on.

"If the fear of death and the fear of competition aren't enough to bury this mad notion, what of the fear of diablerie?"

That word brought a hush. It was broken as the head of the Savior finally fell with a molten plop onto the stone floor. With that sound, a hundred whispers started.

Diablerie: Among vampires, the most feared of their dark capabilities. Feeding off mortals was normal—as normal as such a dangerous and blissful intimacy could be. But when one vampire drank the blood of another and took the last thin drizzle of that preserving fluid, it was possible to go further—to cannibalize the victim Kindred's very soul. That was the greatest sin among those who sinned nightly, the abhorrent crime to those who stole life just to survive.

"An Indulgence isn't a carte blanche to do *anything*," said the Acolyte who'd first made the proposal.

"Yet in the spirit of urgency and license, who is to cry hold?" asked Beatrice, on her feet and glaring.

"An elder who can't stop a diablerist on the one night he knows she's coming deserves to get his soul munched." This heretical notion issued from Scratch's broken-fanged maw. Few others would have been so bold. Beatrice turned incredulous eyes on him, at a momentary loss for words. He grinned, spun his cane around his fingers, and did a brief soft-shoe dance. His playfulness, like his gruesomeness, only made his words more appalling.

"Rather than worry about the deaths of elders who are well equipped to defend themselves, is it not more important to be concerned with the fate of young Kindred?" Tobias Rieff stood smoothly, his words like butter melting off a stack of pancakes, his clothes draped with the perfection usually found only on mannequins, wooden hangers and other inanimate objects. "It's well known that some aged Kindred can slake their thirst only on their fellow Kindred. If anyone in Chicago labors under such a restriction, he—or she—is being sedate about it," he said, with only the smoothest, oiliest glance sliding over Rowen. "But feeding on mortals is so intoxicating that some are led into... unfortunate excess. Charged with the power of our curse, the blood of Kindred is more addictive yet. To feed from our kind and not murder them must take iron self-control. On a night of liberation...?" Eloquently, he trailed off to leave the ensuing carnage to his listeners' imagination.

In the hall of many, only five in attendance had the keen senses required to notice the tiny narrowing of the Prince's eyes when Rieff described elders who could feed only on their fellows. Only those five saw the millimeter dilation of Prince Maxwell's pupils, the way human pupils dilate when they see something beautiful.

"It's a double-edged sword," Mike said. "On one hand, you get elders going paranoid and youngsters getting spooked. On the other hand, you get everyone looking around for someone new to Embrace, some fresh meat for a gang, and you just know that the dumbest of us are going to be sloppy. A citywide string of disappearances in *one night*? You know the dopes aren't going to care if it's someone who'll be missed, either. They'll grab anyone they think is rich or smart or can help them out. It'll be nuts, chaos—every Embrace a potential breach of the Masquerade."

"Are there that many among us who would Embrace purely for political advantage?" asked an emaciated old man with skin as black as night, deeply seamed cheeks, and a floating, snow-white mane and beard. "To create us anew costs a piece of the maker's soul. I *know*. I've done it, in the days before the Tranquility. Discussing it at leisure in Elysium is one thing. Making the sacrifice—cutting off a piece of your identity, whittling the core of your psyche—that's entirely different."

"I agree, this is a tempest in a teapot," said a young, bored member of the Invictus who was dressed in jeans and a silk shirt half-tucked in, his hair carefully mussed as if he couldn't be bothered to primp even for the ruler of the undead. "No one's going to try to assassinate someone the one night they expect it. And few if any are going to expend the effort of *reproducing*."

"Prince Maxwell did."

"That's enough. This discussion is over. You—come with me."

Many in the deadly crowd were startled. They'd been following along and then three words from Rowen and the Prince was on his feet pointing at her. It took a couple seconds for them to realize just what she'd *said*, just what it *meant*, and then she was levering her bulk up off the bench and lumbering off with Maxwell. Her face was expressionless, as was his. They headed off to the left, where a staircase would take them down to the glass walls of the whale enclosure.

The Prince's bodyguard sauntered over and stood between the crowd and their exit. He crossed his arms and lounged, but the message was clear that none were to follow.

The crowd's muttering, then discussion and then debate in turn reminded Velvet of the hiss of wind, the patter of rain, and finally the thunder of an arriving storm.

––––––––––

"Why would anyone want to do it?" Velvet asked Robert as they put away their instruments.

Elysium had finally ended, dawn was scarcely an hour away, and they'd wiped the skull and bone makeup off of their dead and rubbery flesh.

"Challenge the Prince like that? I don't know. If Rowen was making a point, she could have done it... differently. Unless her point was that Maxwell doesn't scare her, that she's willing to call him on it when he..."

"No," Velvet said, carefully locking the clasps on her violin case. "Why would anyone want to Embrace a new vampire?"

He looked at her, his eyebrows drawn together.

"Velvet," he said, "did you know I'd sired?"

"What?"

"It didn't..." He looked down at his instrument as if double-checking it, though they both knew it was perfectly secure. "It didn't last long. Didn't really... take."

"When?"

"1967." He shrugged. "It was such a... a crazy time. Volatile. And I wanted... something that would stay the same. Something that... I don't know. I was tired of everything I lo... everything that meant anything to me, it was all vanishing. That's how it seemed. And I had a... Marí, maybe you remember her? I'd given her my blood, she was..." He didn't say 'ghoul,' he just trailed off again.

"Robert?" Hesitantly, Velvet stood and put a hand on his shoulder. He hunched in further, not looking at her.

"She wasn't going to get older, as long as I kept her supplied. But I could tell it wasn't... I don't know. She was so lively, you know? Do you remember her? I guess not, but... she *challenged* me. Not in an aggressive way, but she was *playful*. With me. Everything seemed new. I needed... well, wanted that and with the blood I was giving her she was becoming..."

"Addicted," Velvet said for him. He twisted away from her and stood, staring out at Chicago's pre-dawn shadowscape.

"Dependent, in any event. I wanted her to be on her own again, but I couldn't stand to see her grow old and die, and I knew that having had the blood she wouldn't..." He sighed deeply and there was something inhuman about that altogether human sound. It was the sound of regret, combined with rot-gas escaping from a drowned corpse's lungs. Velvet put a hand over her mouth.

"I thought that if she started over, as one of us, she'd... she'd recover. I should have known better. I should have known nothing gets better for being killed and brought back. I should have known."

"What happened to her?"

"I introduced her to the matriarch and tried to teach her how to lead her Requiem. After 16 nights she disappeared and I got a suicide note from her in the mail. She said she couldn't stand being between life and death. That she had to complete it."

"How awful."

Robert turned to her. "There are lots of good reasons to do it. You need someone to watch your back. Someone to talk to. Someone to plot with and scheme with. Someone who has a *skill you need*," he said, pointing to Velvet's violin, his finger rigid. "Maybe you just need someone to depend on you, or someone to be more lost and alone and afraid than you are. Those are all good reasons. Just don't do it to make things *better*."

"Robert, I'm sorry, I..."

"It was a long time ago." He looked her in the eye. "Did I answer your question?"

"Yes."

He nodded. "See you at rehearsal." Then he picked his gear and walked away.

She watched him go and did not hear the footsteps behind her. "Velvet? Do you need a lift somewhere?"

She spun and found herself facing the Prince. He offered her a pleasant smile.

"You startled me."

"I have a light step," he said, placing an apologetic hand on his heart. "It must be the ballroom dance lessons."

She smiled at his joke. She dared do no less and besides, he was charming. He was powerful and terrible and had enslaved her horrific Bishop. And now his self-depreciation was warm, impenetrably sincere and completely disarming.

"I thought you'd left," she said.

"I was detained. You may not know it, but once you get Rowen alone you just *can't* get a word in edgewise."

Again, that flawless timing. And the image of Rowen as an irrepressible chatterbox was too absurd. This time she had to laugh out loud.

"Do you think I should grant the Indulgence?" he asked, his tone unchanged, mellow and pleasant, as if he was asking about last night's sitcom.

Velvet blinked. "I don't know. I don't know... anything about it. I'm just a musician."

"You're Kindred. This concerns you as much as the rest of us. You've been around since... since how long? The 1930s?"

"1941," she said quietly.

"So you're old enough to care, old enough to understand."

"If any of us are."

"Hmm." His expression was rueful.

"How... how much did you hear?"

"Of your performance?"

"No," she said. "Of Roger and me."

"Oh." He looked into her eyes and she didn't look away. "I heard everything."

"Why did you do it?" she asked. She hadn't thought the question through, couldn't have or she'd never have asked it. Icy fear shocked her whole body when she heard her own words, and she couldn't imagine what he'd do to her for her temerity, couldn't imagine why she'd asked such a dangerous question.

But she did know on some level that she couldn't face. It was Aurora. Brave Aurora who faced vampires without fear as a scrappy, insolent mortal, and Velvet had responded somehow. Somehow, the witch-hunter had made Velvet sick of being cautious and temperate and modest around her elders.

"Well," Maxwell said, "I suppose I thought I could get away with it."

"You suppose? Don't you know?"

He closed his eyes, then opened them and nodded gravely. "I did it because I couldn't bear not to."

Velvet swallowed, though she hadn't needed to swallow anything but blood for more than 60 years.

It felt like they stared forever.

"I have to go," she said at last, stumbling away, picking up her violin and fighting the urge to run, to use the blood and race away with the speed of a plunging hawk. She was halfway to the door when she heard him speak again.

"Your colleague is wrong. There is no other reason than making things better."

She spun around, but he was already gone.

Chapter Seven

Bishop Solomon Birch pricked up his ears as he walked into the Discarded Image. His alertness was of questionable value, since almost everyone went silent as he entered. The exceptions were Cat, Kitty, and a thin young man the Bishop didn't know, all three sitting at the bar with their backs to him.

"Fischerspooner is *okay*, but I liked 'em better when they were called The Human League."

"Um? I think *I* told you that one? About Marilyn Manson and Alice Cooper?"

"Actually, I *quoted* you that from *Saturday Night Live*."

Solomon bit back a wince. It was going to be a long night.

Other than the bickering trio (who quieted when he walked past) there was Trey Fisher again, one of the Prince's more promising enforcers, an untouched pilsner glass of craft beer warming on the bar and a cool glance raised at the Bishop.

Solomon had once thrown Trey down a flight of stairs, but the Bishop didn't think there were any hard feelings.

Next to the Sheriff sat a glum and slender man in slacks and a velvet jacket. He flicked his eyes up at the Bishop, making the mistake of eye contact, and Solomon grinned.

"Hugo," he said, "any luck finding your gynecological implements for working on mutant women?"

"The collector in Amsterdam won't let the last one go for any price," he said sullenly.

"Tough break. I didn't know David Cronenberg was so big in Amsterdam."

"It's the same guy who beat me to the bone-gun from *eXistenZ*." Hugo shook his head bitterly. "Not being able to bid by day *sucks*."

"At least you got that Romero footage," Trey said.

"Yeah, that's good stuff," Hugo said, perking up. "Did you know George Romero filmed Fred Rogers' tonsillectomy?"

"Who?" Solomon asked.

"Fred Rogers? Mister Rogers? From *Mister Rogers' Neighborhood*?" Seeing Solomon's blankness, Trey just shrugged. "Never mind, not important, just… one of those things. So what brings you to the Image, Bishop?"

"Relaxation?"

"Sure," Cat said, curling around the edge of the bar. "And next week I'll go to your Temple for laugh value."

"You *should* come to Temple, Cat. You might learn something."

Cat languidly presented her profile, but not quite so languidly that anyone could miss her unwillingness to meet the Bishop's gaze.

"Is it true you once forced a man to cut off and eat his own foot?"

"So much for *What happens in Vegas stays in Vegas*," the Bishop said with a smile. "But why have you turned your pretty face from me?"

"The profile is really my best side."

"You're not worried I'll *compel* you, surely? Oh dear child, you… you needn't fear that from me. I don't want mindless obedience, I want you to understand. I want you to come *willingly*."

"We'll get right on that," the young man said. Solomon ignored him, because Kitty had said, "Yes, I understand you have some real problems with compulsion and free will."

"Perhaps you should hold your tongue around your elders," Solomon said. As he'd expected, she pounced on empty bluster.

"And perhaps you should stick to your Temple instead of wondering why you don't fit in here."

"Anywhere I stand is my temple," Solomon said as he shifted his posture to display aggression. (It wasn't something he had to think about.) Then he turned to Trey and said, "Please get Justine."

"Whoa," Trey said, "I'm not her social secretary, I don't…"

"Never mind," Solomon said. He glanced at his watch. "She won't be long."

Kitty laughed out loud.

To understand her mirth, it's necessary to know that 'Justine' was Justine Lasky, a woman who had nearly stolen the throne of Chicago out from under Prince Maxwell, with Solomon's help. Only she'd decided she'd rather serve Maxwell than fight him, so she'd sold her erstwhile power-behind-the-throne down the river. That had been Solomon's first step toward bondage to the Prince.

The Discarded Image was her place, and it was an Elysium, so physical violence was strictly forbidden. But Solomon Birch was not known for an ironclad respect for Elysium truces. That impetuousness had been his second step toward vinculum.

To the youngsters in the Image, his presence was unexpected to say the least. For him to appear and demand an audience with Justine seemed as mad as Hitler showing up at the gates of Downing Street, yelling for Churchill to show himself.

Within 10 minutes, Justine flung the doors open. She wasn't alone. On her left was a stylishly scruffy hoodlum in a black leather vest over cutoff army pants and combat boots. On her right was a shaved, bulging weightlifter whose polo shirt looked painted on. His pants were loose, which to Solomon's experienced eye screamed hand tailoring. He was nearly as muscular as Baines, if not as tall. Birch estimated that her bartender must have called as soon as he entered.

"That took longer than I expected," Solomon said. "I actually had time to order a drink." He shook his head. "Ten dollars for a gin and tonic?"

"There are many options for cheaper beverages," Justine said. She was haughty in green batiked silk, the neckline collarbone high and plunging deep in back. She put her hands on her hips. "My clientele come for the atmosphere."

Solomon laughed—with genuine amusement, as far as even Justine's keen estimation could judge. "What are the muscle-boys for? You weren't planning to have them drag me out and, and... Trey, what's that phrase? You used it last week? Oh yes, 'curbstomp.' Wonderfully evocative. You weren't going to have them curbstomp me, were you?"

"Do you think they can't?"

"I think it would be a dreadful violation of your Elysium, and in front of one of the Prince's officers, too." He turned back to his drink and, violating the unspoken protocol, took a deep drink. Kitty winced and even Trey leaned back as the Bishop smacked his lips. "Mm, that is good gin."

"Why are you here, Solomon?"

He sighed. "People keep asking me that. Very well, I wanted to speak to you, Justine." His wry grin took on a slightly more feral aspect. "You haven't returned my calls."

"Here I am, then."

"Splendid. If you could...?" Delicately, his glance encompassed her bodyguards, the trio at the bar, even Trey. (Hugo seemed to have made himself scarce when no one was paying attention.)

"Oh, is this a *private* matter?"

"You don't think I'm going to get you alone and then, what, 'ravish' you or something?"

She raised an eyebrow. "Your temper is notorious. I'm afraid you're mad at me."

"I swear upon the Holy Spear of Longinus and the sacred blood it spilled that you have nothing to fear from me here tonight."

Justine nodded and murmured to the two thugs. With one shrug and one sneer, they departed.

"Sorry, everyone," she said. "The bar is closed. You don't have to go home, but you can't stay here."

At her words, they slowly rose and left, untouched drinks warming behind them. Cat spared the Bishop one incredulous backward glance before the door closed.

"All right," Justine said when they were alone. "Talk. And make it quick. Some of us still have futures."

"You wound me, and impatience sits awkwardly upon an immortal. But, to cut to the chase, my position is threatened."

"Oh, I know. I've been observing the situation with much amusement."

"You should help me retain my Mask."

This time, she laughed.

"Solomon, you're so brazen it's almost… dashing. Last time I checked, you hated me."

"The last time *I* checked, I was striving heartily to make you *Prince*. Or Matriarch, or however you'd have it. You spurned that favor rather cruelly, and the results have been disastrous. From where I sit, I'm the wounded party."

"Maxwell might differ."

"Maxwell forced his blood upon me before the gathered court. I don't think he needs *you* sticking up for him."

"Very well. I've injured you. Now explain why I should give aid to one who bears me a grudge, rather than finishing him off."

"*Finish me off?* Oh my love, I don't think you can. You aren't going to resort to fisticuffs in your own Elysium. Besides, you dare not violate the Tranquility. Your last-minute change of heart may have kept Maxwell in power, but don't think it escaped him that you went along with me as long as you did."

"There's talk of an Indulgence," she said, smiling gently.

"No one of consequence has more to gain than lose from *that* toss of the dice. And speaking of gain and loss, you stand to lose a great deal if I'm removed from my office."

"Exactly what is that, then?"

"All sparring aside, you accepted my oath. Would you be so trusting of Beatrice Cartwright's word?"

Justine shrugged. "I'd probably trust Sylvia Raines as much as you—if not more so. Wasn't she a nun in life?"

"Sylvia Raines isn't going to become Bishop. If you trust me with anything, trust me to analyze Lancea Sanctum politics in Chicago." He leaned in. "You swing a big stick with the Sanctified."

"I swing a big stick with everyone."

"Yes, yes, but the Sanctified. Many listen when you talk, despite your agnosticism."

"We don't talk religion."

"As Bishop, I've been busy weeding out the sort of sheep mentality represented by Miss Raines. Many are weak and I have antagonized them. That's fine: Being weak, there's little they can do about it. But I know you have not yet expended your political capital recruiting the indecisive or waffling. I can't fight Sylvia's mewling battalions and your allies within my own faithful. Most, I think, would side with me, but your opposition would put some on the fence and take some off the fence into the enemy camp."

"You credit me with much."

"Justine, please. It's too late to try to play at being humble. As long as I'm Bishop, I can't open a second front against you without risking my position against Sylvia. As much as your personal betrayal grieves me, my first duty is to ideological purity."

"Ah. So if you're removed from office?"

"Well then." Solomon sat back and folded his hands. "With no political power, I'm just one lone individual, out in the open. Just me and my web of mortal contacts, and my millions of dollars, and the fanatics I'd be able to pull aside into a splinter sect. Just me, a few incorruptible, dedicated headcases... and my anger. I'd be an angry, bitter man with nothing left to lose, if they took away my mask."

"With nothing but the faith that keeps you from killing other Kindred."

"I don't think God will let me lose my position. If I did... well, even my faith might be shaken. Who knows what could happen? I don't think God would permit an Indulgence, either, but you seem not to share that view."

"I see where this is going. I help you, or else you lose your job, become an angry loner, and then the Indulgence turns up just in time for you to vent your notorious wrath on me. Is that the scenario?"

"It's not a very pleasant one, is it?"

"Try this on for size: You lose your bid to be Bishop and without a strong hand on the tiller, the Sanctified begin to drift. Without their opposition, the Circle and the Order push through the Indulgence."

"The Order doesn't have the will and the Circle is disorganized."

"The Circle has Bella Dravnzie. You get deposed and she'll

have more pull. Ooh," she said, making a sour face, "that's gotta be a bitter pill."

"Mm, yes, let's take it as read that I'm writhing inside with concealed misery."

"You don't need to hide it with *me*, Solomon. Go ahead and cry if you need to."

"I think I've forgotten how. Anyhow, where were we? Oh yes, the elders of the Order decide they want their envious underlings off the leash, and the Circle overnight becomes disciplined and orderly. Setting aside generations of mutual contempt, they push the Prince—a Prince who's just fought off an ouster attempt and is stronger than ever—into making the one decision he least wants to make, the one that puts his carefully designed social order in complete peril. I die in this little fantasy, somewhere?"

"Only if you've made enemies. Sylvia Raines is quite the sorceress, isn't she? I heard she was the one who eventually killed Old John, scorching him to cinders from across town with Theban Sorcery."

Solomon's nostrils flared. "She didn't," he said curtly.

"Oh yeah, you had some... some kind of *connection* to Old John, didn't you?"

"Water under the bridge. Nonetheless, you've convinced me."

"Have I?"

"Oh yes. I can clearly see the terrible peril that faces me during Indulgence if I lose my position. That's why I'm *telling* you that, should those events transpire, I will kill you or die trying."

"This despite your faith in Longinus? Your belief that no Kindred should slay another under any circumstances?"

Solomon's grin and eyes turned eerily vacant as he said, "Ask yourself this: If I lost all that, would I be able to stop myself?"

———

While Solomon was plying his wiles, Velvet was working hers. She played with the Four, absentmindedly thrumming along with the drummer and only really focusing when it was time for her solos. She was scanning the audience, looking for Steve, but he wasn't there.

Did that penny-top bitch steal him away somewhere? She frowned as she plucked her strings and gave the body of the bass a halfhearted pop. She tried to tell herself that there were plenty of fish in the sea, that it wasn't some kind of *defeat* that this 'Aurora'…

"It means 'the dawn.' Dawn kills your kind, doesn't it?"

…that this sad and obsessed little witch-hunter had pulled Steve out of the frying pan.

Not that she has. I've still got his phone number. I could call him, I could crook my little finger and he'd come running. The hook's in his cheek good and deep.

But that wasn't really the point. The point was, Steve was supposed to want her. He was supposed to be obsessed with her, was supposed to desperately follow her and make her his idol. From what the band's manager had said, it sounded like the plan had been working perfectly until Aurora came along.

It was so much easier to harm someone who was asking for it, begging for it.

Never mind, never mind. Just find someone uncomplicated, someone boring… that guy.

'That guy' was in his 40s, beard neatly trimmed, clothes a little too new, posture a little too awkwardly stiff, and after three songs and two whisky sours, posture a little too awkwardly relaxed. Velvet figured him for recently divorced. She'd had dozens.

God bless the no-fault divorce, she thought idly, though she knew older vampires who cursed it, cursed the liberal modern mindset in general, vampires who'd worked the homosexual subculture of the '40s and '50s and who now bemoaned an openness that prevented them from blackmailing their victims into silent compliance.

She blinked and focused. Him. That guy. He'd be easy.

After the set, she flexed her fingers and was tired. She could feel her façade slipping. The blood she'd flushed through her cheeks to look vivid was turning weak and sluggish. She was corpsing up just as Mitch, the band's more-or-less leader, came up to her and said, "You were kind of on autopilot, don't you think?"

She looked at him and he looked back, and even in the backstage shadows he saw enough to blanch. "Um, I gotta... forget it."

Focus.

She forced the blood through her veins again and she'd probably leave that guy pretty sick, pretty weak and woozy, but he'd blame it on the whisky sours. Give him a week and he'd be right as rain. Two weeks, tops.

She walked out to the bar and spotted him at his same table and smiled as she walked past, heading to the bathroom she never had to use anymore. He smiled back, pitifully grateful.

And Velvet thought, *Oh fuck it.*

She kept right on walking past the bathroom, back to the storeroom. She levered open the backdoor and went into the night thinking about Aurora, about the fearless huntress, so frail and weak and living a life less frightened than Velvet's 'Requiem'—Velvet's half-life hedged by caution and prudence and self-control.

Velvet walked out of the alley and into the street, looking around at the people lounging before the clubs, seeing and being seen, the people sitting in their evening, open-air cafes, drinking lattes. She was just tired of it. She had a second set soon but she was tired of that, too, and went to the train station.

It was busy. She rode the rails a while, switching trains to get away from the wealthy, the well dressed, the happy, the successful and the drunk. She was looking for something else, for someone you'd find alone in a subway car, maybe someone wearing a crappy polyester fast-food uniform. Someone who wasn't content.

It took her 20 minutes to get herself alone in a car at the back of the train, alone but for a man in his 30s maybe, perhaps older, or younger and just hard used. He was wearing the ubiquitous coveralls of a maintenance worker and he spared her a single sullen glance from his newspaper as she entered.

Typically, the etiquette of a late-night train ride broke along gender lines. The man gave the lone woman enough of a look that she'd know he'd seen her, and she'd look back, a little wary, and he'd nod or give some other acknowledgement, a tacit, "I won't hassle you if you don't push your luck" stare. The woman would demurely lower her eyes and sit with her posture closed and modest and no one would even have to speak, the roles of "nothing to each other" silently established and carefully maintained.

The janitor's look had been textbook, maybe a little on the forbidding side but certainly well within norms. It was Velvet who broke tradition. She stared boldly back and didn't sit down. Instead, she walked toward him.

She passed two rows of seats and he ignored her. Two closer and he looked up with a flat, weary glance, trying to gauge if she was going to panhandle or talk to him about Jesus.

She kept walking steadily. She had grown tired with the mask of humanity and she wasn't breathing, she was paper pale and unblinking, lacking the tiny balancing movements of a living creature and instead walking with the smooth articulation of a *thing*.

The man got to his feet and stepped into the aisle. He didn't know what he was doing or why, he just responded to some throwback urge telling him that you don't want to be cornered when a predator comes close.

When he stood, Velvet could see a name-patch that said "Marcus" and she grinned and pulled out her new knife. It wasn't as good as her old one. It was a double-edged butterfly. She didn't bother with any fancy one-handed flicker opening. She unfolded it with the quick, practiced purpose of a plumber reaching for a wrench, of a cook who knows exactly where his pan is hung. Then she grinned. Seeing the fangs, Marcus didn't speak, he just picked up his metal thermos and held it like a baseball bat.

She paused. She locked her eyes on his, waiting to see what he'd say, willing him to say something. But he just waited.

Then his nerve snapped and he lunged in, swinging.

Velvet could have made herself fast, but she didn't. She

could have given her muscles a brief burst of strength, but she didn't. It all came down to blood. All those tricks that made her body more than human required her to overcome humans and steal life from them. She'd known too many vampires who became lost, using more blood than they could harvest in fights like this. She needed to fight…

…and more, she needed to fight like Aurora did, no unholy death-tricks, just her own skill and will and fierceness.

He swung and she turned the knife in her hand, shifting from the probing forward grip, where she held it like shaking hands, to a downward spike, like a chisel. She didn't dodge his blow, she met it with the base of her hand and the full length of her blade. She met him force-on-force, only her hand was dagger-tipped and the knife hilted itself in the meat of his forearm.

Marcus howled and staggered as he jerked back from the stinging pain, but Velvet moved in to flank him. Her empty left hand slid behind his head to grab his left ear and a good hank of hair. She pulled his head to the side to bare his neck.

Marcus had some fight left, though. She felt the bones of his right arm grind against the knife blade as he pulled free, whipping his thermos up and back. It was a heavy steel one and he knew just where her face was going. He could feel her dry lips gliding along his neck as she went for the jugular, her face right between his head and his shoulder, where he bashed her.

It hurt, but Velvet didn't cry out. She just jammed the knife into his belly, twisting it as she pulled it free and struck again and again, a circular turning movement that somehow reminded her of stirring stiff bread or cake dough, how she'd hold the bowl by her hip so that her wrist wouldn't stiffen. Now Marcus was sinking down and she took the knife to the side of his neck and slashed, pausing only so that first arterial spray wouldn't paint her face and hair, and then settled her mouth over the red fountain to drink deep, racing against the holes in his stomach to bleed him out.

The train was starting to slow down when he died. She pushed the corpse forward and looked at her blurred reflection in the dark window.

Not bad. Blood all over her mouth, but a big ol' wipe on the back of Marcus' coveralls took care of that. Likewise her red right hand. She wedged it in the back of his knee and pulled it out cleaner. Her left hand was less smeared. She could rub it on his shoulder and she still looked dirty, but she no longer looked *gory*. There was a bit of blood on her shoe tips, but who would notice? Rolling up her sleeves would mostly camouflage the stains on her cuffs, she'd been behind him and he'd mostly bled forward. She would hold up to casual inspection. She carefully smudged her tracks as she went to the back door of the train. It was locked, so she popped the emergency window and lowered herself out. The train was still moving fast, but now she could use the blood, she had plenty. A jolt of inhuman speed let her match the train as she hit the ground running, and if anyone was watching, all they saw was a blur of black and white in the dark, a flash into the weedy ditch by the tracks, and then nothing.

Crouched among the crickets and cicadas and stagnant rainwater, Velvet felt empty, but it was a pure emptiness. She thought of Aurora and she couldn't help it. In the dark, Velvet started to giggle.

———

Aurora was filing her nails to keep from biting them. She hadn't been able to afford a manicure lately. Even with the windfall of eight grand, she didn't feel right spending cash on her nails. So she filed, rasping off the numb flesh. She couldn't handle having it on the ends of her fingers, dead skin. It gave her the creeps.

She was on break at her cocktail waitress job. Speaking of the creeps, she'd just gotten a heavy dose from a lone drinker in a corner booth. He was nondescript—intensely average, except that his eyes were a vivid, Elizabeth-Taylor violet.

"Have you ever been to China?" he asked her when she came by to get his order.

"Can't say that I have." She hadn't gotten the creeps yet, so she was being pleasant, a professionally balking smile to encourage a big tip, but not any kind of drunken confidences or propositions.

"There's a little village there called Yurfa," he said, with a little smile. Ordinary teeth.

"Never heard of it."

"Well, I hope there haven't been too many people there before me."

"Hmm, sounds nice. What're you drinking?"

"I'll have a Scorpion," he said. "You know how to make one?"

"I'm sure the bartender does."

"Yeah," he said as she was turning. "I'd sure like to get a good look at Yurfa, China."

It took her a couple steps to get it, and she'd avoided eye contact delivering his drink. She'd also checked him out in one of the many mirrors—her favorite thing about this place, beyond the paychecks—but he scanned normal. Just another freak on the make.

Then her phone rang. The *special* phone.

"Talk," she said, whipping it open.

"Are you healthy?"

"What the hell kind of question is that?"

"Your well-being concerns us, Ms. Barclay."

"That's real sweet. Is that why you send me to..." She turned her back as another waitress walked by, Jenna. Jenna seemed completely unable to be interested in anything, but Aurora didn't want to test it by saying 'Kill vampires' out loud. "I'm fine, I'm healthy," she said. "Why? You have something for me?"

"We think something big is coming down. We've got a number of..."

"You know what? I'm about ready to toss this phone in the toilet."

There was a pause.

"I'm sorry?"

"I appreciate the money and the 'gifts,' but come on. I'm putting it on the line here and I don't even know who you are. I don't know your name."

"You can call me Agent Black."

"I don't care if you're Agent Orange. I don't know who you are, who you work for... even *what* you are. That first call was by day, but so what? Thanks to what you've told me, I now know *they* can move around when the sun's up."

"I can only assure you that I am, in fact, a human being."

"Oh, well, the word of some kind of..." Another pause as the token male waiter walked by, probably about to do another coke transaction in the storeroom. He looked down his nose at Aurora and she glared back until he went by and then "...*spy,*" she hissed. "That's something to take at face value."

"What do you want from us, Ms. Barclay?"

"I want to meet you. *You.* Tomorrow, Millennium Park at high noon."

"High noon. Very well. You want to meet by the spitting fountains? Or how about under the Cloud Gate?"

"Cloud Gate? Is that the big 'supreme bean' sculpture?"

"That's the one. Twelve sharp. I'll mention the place where you blew your cover."

"What?"

"Same place you got on *their* radar. If it's not safe to talk, use your current pseudonym, Barclay. If it is safe, greet me with your *real* name. Don't worry, I'll recognize it."

Then there was a dial tone.

Aurora checked her watch the next day. 11:57. She felt ridiculous. It was a sunny day and vampires seemed stupid. Just thinking that they might be real as she stood under a giant chrome *bean,* surrounded by tourists and kid-herding couples who were admiring it, she had to question her sanity.

How convenient for you that they just 'fade to ash.' The voice in her imagination sounded like Valerie's psychiatrist. *Is it easier to face the undead than to confront your failures as a parent?*

The cloak and dagger routine only added another layer of gloss to the ridiculousness of it all.

"Excuse me, didn't I meet you at the Jade Room?"

"Yeah," she said, shaking his hand. "Aurora Graham. I missed your name."

"Adrian Black," he said. "Can I buy you a lemonade?" With that, he stepped out into the sunlight.

He didn't look like a secret agent, but then she supposed that he wouldn't. He was bald except for a thin, fine fringe of brown and gray. There was a wine-colored birthmark on his neck. He was wearing bulky sunglasses, a JC Penney suit, and had a shopping bag in his left hand. He carried it like it was heavy.

"Okay, Adrian," Aurora said as they walked toward the drink cart. "What's going on?"

"Play along," he said. "We could still be under surveillance from parabolic microphones... or God knows what else."

Something about the haunted way he looked around when he said it gave Aurora a little chill.

With drinks in hand they got in his car—the same car she'd seen outside her apartment when she got the briefcase of guns and money. Inside, he seemed to relax.

"We swept the vehicle before coming here. If it's still not clean, well, to hell with it." The radio was playing WBEZ as he turned the ignition, but he switched it off as he pulled out into downtown traffic. "What do you want to know?"

"I want to know about... about *you*. Who do you work for? Who's funding this... what did you call it?"

"The Counterinsurgency?" Black gave a little laugh. "Okay. Imagine that you're a cop or an FBI agent on the serial-killer beat, or you're INS border patrol. You come up against something weird, something that doesn't add up, doesn't make sense."

"A vampire," Aurora said.

Adrian nodded. "Maybe you follow protocol and it becomes a cold, open case, and eventually no one but the victim's wife or his parents remember it. No one but the witnesses ever wonder how the hell all those guys with guns busted the border or how the bank robbers avoided being ID'd from security cameras. Maybe you're lazy or not very imaginative and you let it go. Nothing happens and you maybe have a little professional setback but, shit, even Barry Bonds strikes out more often than he whales a homer, right?"

"But what if you don't?"

"Yeah. You start poking and you keep poking and maybe you got a dumb one. Vampires aren't any smarter than you or me—just tougher and faster and stronger, and some of them can do crazy shit like you wouldn't *believe*. Maybe you get a dumb one and catch him with his pants down and you shoot him and he turns to ash. Just what do you put in your report?"

"I don't know."

"You have two options. You can cover it up and become part of the problem, because that's just what *they* want you to do. They want to stay hidden, so they've created a culture where anyone who tells the truth about them gets painted with the loony brush. So you cop out and keep your job and that dead one's creator, or its offspring, keeps on killing."

"Or?"

He took a deep breath. "Or you tell the truth. You write down exactly what happened and you trust the system and you take that blind, faithful step over the edge." He swallowed hard. "And you fall."

"That's what happened to you?"

He nodded. "You fall and you hit the rocks and you get quietly drummed out of your job. And the cover-up, Christ. They bury your report deeper than you could ever dream. And when you're lying there, professionally dead, the Counterinsurgency comes for you and your real work begins."

Aurora blinked. "Where do... where are they from?"

"They're part of the government. Hell, they're *older* than the government. You ever hear all that crazy talk about the Masonic seal on the dollar bill? Freemason symbols in the layout of Washington?"

"No."

"Hmm. Well, it's not so crazy. Vampires always seek out power, the more one-sided the better. Taxation without representation... British governors in the colonies... lots of power in one place. Lots of opportunities for victimization."

"You can't seriously be telling me that... what, that Washington and Paul Revere were vampire hunters?"

"I suppose it doesn't much matter, does it? Maybe it's just

some patriotic bullshit they told me to stiffen my spine, to make me feel better about going rogue. If your authority is older than the Constitution, it makes it feel better to ignore all that inconvenient Bill of Rights stuff, huh?"

"I never paid much attention in Civics class. It's all the same to me."

"That's the spirit." He took a deep drink and made a little face. "Hey, when the bad guys turn to ash and you've given up writing reports, it's almost *easier*."

"You don't have to bother with evidence or juries or the rest of it."

"No, you just have to go balls-out against the worst the night has to offer."

"Where do I fit in?"

"We're always looking for talent. We're like the CIA that way. You find someone with skills, you get her inside the tent. Congratulations."

"Gee, thanks."

"I'm serious. You've got no training, no experience, and you've smoked one and escaped one."

"I've 'smoked' two."

"That's very impressive. I knew a guy, Delta Force type, bench-pressed twice his weight and ran 10 miles a day, crack shot with everything from a rocket launcher to a slingshot, trained for a year to take out a pack along the Pakistan border and got iced on his first mission."

"What did he do, try to go man on man at night or something?"

Black shrugged. "No, he went in by day. All we know is he went in armed to the teeth, ducked under the tripwire at the cave mouth, and 20 minutes later came out running, screaming. He hit the wire and set off a booby trap. Boom. Dead, and the target was buried. Buried, that is, until intel sighted him four weeks later in Baghdad."

For a moment, they just drove in silence.

"I'm a fucking *cocktail waitress*," Aurora said. "What the hell am I supposed to think after hearing that?"

"That training to be a combat badass doesn't necessarily

help much. Maybe he thought he was ready. Maybe you know you're not."

"And yet, here I am."

"Yeah." Black glanced over again. "Look in the bag."

She did.

"You know how to fire one of those?"

"Pull the trigger?"

"The variable rate of fire should explain itself. White bullet is one shot. Red bullet is a burst. Three red bullets is full auto."

"Yeah, I grew up with guns," Aurora said. Seeing Black's raised eyebrow, she said, "Dad was a hick, okay? Rack in the pick-up truck and everything. I had three older brothers, I tagged along. Them telling me hunting wasn't for girls just made me want to do it more."

"The bullets are… special. And so far you've been up against small fry."

"That you know of. What about that jazz bitch?"

"Leave her," he said sharply. "You are off that assignment."

"Suddenly it's an assignment?"

"*Listen.* She knows you. She's seen you, and once is all it takes for some of them to…"

"Twice."

"*What?*"

"Well, she performs in public. What did you expect me to do?"

"I expected…" He changed lanes, slowed, then braked at a red light. He took a deep breath. "Never mind what I expected. Stay away from 'Velvet.' Now, seeing you coming, you're way out of your league. Hit targets who don't know you, don't expect it. That's the smart move—the one that'll keep you alive to fight another day."

"Hmph. What about Steve Quartermain?"

"Who? Look, Velvet is on the sidelines, anyhow. She's a minor player. We may have a chance to point you at someone bigger, someone worse."

"Like who? The Bishop?"

This time, his antilock brakes jerked and stuttered. Horns

blared as he pulled off onto a side street and parked. He turned to her with wide eyes.

"What do you know about the Bishop?"

"Why don't you go first?"

"Do you think you could get a shot at him? A clean shot?"

"At Solomon Birch?"

Black turned off the ignition and pinched the bridge of his nose. He looked at Aurora, who gave him an exquisitely blank look in return. She could not have been clearer if she'd spelled out "AFTER YOU" in sign language.

"Okay. The Bishop." He sighed. "He's at least a hundred. At least."

Aurora kept her face blank, but suddenly felt much less like being a smartass.

"There's this… this vampire religion. I don't know if they're Satanists or something else altogether or… we haven't been able to get into the temple. No man on the inside unless we wanted to get a wire on a human sacrifice. Hell, we don't even know where they get their victims, or how or… Anyhow, Solomon Birch is the Bishop, the leader."

"They do what he says?"

"I guess. I don't know if it's like a cult where you do whatever the guru commands, or if it's… I just don't know. But there's some kind of trouble brewing with them."

"You've been picking up chatter."

"More meetings, yes. Vampires seem to be solitary creatures, but the church honchos keep going off into little groups. Something's coming. Something called 'Founding Day.' We think something's going to happen then. If it's some kind of push, some kind of coup or… or *anything*, we want to be ready to strike." His mouth quirked up. "We want to be ready to make it worse."

"And that's where I come in."

"Sure. You don't know much, excuse me for saying."

Aurora bristled and Black held up his hands. "I mean—you don't know much about the Counterinsurgency. You've seen me, you've got the phone… you banked the money, right?"

"Some of it."

"I don't think they can trace the bills normally, though there are rumors about... hell with it, never mind..."

"No, what rumors?"

"They may be able to, um... see into the past."

"Huh?"

"Like all those serial-killer movies, where the profiler goes to the scene and sees it through the eyes of the killer?"

"You're shittin' me."

"Maybe they can't. You probably don't want them to get hold of any of your stuff, though."

"Too late."

He rubbed his head.

"Well, if they could do anything about it, they'd have done it, right?" she said.

"Not necessarily. When you're a hundred years old, you can afford to take your time with your problems. But there's not much we can do that we haven't already done. We already assumed you were under surveillance."

"I don't think I've been followed. I've been keeping an eye out."

He shook his head. "You haven't seen *our* people, and they can't even cloud your senses or make you forget what you've seen."

"Jesus Christ! You want me to go up against them with *this*?" she asked, shaking the paper bag.

"You're... I don't know. They don't seem to have a handle on you. You don't do what they expect. They've been secretive predators for generations, and they know how to think like spies and cops, but you... I don't know."

"They don't know how to predict a batshit-crazy cocktail waitress with nothing to lose."

"If you say so." He sighed. "Please don't think I like using you the way we are. But tracing us back through you is harder than finding us through a former government agent. The worst-case scenario is that they catch someone like me, who knows names on top of faces, and they... turn me or torture me or suck out my brain, and then they roll up the whole operation. Night-night, that's it for organized resistance to vampires in America."

"And if they catch me, they get your face and a fake name and this car."

"Yeah. And my face is pretty unremarkable."

She wondered if the birthmark on his neck was fake. Probably.

"Wow, I'm really a great deal to you guys. A disposable assassin. Might do some good, can't do much harm."

He clenched his jaw, looking away, and when he turned to her she could see the pain on his face, despite the thick, dark shades.

"I hate to do that to anyone," he said. "It'd be easier if you were a scumbag, but you don't seem to be one. Look, are you okay for money? I can—"

"Save it. You've done plenty. I'm using you as much as you're using me. What does this Bishop guy look like?"

"Tangling with the Bishop could be a death sentence."

She gave him a long, level look and then started lighting a cigarette.

"Okay," Black said. "He's medium height, muscular build, bald. Usually well dressed, sometimes has a goatee and moustache. His head and arms are covered with scars."

"What kind of scars?"

"Like someone tried to hack him up with an axe and didn't quite get the job done. Those kind of scars."

"Thanks." She unlocked the door and opened it.

"Aurora… be careful. If you have to go at him, *make sure you kill him*. You won't get a second chance. And you don't… none of us know what he's capable of."

———

"It's time," Solomon said.

Margery Brigman wouldn't look at him. She sat on the edge of her bed, perfectly still. Then she rose. There were no wasted movements as she got to her feet. She moved with the glacial efficiency of someone who is very, very tired.

It wasn't just that Solomon had worked on her. Her father Ian, her grandfather, everyone in her family. They had all been in on it. They had shown her, in a hundred small ways, that her resistance to Solomon was making them sad, or confused, or disappointed. Their disappointment was the worst. Every day she ingested their eugenic fervor with her breakfast, and every night the desirability of her pregnancy was discussed over supper.

The sick thing—to her, perhaps the most perverse element—was that in the evening, when her aunt was browbeating her about it, Solomon had come in and *defended her*. Sadly, his tone full of regret, he'd mouthed pious platitudes about her free will, her right to determine whether her body would be the crucible for mankind's betterment or if it would lie fallow, unused and purposeless. He gently chided Hortense for pressuring her, as if he was not a thousand times more guilty of the same exact sin.

Hortense had collapsed before his displeasure, apologizing to both Solomon and Margery (though to the vampire first, of course).

Ultimately it had gotten to be too much and Margery had agreed.

Solomon had come to her bedroom late one night to feed from the tender vein of her wrist. She had shuddered when his cold lips brushed her skin, shuddered and bitten her lip but something in her had made her inch closer, had made her open her hand in welcome, had made her lie in a deliciously subservient lassitude as he drank, and drank, cherishing her violation even as her stomach clenched and a wild, beating desperation inside her tried fiercely to resist.

That small free part tried and failed, and she knew it was getting weaker each time he came to her. She knew that if it went on much longer, she would come to want it, to be impatient for it, and then she would be his creature and desire him as much as she now despised him. Somehow she felt that when she was broken, when that tiny fluttering resistance died, she would hate him even more, but not so much as she would hate herself.

So she said yes. She bought herself nine months of freedom, close to a 20th part of her life. He'd even hinted that he would back off after the child was born, that he'd want her to stay robust and healthy while she was nursing.

She didn't believe that. She was pretty sure he'd take it easy on her post-partum—let his little brood sow get her strength back—but pretty soon she'd have *two* dependent mouths pulling at her, drawing the life out.

Solomon led her down the hall, down the steps. They didn't speak as they went out front and got in the minivan. Margery's mother, Diane, drove. Solomon sat in back, as he typically did.

"I'm very proud of—"

"Mom, could we please not talk?"

They left the radio off and drove to Dr. Gupta's office.

In the exam room, Margery slipped off her jeans and her track team T-shirt. She left her socks on as she put on the gap-backed hospital gown. Pulling her white cotton panties down and stepping out of them, she felt a wash of despair, felt it physically, stirring the downy hair on her arms and on the back of her neck.

She had a brief moment of hope when Dr. Gupta vehemently refused, declared that he'd been misled, that he couldn't do this to a teenaged girl, that it was unethical and he could lose his license.

And then Solomon locked eyes with the gynecologist and spoke in those grating, booming tones that brooked no resistance. Then the doctor was silent, and moved like a zombie, tonelessly directing her into the stirrups while behind his eyes she saw something desperate and miserable, something she recognized from those nights with Solomon, alone in her bedroom.

She closed her eyes. She didn't want to see the implements Dr. Gupta was using, but she could feel them. He'd warmed them, but the slime he used to ease them into her was cold and she could smell it. No one spoke as she clenched her fists. She felt something cold in her ear, and realized it was a pooled tear.

When it was over, she started to sob in earnest, though she'd hoped she wouldn't. She'd tried to make herself dead inside and not care. Her mother stayed with her and held her and stroked her hair. Margery tried not to take comfort but it was her *mom*. She hated herself for that instinct, for still loving a mother who had been a party to her defilement. She hated her mother, hated wanting comfort, but she needed it and she sobbed and clung as Diane said, "Shh, it's all right. It's over sweetie, it's all right."

But Margery knew it wasn't all right and it wasn't over, that she was another part of the Bishop's plan and she hated the life now growing inside her.

She heard Solomon Birch talking at the doctor, reprogramming him and stealing his memories. As her mother gently helped her put her clothes back on, Margery hated Solomon most of all.

⸺

Pollidori's Spa had no number in the phone book, did not run ads on the radio, and was not even listed among the other businesses on discreet bronze plaques in the lobby of its building.

It was on the 47th floor and during the day its personal trainers, fitness experts and masseurs alternately pushed and pampered a variety of excessively rich white Chicago men. Pollidori's didn't have any kind of racist *policy*, it just worked out that way. Michael Jordan would have certainly been welcomed as a member, had he somehow found out about the spa's existence.

By day, Pollidori's was a retreat where an elite section of society could get away, tend to their needs and relax among others of their kind. Billions of dollars in casual business deals had started at Pollidori's, as had a fairly large and quiet wife-swapping ring.

But its wealthy clients stayed away after dark. Those bold corporate plunderers, neurosurgeons and white-shoe lawyers… they didn't go to their health club after sunset.

Or rather, if they did, they didn't do it again. They wouldn't say why or couldn't. Many couldn't even think of a reason. But after their first evening workout, most just found they didn't *want* to go back again.

Almost universally, they found themselves sick and listless for a week or so, too.

In the dark, the delicious joke of Pollidori's name was appreciated by members of the Invictus, a society that looked down on its fellow vampires with as much disdain as the

Pollidori day-clients had for the people who hauled their trash, cleaned their homes, and made their prosciutto-and-mushroom sandwiches at the country club.

"So," Alex Armor said to his companions. "The Indulgence?"

Once Armor had spoken, the others felt it was acceptable to speak as well.

"Not going to happen," David Ingebord said. "Lancea won't have it."

"We'll see," Armor said. "I've asked a guest to address us on that issue."

With that, he gave an imperious nod at a towel boy standing nearby. The boy bowed and left, returning moments later leading a fourth vampire—one with a long nose and chin like the Wicked Witch of the West, long ears like Spock, and long fingers like the boogeyman of countless nightmares.

"Gentlemen," Armor said to Ingebord and the other. "Allow me to introduce Vadim Siorkov."

Siorkov was dressed in nothing but a towel and looked distinctly uncomfortable. His pale and scrawny chest was pocked with dark blots. Birthmarks or liver spots, it was impossible to tell.

"Nice view," he said, and it was. The floor-to-ceiling glass was carefully Windexed every sunset, and the Chicago panorama was stunning.

"Get in," Amor said without preamble. With momentary hesitation, Siorkov took off his towel and did.

The three members of the Invictus soaked in a hot tub. Ingebord edged away with a scornful move as Siorkov lowered himself into the water.

The boy silently vanished. With the steam condensing on their clammy dead flesh, it looked almost as if the vampires were sweating, as if they were alive.

"Tell us how things go for our... colleagues in the Sanctum," Ingebord said.

"First, let's just make sure we understand each other. I give you this report, and our little problem in Skokie ceases to be an issue?"

Ingebord looked at his nameless colleague, who airily waved

a dripping hand. "That's correct," Ingebord said.

"Okay," Siorkov said, and shifted his weight to get a bubble-jet onto his back. "What do you want to know about the Lancea Sanctum?"

"We've heard noise about a coup," Ingebord said.

"What kind of coup, against Maxwell? You know that's ridiculous."

"Against Solomon."

"That's pretty ridiculous, too."

"Is it?" Armor asked. "Solomon's long agitated against the use of vinculums on Kindred, arguing that they make us unstable. Now he's under one. Is not his own stability in question by his own words?"

"Hey, there are always gas bags and troublemakers, and yeah, the Bishop's made a few enemies. Who hasn't? But I don't think there's any serious challenge brewing. Sure, some knucklehead may try something, but you know what George Bush said."

There was a pause, and then the nameless and previously wordless soaker said, "'I want to be the edjamacation president?'"

As soon as he spoke, it was clear why he'd been silent. Despite his size there was a high, fluting whine to his voice that made it very difficult to take him seriously. Siorkov turned a withering glance on him.

"Valerian..." Armor said. As the presiding Invictus squinted, the third Kindred's face—which previously had looked lordly, contemptuous and handsome—wavered like the bubbling water's surface and became smaller, plainer, less impressive.

Vadim shook his head and continued, "The *real* George Bush, the first one. He said 'Coups fail.' I think that's just what's going to happen to anyone who tries to pry the mask off Solomon Birch."

"But by his own doctrines, he doesn't have a leg to stand on."

"Does Solomon strike you as the kind of guy who relies on *doctrine*? The Lancea in Chicago is not doctrine-based, it's *Birch*-based. The Bishop's like... like that Waco guy, or Jim Jones. It's a cult of personality. Now, sure, Solomon wouldn't have gotten

nearly as far without the established Lancea church, and it
doesn't hurt that he's got the *Testament of Longinus* for legitimacy,
but he's not going to let some friggin' point of dogma pull the
bone out of his mouth."

Armor raised an eyebrow. "All this time, I thought Mr. Birch
was truly fervent about his ideology. How many of your fellows
feel that he's only using it as a means to—"

"Don't," Vadim said, raising a finger.

Armor's other eyebrow went up.

"Don't…" Vadim repeated, "Assume that Birch is a hypocrite.
Fuck, don't think I am, either. I believe. The *Testament* makes
sense and Birch makes sense. I personally think he's got a hell
of a lot more on the stick, perspective-wise, than you Invictus
guys. No offense."

"None taken," Valerian sarcastically replied. The others
ignored him.

"Solomon Birch sees his religious beliefs and his ambitions
as being… they're like the same thing, see? He succeeds because
he's right. He's right because he's succeeding. It's not a question
of one moving the other or one being more important. They're
exactly the same. That's why he's got so much power, because
you can't spend 20 minutes with the guy and not *get it*, not
understand how deeply he believes. The rest of us have our moral
quandaries and moments of weakness and hesitation. Not him.
Birch doesn't do angst."

"His record certainly bespeaks a great deal of passion and…
mm, decisiveness."

"Sure. Look, you may think you're right, but Birch *knows* he's
right. And he knows anything he *does* is right, because he's the
one doing it. That's why he'll never get the boot. There's no one
else with that kind of rock-hard, rock-headed belief. Even the
people who don't agree with him, half of them follow because
they're not *sure* they disagree. They aren't certain he's wrong,
and if there's a 10-percent chance he's right, they don't want
to get in his way. Anyone else takes over, the Sanctum's going
to start splitting, just like the Ordo Dracul with, with Marana
versus Mullner and all that crap, or the Circle with Rowen and

Bella Dravnzie throwing down. That's *another* reason. A lot of people who don't agree with his fundamentalism, hell, they still really like having a covenant that's all together, a covenant that's got your back against the Carthians or whoever. Even if you think he's a nut—and I don't, for the record—people still think he's a nut who makes the trains run on time."

For a while, the only sound was the bubbling water.

"If there was to be a coup attempt," Armor said at last, "Some 'gas bag' or other... who do you think would do it?"

"Sylvia Raines is the obvious candidate. I got nothing against Syl, she's respected and she's earned it, and she thinks Solomon's ideology is off the map. But even though she probably speaks for the majority, it wouldn't work. If she can get the mask, she won't hold it. Too moderate. You guys in the Invictus would eat her alive, and anyone in the Sanctum with a brain knows it. Except maybe Sylvia herself. She's smart but—"

"Vulnerable?"

Siorkov shrugged. He seemed to be relaxing into the water. He rolled his neck to stretch the muscles in it. "Not necessarily in the physical sense, if that's what you're thinking. She's got the *eye*. She'll see it coming. When it comes to Theban Rites, no one in the city even comes close. But it's all book learning. While Solomon's been out twisting arms and gathering debts, she's been inside learning how to turn lead into gold or whatever. She's one of those smart academics who can't understand why people don't listen to reason."

"What about Beatrice Cartwright?"

Now it was Siorkov's turn to raise an eyebrow. "What've you heard?"

"You tell me."

"She's a true believer, all right, but... man, I don't think she'd have the guts to cross Solomon. She might plan it, but when it came time to drop the hammer?" He shook his head. "She's spent too many nights saying 'yes sir.' If she still had to pee, she'd raise her hand and ask permission."

"Even if she had the assistance of Xerxes Adrianopolous?" Ingebord asked.

"They've been seen together," Valerian added.

"I bet they have," Siorkov replied. "They're probably talking about how to *keep* Solomon in charge. Beatrice admires the guy, and Adrianopolus is Inquisitor—the Bishop's kept his security chief *well* fed, believe me. Why would Xerxes toss the dice with a new Bishop when the one he's got is treating him right?"

"Why indeed?" Armor looked meditatively into the swirling water, then shifted his gaze to the lights of the city beyond.

"You have any more—?" Siorkov's question was cut short by an imperious gesture from Armor's perfectly manicured hand. The Invictus leader didn't say a word or turn his gaze to his guest for a few more silent moments. Finally, without looking, he spoke.

"No... No, I think you've answered our questions to my satisfaction. You're dismissed."

"And we're...?"

"You're dismissed," Armor said, his tone gentle, but the subtle stress on the second word was unmistakable. Siorkov's lips tightened briefly at the dismissal, but then he shrugged and stood.

"Have a nice soak," he said.

Vadim looked, in vain, for something to cover his nakedness, but the towel boy did not return. None of the others bothered to reply to his words, or even watch as he walked off.

"That's that, then," Ingebord said, and Valerian snorted.

"If you trust the judgment of Vadim Siorkov, that's that. He's hardly infallible."

"Mmm," Armor said, and the others quieted, waiting for his words.

"There are a number of possibilities," he said at last, still staring out at the city. "One, Solomon remains in power and squelches the Indulgence. That is our status quo scenario. Two, he retains his mask but fails to prevent the Indulgence, perhaps because he has to spend half his political power to preserve the other half. That is the spike scenario—a surge of chaos during the Indulgence night, but within a context of larger political stability. Three, he is deposed and the Indulgence is nevertheless prevented. We can call that possibility 'gathering chaos,' as it avoids immediate disruption but still indicates greater political movement in the future. Four, he is deposed and the Indulgence occurs. This is the maximum-chaos outcome—experienced Kindred killed, replaced perhaps by a slew of neonates, and with one of the five covenants less able to absorb and channel its energies.

For a moment, the trio thought about that.

"Rank the scenarios," Armor said, nodding at Ingebord.

"Most likely is status quo. Siorkov confirmed my feelings about the uselessness of the challenge, and if both the Sanctified and the Carthians oppose the Indulgence, they can probably undermine it. Second most likely is maximum chaos. Somehow Solomon loses his position, possibly by being pushed until he snaps and kills one of his fellow Kindred. With the main supporters of the Tranquility in disarray, the Circle can push hard and widen Carthian divisions to prevent a successful Carthian opposition. Gathering chaos is unlikely—I don't think Solomon is going to lose his mask, but if he does it's going to be both symptomatic of a larger unrest and a catalyst to intensify that unrest. The least likely is the spike. Solomon isn't going to let the Indulgence happen on his watch."

"You're not taking the Ordo Dracul into account," Valerian said.

"They're as conservative as we are, if not more so," Ingebord responded. "They think *they're* the elite, smarter than everyone else, so they have no reason to kill vampires. Their enemies are too stupid to bother with. They have no reason to Embrace, either, since their goal is knowledge, not numbers."

"Your theory is flawed by assuming the Order's motives are pure," Valerian insisted, his whining voice tiresome. "However they pose, they hold grudges just as tightly as anyone, and they're no more resistant to the lure of the Embrace than any other Kindred."

"Even yourself?" Armor asked.

From the haunted look that crossed Valerian's face, it was clear that he would have blushed if he could. He sank lower into the water.

"Does the Invictus stand to gain from the Indulgence?" Armor asked.

"Only to the extent that there would be a larger pool of confused and vulnerable young Kindred to… guide," Ingebord said. He shrugged. "I've got plenty of those."

"And the natural envy other covenants have for their superiors would lead us, I think, to suffer more assaults under Indulgence conditions," Valerian added.

Armor nodded. "We are in agreement."

Valerian smiled, a small but genuine smile. He was truly pleased that Armor agreed with him. Ingebord was pleased, too, but was more crafty about concealing it.

"With that settled, how are we to prevent the Indulgence?"

"Petition the Prince. He's one of us, for Christ's sake," Valerian said.

"Mmm." In that minor sound, Armor managed to communicate how unimpressive that suggestion was. "The Prince has his own motives. One might almost suspect he views the Invictus as a prop for his power, rather than regarding himself as one support—albeit a crucial one—of Invictus authority. In any event, I have reliable intelligence that those dreary fools from Fields are actually in *favor* of the Indulgence. In terms of pure Invictus influence, they offset us somewhat in the Prince's ear."

"What of his own offspring, young…" Ingebord's mouth twisted with disgust, "Persephone?"

"What of her?"

"Surely her disobedience and willfulness should suffice to poison his opinion against neonates?"

"Unless he wants more new Kindred," Valerian said, "As a disguise for his own error of judgment?"

"Hmm." Again, one note from Armor silenced the other two. "I think there is no silver bullet argument to sway the Prince. Rather, we need battalions, preferably from a variety of political positions. If he can cloak his own desire for Indulgence in the guise of appeasing all the covenants, he has no reason to do anything else. The most vehement opposition is likely to come from the Lancea, as embodied by Solomon Birch."

"The Prince's slave," snickered Valerian.

"The Prince's ally," Ingebord said.

"The Prince's colleague," Armor concluded. "In him we find our best bulwark against this… unpleasant possibility."

"Are you suggesting we try to keep him in office?" Valerian asked.

For the first time in the evening, Armor smiled. "If he asks."

When their laugher had died down, Valerian continued, "But realistically, I think our efforts are best spent preparing alternatives if he does fail. Without the Bishop, who *will* stop this folly?"

"The Invictus, of course. As we always have."

Chapter Eight

Margery Brigman stepped lightly across the dust-strewn floor. She didn't want a wayward creak to give her away.

"I hear you, Margery," came a cooing, taunting voice. "I can *smell* you. Delicious."

She didn't let it get to her. An old trick. A psych-out. She was way beyond that.

The gun in her hand was a Colt Delta Elite. Solomon had given it to her, describing it as 'the Cadillac of semiautomatics,' on her 16th birthday. Now she was trying to shoot him with it.

Something stirred behind her and she spun in time to see him charging, hands hooked like claws, and she snapped off two shots toward his chest. He flung himself to the side, rolling into a passageway. She stepped quickly after him, though she knew that if he was moving at top speed she wouldn't catch up. No human would. She maintained a safe space from uncontrolled tactical areas and she held her gun alertly, ready to fire. Like a well-trained cop, she ducked in and out, checking the corridor.

"One hit, one miss," came his chuckling voice. "Not bad, but you'll need to do much better to put down one of the Kindred. Let's escalate, shall we?"

The pair was on the fifth floor of what had once been a thriving office building, long closed and decaying before finding a bizarre second life as a maze for paintball enthusiasts. Solomon had rented out the entire facility and permitted Margery to hunt him with live rounds.

It wasn't the first time. She'd had her first game of "cat and mouse" when she was 13, prepared for it by her father and grandfather taking her to a shooting range and regaling her with stories of their 'training' exploits with Solomon in Illinois' wildlife preserves.

All her life, Margery had been told that she was special and superior—that others would envy her gifts and that she might need to save herself, possibly with force.

She'd been a terrible disappointment the first time. She'd cried and hadn't been able to shoot at him until he was inches away, screaming at her to do it, telling her he'd kill her if she didn't pull the trigger, and when even that hadn't worked, he'd slapped her and she'd fired.

Now she was more motivated.

Carefully stepping from the outsides of her feet inward to transfer her weight smoothly and quietly, she came to a staircase. There was dust in the air and paint spatters everywhere from more frivolous contests. She knew the terrain, and besides could tell from the density of color that this was a good choke-point. She was staying away from action zones, but she was confident that Solomon was smart enough to do the same.

Can you really smell me? Smell this then, she thought, stepping out of her shoes. She peeled down one sock and dropped it down the stairwell. If he thought she was a few floors lower, good. If not, well, she could walk without a sock.

She heard a door creak behind her and decided instantly. She bolted down a few steps, rejecting stealth for speed, and then vaulted the rail at the turn to clatter farther downward. Her plan was to get below him and shoot up through the floor, or maybe catch him on the stairs.

She was five feet into the corridor of the fourth floor when Solomon's hand smashed through the ceiling above her. He started tearing a hole and she raised the gun and started shooting.

The hand zipped back and she saw a little blood dripping through the hole. A little, but not much.

Did he retreat or go to the stairs? Even with a silencer, the gun was loud enough to deafen her, or at least to keep her from picking up footsteps and stair-creaks.

Instinctively, she'd been counting bullets and knew she had one left in the chamber. She pulled a fresh clip from her left back pocket, and crouched to eject the empty so that it would fall in her lap and not clatter on the floor.

In a rush, he exploded down the hallway. He must have gone to *another* stairway. So fast, and without her hearing, he was coming at her like a freight train. When she pulled the trigger nothing happened, because the clip wasn't all the way in. She slammed it and raised it and felt it click home. She pushed the gun up and forward even as his hands closed on it from either side, bracketing her own.

The muzzle was an inch from his face, his grinning face. It was pointed between his eyes.

"Very good," he said. "When fighting Kindred, keep your cool and aim for the head. But you should have fired sooner."

His eyes were locked on hers and he saw it. He couldn't read her mind, but he'd known her since infancy and he'd fought a lot and when her pupils dilated, he instantly knew that she was going to shoot him and that he didn't have time to command her (even if he could). For all his strength, he wasn't sure he'd be able to shove the gun away before it went off. All these factors flashed across his mind in an instant and he responded even before Margery realized she was going to pull the trigger.

He reached out with the cursed part of himself, blood called to blood and the pistol melted away in her hands, turning crimson. Her eyes widened as the blood did not drip, but *crawled*, crawled to Solomon. The fine veins in his wrists opened, like tiny lips drinking. She saw the blood flow into him and she was left holding the full clip. It was dry. Her hands were dry, too. The pistol was gone.

"Sorry, my dear," he said. "But for a moment there I thought you were going to do something foolish." He was still holding her hands and she pulled them away.

"How did you do that?" she asked.

"Not every Kindred can," he responded. "And I'll admit it, the gun was prepared beforehand."

"What do you mean, prepared...?"

"It doesn't matter," he said. "You played the game well, as well as any mortal. You are a credit to your lineage. Would you like to go get ice cream?"

"No," she said, drawing away from him. "I want to go home."

For a moment she thought he almost looked *hurt*, but then her mind was too busy wondering what had happened to her gun, how and why, and had she really been about to blow his brains out?

Would that have worked? She wondered. She didn't know, didn't know anyone to ask. She didn't know anyone who had killed a vampire.

Aurora drummed her fingers and filed her nails, but they were already short, so short the rasp of the emery board stung. She knew from experience that if she kept filing, she'd hit live skin and it would burn and itch and swell. She instinctively reached for the file anyhow, then stopped herself.

She was waiting.

Juggling two jobs and the avocation of "vampire hunter," not to mention traveling to Joliet to see her daughter whenever possible, Aurora did not have a lot of free time. Every now and then, however, she'd get a night when neither the lounge nor the restaurant scheduled her. Usually, she'd hit the bars and clubs, sunglasses at the ready, looking for *them*. But she didn't want to do it, not with Black's promise of 'something big.' She didn't want to show herself too soon, tip her hand, lose her shot at 'the Bishop.'

So she waited.

She'd called about seeing Valerie, but no dice. It was short notice and she couldn't make the normal visiting hours. The hospital was already just about fed up with her and Aurora didn't want to push her luck, draw attention, and maybe get some smartass social worker to declare her a 'bad influence' or whatever. No, that was too risky.

Aurora clicked on the TV and watched for maybe 10 minutes, but it was some reality show where this guy was doing some symbolic gesture thing with this tall plant in a bowl. All the onlookers seemed solemn and Aurora didn't know what the hell was going on. What was the deal with the plant? What show was this? What were the rules of the game?

She clicked through a family sitcom, a sex sitcom, some drama with doctors, some drama with cops, a weepy movie about a woman who lost her daughter (*No way!*), another reality show with grainy footage of a guy in a bathroom with this weenie blocked out.

Finally she found some sports, watched that for 10 minutes and then hit the clicker again.

Good Lord. With an irritated sound, she turned it off.

She looked at the cell phone, the special one. It was on. Full battery, strong signal, no messages, no call.

She reached for the emery board, picked it up, and put it down.

She went into the kitchen and looked in the fridge and reached for a beer, but no. She'd had one already. She could hold it just fine, but after a second she was pretty sure she'd have a third and that would be just enough to take the edge off. Which, of course, would be great. It was exactly what she wanted... unless the phone rang and Black told her it was on.

"Shit." She closed the refrigerator.

Back in the living room, she looked at the cell phone again.

Keeping her eyes on it, she picked up the other one, her regular phone, and dialed.

"Steve?" she said when he answered. "You want to come over?"

The Ordo Dracul was a collection of scholars. More than that, of course—mystics, vampires, defiant philosophers, and some said lunatics. But first and foremost, they were scholars.

When three Order legislators chose to meet, they naturally did so in a library.

Just as they were atypical students, this was an atypical library. It had no sign announcing it, and technically it was classified as a 'rare book store.' Nameless, it was open by appointment only, to friends of the proprietor, or friends of friends.

In point of fact, while the vampires thought they knew the store's owner, they did not. They knew the counterman, the man who would ring the cash register if anyone ever sauntered in and actually met the price for one of the books. No one had done so since 1955.

The counterman even believed he *was* the store's owner. He wasn't, though. The store's owner stayed down below and in back, with the really old incunabula and clay tablets, in a room where no light was permitted. No one who entered the room remembered him, if indeed they ever came out again.

"So," said Madge Dorfmann. A phlegmatic woman in death as in life, she was aggressively practical, severe in both her dress and demeanor. The pale and slack skin of her neck folded in wattles, pocked here and there with moles, looking like nothing so much as a pile of pale pancakes, with the dark lumps serving as blueberries.

"Mmm," agreed Lonna Cohagan, who was a stunner. Lustrous tresses pinned in a bun, stark spectacles perched upon flawless facial bones, her lush yet athletic body concealed in well-mannered tweed. She was the very archetype of the stern, yet secretly passionate, librarian.

The third member of their clique was named Madeline Diamante, and she had the kind of profoundly average, plain, unadorned face and figure that could look incandescently beautiful one minute in every thousand, and utterly forgettable the rest of the time.

She nodded along with the other two, and for a minute—not just a moment, a minute, 60 full seconds—they sat in silence.

"The Indulgence," Madeline said, prompting Lonna to raise an eyebrow and Madge to actually turn her body partway in her old, comfortable chair.

The others considered Madeline the bluntly outspoken one.

"Yes," Lonna said.

"That," murmured Madge.

Another few seconds of rumination.

"Did you see…? In the paper?" Madge asked.

"The *Sun-Times* or the *Trib*?"

"I meant the *Wall Street Journal*, actually."

"I don't think..."

"You mean the one about...?"

"Mm hmm."

They sat and thought, and then Madeline's forehead cleared.

"Oh," she said. *"Oh.* I *see."*

"Yes."

"Really?" Lonna asked.

"Oh, yes. My, my. Yes." Madeline nodded, once. "Yes, indeed."

The 'indeed' settled it.

"That's that, then," Lonna said, a tidy small smile expressing her satisfaction.

In exactly that fashion, the three legislators from the Ordo Dracul decided their covenant's official position regarding the much-debated Prince's Indulgence.

The boutique was cluttered and the merchandise was not first class. An expensive antique store has no dust, just impeccably tasteful relics, usually without price tags. This store was *all* dust and *all* tags, and the objects were a disorganized hodge-podge. Tin toy guns and tarnished silver cigarette lighters mingled on chipped (but still elegant) glass-topped tables, alongside JFK campaign buttons in cellophane bags and music boxes from the 1920s.

He found her looking through old copies of *Life* magazine.

"I preferred *Look* myself." He was swarthy and stocky. The hair on his knuckles contrasted with his perfect manicure, and the coarseness of his features contrasted with the fine material of his suit.

"It's not just any old *Life,"* sighed the woman. She was birdlike and old, her skin drawn and sallow, her bun of hair gray with wisps escaping the grip of two pencils. She wore a yellowing white cardigan with a tiny moth-hole in one elbow over dungarees. Not jeans, but genuine dungaree pants like you'd see in a photo of Georgia O'Keefe at work. Their lines were somewhat spoiled by the glaring, unnatural white of the new sneakers on her feet.

"It has to be one with a dramatic article," Sylvia Raines continued. "Something that provoked a strong reaction."

"Ah," Xerxes Adrianopolous replied. "So you buy it not to see, but to examine with the Sight?"

"Ghosts and whispers." She shook her head. "Almost always ghosts and whispers. Still, I do enjoy my antiquing. I once found a gun that had belonged to John Dillinger. Once I proved he'd owned it, I turned a tidy profit, very tidy."

"Mmm. Speaking of tidy, what's your take on our current situation?"

Sylvia raised an eyebrow and drifted over to a display of dolls, huddled together unblinking on a musty child-sized bed.

"He who lives by the sword, dies by the sword. That seems to cover it."

"You think the Bishop is only reaping what he's sown?"

"Let's consider," she said. "He's being bullied and broken to heel? Mmm, yes. He was the victim of violence, in the form of public humiliation? That certainly seems apt. A stringent standard of behavior based on arbitrary and idiosyncratic interpretation of scripture is being wielded against him by political foes...?" With that last, she turned sly but twinkling eyes on Xerxes.

"Solomon has enemies?" the Inquisitor responded, with mock surprise.

Sylvia brushed a doll's straw-blonde hair and then paused, her eyes unfocussed. "Oh my," she said.

"What?"

She blinked. "Some old unpleasantness. Very sad." She picked up the doll and turned to Xerxes, her expression suddenly far more frank. "I understand that your friend Benjamin wishes to learn the ritual of Sanguine Exaltation."

"Yes." Xerxes did not comment on this apparent change of subject, because he was fairly certain that it all tied in. "You've seemed far too busy to educate him for... years now, yes?"

"Well, that's true. As the lone Priestess of my little Temple, I find myself constantly busy. And so much of it is busy-work, unpleasant necessities that must get done, things could so easily be delegated to underlings. If I had underlings. But instead, I find myself—the only person in Chicago who understands the Sanguine Exaltation rite—reduced to arranging the cleaning of my church and seeing to the acquisition of mortal participants."

"It's a waste of your talents," he agreed.

"But what can I do? To qualify for some aid from my fellows, I would need to ascend to a position of greater authority, and with my 'questionable theology'—I believe that was the Bishop's phrase for it?—that's simply not going to happen."

"So the city's foremost scholar of Theban rituals is unable to teach them, even to a keen Inquisitor's aide who guards the faith, due to a lack of *time*. It's tragic."

"But what can we do?"

"That's the question," Xerxes said, his eyes lingering on a display of antique jackknives. "Certainly your theology is no more flagrantly liberal than many who are welcome at services."

"Like your own?"

"It behooves an Inquisitor little to take a public stance on such matters."

"Are we in public?"

He grinned and dropped his head. "You remember me from the old days."

"The days before Solomon."

"I serve the church."

"As would Bishop Birch. The question is, can his judgment—so tragically perverted during his political fall—be trusted to discern the best path?"

They walked in silence toward the cash register. "I wish Velvet was here," Sylvia muttered as she brought out her purse to buy the doll.

"I beg your pardon?"

"Nothing, nothing."

The pair emerged into a busy night, with childless mortal couples around them merrily searching for overlooked treasures or maybe just for a place to get tea.

"Are you going to the Temple for Founder's Day?" Xerxes asked.

"I'd have to cancel my own services."

"You should come," he said. "It's a big event. The entire church should be together for it."

He smiled, and this time it was wide and calculating.

"Oh my." Sylvia smiled back, and they parted ways. She turned her steps toward her sensible, reliable Honda, while he stepped into a dim gap between buildings.

Moments later, a huge bat fluttered off into the moonlight. Sylvia was still smiling as she drove home.

The celebration of Longinus' birth—his human birth, not his rebirth as a monster—was a controversial holiday within the global Lancea Sanctum. Not every church recognized the legitimacy of Founder's Day, and among those that did keep it, there was disagreement about the date. Solomon Birch was better known as a passionate scholar than a thorough one, and his research position on the Dark Messiah's birthday was not universally or even widely accepted. But in Chicago it was law, and perhaps more importantly tradition. It set Chicago's faithful apart and made them unique rather than embarrassed, so they took great pride in their difference from their fellows.

Thus, the dark festival was not only a monument to the Dark Messiah, it was very intimately associated with Bishop Birch himself.

Earth Baines contemplatively massaged the skin of his scrotum through the rough blue fabric of his tent-like blue jeans. His expression was sour and petulant.

"It's bullshit," he said.

"Uh huh?" Trey Fischer replied, trying hard to seem interested, but not *too* interested.

"I mean, the Bishop gets on me and he's all fired up to find this bitch with the stake, but he don't, y'know, actually have any *ideas* or *plans*. Other than his plan for buggin' me until I find her. But what am I supposed to do?"

"I thought you had... mm, connections," Trey said.

Earth cut his glance sideways, cagey. The two of them were in the nosebleed seats for a night game at Wrigley. Attendance was okay, but hardly crowded since the Cubs had recently imploded, dashing even wild-card hopes. The fans had drifted forward, hoping to catch a foul ball at least, while the two Kindred had moved back to sprawl on the bleachers in open solitude.

Even if it had been crowded, the more sober Cubs fans might have given space to the sullen giant wearing an unzipped hoodie over his naked barrel chest. Well, naked except for a pawn-shop's worth of jewelry, of course. Especially since the giant was sitting next to a whip-thin man with intense eyes, a man in black jeans and a denim vest adorned with patches from a dozen different punk, goth and hardcore bands.

Since the two were vampires, and even to the drunk gave off a vague impression that they might go predator-apeshit at any moment, they would have had their space regardless. But tonight it wasn't even an issue.

"Well, *them*. But that's not a number I want to call too often."

Earth Baines was known for associating with a group of creatures who weren't Kindred, but who couldn't be dismissed as 'mere mortals,' either. Not by any vampire who wanted to see the next sunset, anyway. They walked in human shapes... most of the time... and the Prince was known to have dealings with them. Elders like Justine Lasky and Norris were reputed to negotiate with them as well, but it was uncommon for someone as relatively young and inexperienced as Baines to have contact with their kind. Or at least, contact that involved anything other than posturing and mistrust.

Baines was tightlipped about how he'd met them and just how intimate his relationship was. Trey suspected the big guy was passively allowing the Legend of Baines' Contacts to grow wild. That in turn had given Trey a little more respect for Earth's brains. He might not be a genius, but he probably wasn't quite as dumb as he seemed.

"I've heard they're formidable trackers," Trey said.

"Yeah, well, sure, but what have I got for 'em to track with?

Any of the stuff from the night of, it's old and stale by now. More to the point, why should I put myself in a position with the fuckin' moon people just because *Solomon* has a bug up his ass? I ain't his thrall, I ain't his employee, I ain't his fuckin' pissboy. What *I* don't get is why he doesn't have his own people on this thing. If he's so hot to find this ho, this 'Aurora'? Shit. There's that Raines woman. She's got that whole look-to-the-past bizniz working. How come he ain't asked her to do it?"

"Didn't she already try?"

"Well, I'm just giving an *example*," Baines said. "They got all that Theban Heebie-Jeebie witch crap. How come he doesn't just use that shit to find her?"

Trey shrugged. "By logic, there are three possibilities."

"Say what?" Earth looked at him like he'd just started speaking Arabic.

"One, he doesn't do it because he can't. Either Theban Sorcery doesn't work that way or because he's not good enough at it. Have you seen him use it a lot?" Trey asked it in a casual, rhetorical tone, but this was the kind of thing he wanted. It was his payoff for coming to a stupid baseball game with a stupid wannabee gangsta. He'd managed not to roll his eyes the first time Earth said 'fo shizzle,' but he wasn't sure he could refrain if it happened again.

"Nah, never. Not that I know of."

"Possibility two is that he can, but doesn't want to. Theban Sorcery requires sacrifices, right? Maybe the price is too high."

Earth grunted.

"Possibility number three is that he could, and he doesn't want her found, but he wants it to *look* like he wants her found."

"What?"

Trey shrugged. "You know, like Uncle Tom. He puts on a show of finding the scary witch-hunter. He even enlists a big guy who gets a lot of attention—no offense, man—but really, he doesn't *want* her found. He wants her running around wacking vampires so that everyone's scared. Has he done anything that might actually *prevent* you from finding her?"

"Other than hasslin' me all the time, no," Baines said, as if Solomon had forced him to the ball game when he'd prefer to be pursuing the mystery. "Why would he want a witch-hunter running round, though?"

"Beats me. Maybe he figures people are more likely to come running to him if they're scared, or less likely to boot him from his job. You hear anything about that?"

"Mmm. The Bishop talks a good game about not being 'fraid, but he sure has his people around him all the time. All the time he's got his celly ringin', talking shit, hangin' up, then it rings again. Oh yeah, I think he's nervous." The thought made Baines grin, and then he lunged to his feet yelling, "Throw his ass out! Throw it! Throw the fuckin'...! Aw man," he said, and sat down in disgust. "Fuckin' Cubbies."

"I thought you were a fan."

"Only a fan's allowed to hate 'em like I do."

Trey blinked. "Okay," he said. "Um... what about the Indulgence?"

"What about it?"

"You think Solomon cares?"

"Oh hell yeah! You want to see him get up a big head of steam, you just mention that thing. He'll sermonize you into a coma and wake you from it yelling." Baines scratched his chin. "Now that's something. You figure a witch-hunter would make people more or less likely to want the Indulgence?"

Trey sat back, nonplussed. Baines had made a connection he'd overlooked.

"I can see it," Trey said. "Yeah, any hunter who knows what's going on is a threat to the whole show, right? And if there are a bunch of newbies, wet behind the ears, they're more likely to get caught and crisped. That, in turn, is more likely to give away the whole charade... I think you may be onto something."

"Plus, if people already be worried about some psycho redhead killin' 'em, they ain't going to want to give their undead enemies a ticket to even any scores."

"Uh huh," Trey said. "If that's the case, he *really* doesn't want you to succeed. At least, not until the danger of the Indulgence is past. And who knows when that'll be?" Trey kept his tone breezy, philosophical, watching the game and waiting to see if Baines followed the bouncing ball...

"Shit, he's fuckin' *playin'* me!"

"Well…"

"He don't want me to find her. He don't give a shit how much it hurt my career. He thinks I'm just some big, dumb farm boy he can hide behind!"

"That's only one possibility now…"

"Naw, it all fits. Fuck. *Fuck* dat!" Baines was fuming and glaring at the ball field like it had personally offended him, and then he leapt to his feet, pulling out a vibrating cell phone.

"Shit!"

"What?"

"It's *him*." Baines muttered curses as he stomped toward the exit.

Trey smiled and stayed to watch a late-game rally that did the team no real good at all.

———

Steve shifted his weight and inched closer. The leather of the sofa creaked beneath him. He had a glass of wine in his hand and music was oozing out of the stereo as he slid his hand along her shoulder, feeling the smooth fabric of her shirt and, beneath it, the firm softness of her skin.

She pulled away and stood.

"So this is your place, then? It's nice," he said.

"Have you seen her?"

Steve set down the wineglass and fixed his eyes on it. "I didn't think you asked me here to talk about her.'"

"That's no answer."

"Okay. Yes. Since that time at the club I, yes, I've seen her." The wine in the glass was a deep, rich merlot.

"Did she ask about me?"

"You know, I work at an elementary school, so I hear 'Is so and so talking about me?' all day long."

She turned with a sweep of dark hair, and under Velvet's glare, Steve raised his hands. "Okay, that was a little mean, I'm…"

"She wants to *kill* me."

"I'm sorry."

"She *tried* to kill me."

"And didn't you try to kill her? Haven't you threatened to kill her?"

Velvet turned away and went to the window, moodily posing with an arm up on the sill. For a moment Steve was quiet, just drinking in the elegance of her silhouette.

"Maybe I should let her do it," Velvet murmured.

Steve said nothing.

"What good am I, anyhow? What's my excuse for existing?"

"I could ask the same thing about myself." Steve stood and came up behind her, close. "Is the world really worse off if a few fifth-graders don't learn to read sheet music?"

She leaned back, just a little. Just enough for her hair to be inches from his face, for him to smell lilac perfume and, under it, a dry aroma like an old library book. The scent of age, of dust.

"You don't have to hurt people," she said. "You aren't driven by needs you can't control."

"You don't know that," Steve said, then seized her shoulders, spun her around and kissed her.

She permitted it.

When it ended and there was a gap between them, her eyes seemed gray in the luminous streetlight.

"I'm playing on that recording," she said.

"Really?"

"Violin. Chicago Symphony. Reissued from when I was alive." Her gaze was steady as she said it, and his didn't waver. His hands were still on her shoulders.

"Maybe that's your reason then. Music."

"Is music enough to forgive what I take? My violin pays for my violence?"

"It depends on the music. What's the price of pleasure?"

He kissed her again, kissed her like he couldn't help it. He couldn't.

She withdrew. "Don't."

"There are lots of people, living people, who do much more harm and give back much less. You have needs? I have needs, we all have needs."

"It's not the same." She turned halfway.

He stepped in again, took her in his arms, but this time his hands rose to her breasts while he whispered in her ear. "What is life if not the negotiation of need?"

She leaned back against him, closed her eyes, put her hands over his and they swayed, gently, moving their bodies with the music's rhythm.

"You need to take it," he said. "I need you to take it from me."

He turned her and tilted his head, presenting his jugular. Once again he smelled her hair as he pushed his neck to her face.

Velvet said, "No."

"You have to," he said. "You need it."

"No." Suddenly, she was like a statue in his arms and the intimacy popped like a soap bubble.

"Don't you need it?" he demanded.

"I can't." Her cold, pale hands came up and broke his embrace as she stepped back. "Not while you're involved with *her*."

"I'm not." He smiled, eyes half-lidded, voice warm and confidential.

"You are," Velvet said flatly. "You said yourself you met her again."

"We… we split a pizza and rented *Pirates of the Caribbean*," he said with a chuckle. "It wasn't even a date, let alone some kind of treacherous conspiracy."

"You know what she is to me, and what I am," Velvet said.

"I know what you are and I accept it," Steve said. He stepped close again, reaching out.

She blurred away and he froze. He'd seen a smear of motion and then she was across the apartment from him, on the other side of all the furniture, partway down a hallway.

"Go," she said.

"I can't. And I don't think you really want me to."

"I don't," she said. Her eyebrow rose fractionally even as a desperate tone entered her voice. "But I *need* you to. I have to be safe from her, Steve. And I don't want to give you up, but if I must…"

"You don't," he said quickly, and started down the hallway.

"Stop," she said, and he did. He didn't have to obey, but he was starting to feel panicky. He wasn't sure what he wanted, wouldn't let himself think about what he wanted, but he knew she had it and that if he wanted to feel it again, then he needed her.

"There has to be a way," he said.

"Go." She pointed at the door and suddenly she didn't look like the pale, unearthly heroine from a gothic romance. She looked *dead*, fresh dead, lifeless and morbid, not only cool but quite cold.

He didn't take his eyes off her as he obeyed, nursing the slim consolation that she had not denied his last words.

Steve went to a bar where his callousness and bitterness attracted a nice college girl from Minnesota, a beautiful girl who didn't realize that her desire to find a bad boy was pathological. She got his attention and he insulted and condescended to her. She found it strangely thrilling and he bullied her into driving him to her apartment. She didn't really want to, but did it nonetheless and he fucked her selfishly, rudely, three separate times. The third time she was saying, "Ow, ow, OWWW!" She didn't really know if it was from discomfort or from being overwhelmed. Steve didn't care.

As he walked to the train, Steve crumpled up her phone number and tossed it to the sidewalk. His little shudders of physical pleasure had been nothing. He needed more. He needed something that would quake his soul.

"Mr. Quartermain, I still can't get it!"

"Did you practice?"

"…yesss…"

"Then maybe you're just stupid."

The child looked at him for a moment, jaw slack, then burst into tears.

"Who is it?" Aurora asked, her mouth close to the intercom.

"I made a child cry today."

She buzzed Steve up, gritting her teeth. She didn't have time for this. She had to get ready for work.

When she let him in, she paused. She had to move, but she paused. He looked that bad.

"You went to see her, didn't you?"

"Jesus Christ, you two are both fucking crazy!" he shouted.

She grabbed him by the sleeve to pull him into the apartment, then looked up and down the hall. No one watching. Good.

When she re-entered, he was toying with her bracelet on the counter and she felt a brief flash of irritation. "What do you want, Steve?"

"I don't know," he mumbled, his eyes roving aimlessly over the disarray. She was in stocking feet and had been putting on makeup when he rang the doorbell.

"Well, we're fresh out of it here," she said. "Are you okay?"

"Do I look okay?"

"Could we have a conversation where every question doesn't get answered with another question?" She shook her head. "No, honestly, you don't look okay. She did it, didn't she? She got you again."

Then suddenly he was in her face, his hands on her shoulders, yelling, "I should be... SO... LUCKY!" from inches away. She flinched back, feeling his breath on her nose and spittle flecking her face. Shoving herself away, the slippery heels of her pantyhose lost traction on the linoleum and she stumbled, falling hard to the floor.

She looked up at him, his back to the door. Both of them were breathing heavily.

"Steve," she said. "You're scaring me."

"Good! Maybe it's time someone was a little scared of poor ol' Steve, the fucking hockey puck in this crazy game you two are playing! Christ, why can't you just leave her alone?"

Aurora edged away. "I'm not sure I get what you're..."

Steve saw her eyes dart to her purse, she saw his reaction, and then they both lunged for it. But he was already upright, and those damn pantyhose betrayed her again. He got there with a half-yard lead, picked it up, and shoved her back down to the floor.

"What's in here? Oh, of course." He pulled out the gun, the semiautomatic.

Aurora got her back against the couch and used it to get to her feet. As she did, Steve raised the pistol.

"I don't know what you..."

"This isn't the one you used on that poor bastard in the hole, is it?" He pointed it at her. "Where's the other?"

She said nothing.

"Well, it's not under the couch or you'd have it by now, right? So why don't you just sit?" He took his eyes off her for a moment and leaned a bit so that he could look at the gun while still aiming it at her. He gave a little grunt of satisfaction as he found the safety and clicked it off. "Get on the couch there."

Aurora sat. "Steve, what do you want?"

For a moment, he was silent.

"You don't know what it's like," he said. "When they do it."

"Why don't you tell me?"

"It's like..." He swallowed hard. "It's like everything makes sense. Just for a little while. No, that's not it. It's like nothing *has* to make sense, that making sense doesn't matter. Do you understand?"

"Sure," she said.

"No you don't. You're just humoring me."

"Okay, you caught me." She gave him just a tiny hint of an eyebrow-raise and it worked. He laughed. A weak, half-laugh, but the emotional atmosphere got a shade less deadly.

"I did, didn't I? All my life, I've been looking for the woman who would make it all fit together. Instead, I found the one who..." He trailed off.

"The one who what?"

"The one who showed me that it's most beautiful when it's pointless."

"Steve, don't you think—"

"Could you just *shut up* a minute?" Suddenly, he was yelling again and Aurora tensed up once more. She felt her hands shake and she hated it. "Do I *ever* get a chance to think things out on my own? No! And what's the point of it anyhow? Nothing ever adds up. It's all just madness and bullshit, and she's *right*. What she showed me is right, Aurora, it's what's real, just a moral void where nothing means anything so why even give a fuck?"

He looked at her like he expected an answer. She had no idea what to say.

"Well?"

"What happened with the kid?" she asked.

Steve sighed.

"Yeah," he said, and the gun drooped. "The kid."

Aurora took a deep breath and tried to calm herself, tried to still her hands.

"Steve," she said. "Come here." She patted the cushion next to her on the sofa.

He turned his head, looked at her sideways.

"Come here," she repeated, and patted the spot beside her again.

Slowly, he did.

"I don't know what... anything about a 'moral void,'" she said. "I don't understand that stuff. Here. Sit." She put an arm around him.

He was on her right side. The gun was in his right hand.

"I know you're sad," she said, and with her left hand she brought his head to her shoulder. Gently, she stroked his hair, just like she'd done with her daughter. Her voice was smooth and low and soothing. She kept the trembles out of it.

"I know you're pretty mixed up," she said softly.

He started to cry.

"Give me the gun, Steve."

Mutely, he handed it over.

Aurora put the safety on and set it aside... almost. She cooed at him and calmed him and tried to understand how he could want Velvet, want what she offered… almost.

Almost, but not quite.

When she felt the gun in her left hand, the anger surged back. It ran down to her fingers and her right arm, the one behind his head. She held him with it while she whipped the butt of the pistol right into his forehead, as hard as she could.

"AAAooooow!" he wailed, pain and fright mixing with confusion. He flung his arms up to protect himself, but she got the next one on the crown of his skull. He dropped off the couch onto his knees as she stood, backed up and chambered a round.

"I don't know what she did to you," Aurora hissed. "I don't know what crazy poison she put in your brain, but you know what? I don't like being threatened by some whiny piss-ant who can't even figure out what the hell he *wants*. She is death, you fuckin' moron. *Death*. You like that? You think that's your answer? Well, go ahead. Be my guest. Go let your hot little tramp kill you. And if you come to see me again? *I'll* kill you."

"I'm sorry," he blubbered and that made her see red. Her knuckle whitened and it was lucky that she'd kept her finger outside the trigger guard. Otherwise she might have shot him before she got under control.

"Get out," she said. "Go."

He stumbled to his feet, a big red bruise already starting to swell and darken on his face.

"Get out," she told him, aiming the gun at him as he scuttled away. "I've got to go to work."

———

Solomon Birch prayed. Kneeling in a small chamber, kneeling on stone before the mask and the robe and the clawed gauntlets, he prayed.

"Oh Lord," he whispered. "You have guided me into this dark place, this dark eternity, as part of Your holy plan. Help me, my God. Help me accept my punishment. Help me be damned in humility before You, and to guide the damnation of others. Oh Lord, Your flails of justice and fear are weakening.

Your punishing rods bend beneath selfishness, weakness and fear. Help me make them strong. Help me be strong, though the curse of my blood is compounded by the bondage of the Prince." But even as he said it he couldn't find it in himself to hate Maxwell. No, the Prince had saved him. If Maxwell had not bound him, humiliated him, the only alternative would have been destruction. That or the failure of Maxwell's reign, and Solomon knew his friend was the only one who could govern Chicago. Had not Solomon's own test, his own treachery, proved Maxwell's fitness?

"Let me test mankind as I have tested the Prince, and Lord let them pass."

Margery Brigman was another disappointment to him. How easy it was to use her with contempt as he had her father, her grandparents, so many of her ilk. The strongest and best of mankind, he had hoped, but still weak before the naked force of the Kindred curse. She had submitted. She had given in. He despised her.

"Lord, bless the child Margery Brigman. Let the weaving of strength between her blood and that of Father Fontaine yield a better hybrid, a child who will rise up above the slough of moral vulnerability that grips humanity! Let her bear a child who will resist me! A child worthy to truly worship You!" As he prayed, he thought of Father Fontaine, who had fought him—as Cass' pawn, of course, but still fought with strength and conviction, until Solomon had met his eyes and broken his will and sent him home with only the tamest memories of Chicago.

Yes, as long as Margery Brigman's child was safe, he had hope for humanity. But his wayward flock was another matter.

"My Lord, through the intercession of your Dark Messiah You have shown the cursed Kindred how even our darkness can be a counterpoint to Your unstained light. But Your flock has lost its way and would repudiate its true shepherd. Oh Lord, let the hardness of dead hearts give them strength to do wickedness justly, to tempt and terrify by Your design! Do not let them fall into indolence and selfish ease! Do not let righteousness be used as stage dressing upon a drape of shameful cowardice!"

"Bishop?" The voice belonged to Emily Morris, the Bearer of

the Mask. The Bearer of the Claws, Chet Berman, stood behind her. "It is time."

"Please, Lord, do not let them take my authority."

Then he stood and raised his arms, while Chet and Emily dressed him for the ceremony.

While Solomon was ensconced in his inner sanctum, Sylvia Raines entered alongside the masses. She was greeted with surprise, deference, well-hidden dismay (hidden from others with duller senses, that is), but always with respect. Her keen ears picked up fragments of conversation, even in low tones.

"He went crazy when the Nazis buttfucked him. And when I say 'crazy,' I'm not exaggerating. 'Buttfucked' is not any kind of euphemism. 'Nazis' isn't a metaphor, I mean real goose-stepping racists who voted for Hitler in the 1940s..."

"I'm out of touch? *I'm* out of touch. This, from a guy who as late as 1995 thought The Clash was singing 'Rock the Cash Bar'?"

"...It got so bad? I went up on the deck, and there was this family of Mennonites? They were *smoking*."

"...Whole Indulgence thing is just a cover for the Circle to replenish their numbers and the Invictus to throw down with the Carthians. Don't believe we've got any pull, not with the *Bishop* tidily dealt with. Nah, if the Invictus thinks they can win the war, they'll do it. If not, no amount of debate is going to sway them."

She gave a small, distracted smile, then saw Velvet.

"Expecting excitement?" Sylvia asked.

"Always," Velvet replied. "But tonight especially."

"Well, I'm sure Mr. Birch will put on a good show."

"Don't you mean Bishop Birch?"

"Of course. How could I forget?"

"Sylvia!" Both women turned as Beatrice Cartwright came to greet them. She wore a big politician's smile. Sylvia's expression was far more restrained.

"Beatrice, you're looking chipper."

"I'll take that as a compliment," Beatrice said, her grin seeming a shade less warm and a shade more artificial. "Say, can I speak to you in private for a moment?"

"If you wish." Sylvia leaned in and added in a low voice, "Was that a collective 'you' or did you want your childe to remain behind?"

Being dead, Beatrice couldn't blanch, but her expression was the next best thing, just for a moment. Then she tightened and looked to the left and right.

"No one heard us," Sylvia said tranquilly. Teeth clenched, Beatrice put an arm on the other priestess' sleeve and pulled her into the Temple. Velvet followed along as the two women quickly stepped past the altar into the corridor through which the priests entered. Beatrice moved swiftly and with complete confidence until they were in a stone cell. It was empty except for shackles and some old torn-out fingernails on the floor.

"I didn't tell her," Velvet said as Beatrice gave her a glare.

"It was a long time ago," Beatrice said. "Before I got Sanctified..."

"You don't have to justify yourself to me." Sylvia's tone, like her expression, was mild.

"Who else knows?"

"I'm sure I couldn't say. I didn't tell anyone, but as you should know the Sight isn't hard to conceal. Not everyone who possesses it is as open about it as I am."

"I was Invictus then. The Prince had seized on Old John's idea for Kindred musicians... I had to talk him down to a quartet, he wanted a full orchestra."

"All water under the bridge, I'm sure. You found religion and so did your progeny, so all is well. Or, at least not as bad as it might have been."

"You're very understanding," Beatrice said, giving Sylvia a look that was part skepticism, part resignation.

"Would that all were so. Do you think you could carry off a bid for Bishop if it was widely known that you had such a... violation in your past? Especially challenging Solomon, so widely respected. Feared, even."

"And you think you could? You think dragging me down

will make you any stronger? The Sanctum isn't ready to go from Solomon to you, and you know it. The stress would fracture it, and then once divided, the apostates would conquer. I'm not your enemy, Sylvia. Even Solomon isn't. Your enemies are the Circle and the Order and all the other unbelievers who want to see us, you and me, do what they cannot—shatter the faith of the Lancea Sanctum."

"So then even you believe it?"

"What do you mean?"

"You believe Solomon is the only one strong enough to keep our covenant whole." Sylvia shook her head ruefully as Beatrice struggled with her expression. "Don't try to hide it from me, Beatrice. You know how I see."

"I'm the only other choice. Can you not see that?"

"I see that you believe it. I think you'll even keep the mask warm for him, waiting for the day that Solomon once more presses it to his face." She tilted her head as her eyes went starry and distant. "No... you *think* that. But once you taste the power, will you give it up? You think so, but I do not. And neither does the Bishop, whom you admire so. You're afraid, aren't you? Afraid he'll restore himself by force. Afraid he'll fail and you'll be without him. No matter which way you turn, you betray your beliefs, because your strongest faith is in him. And he has betrayed himself."

"You're talking nonsense," Beatrice snapped. "Tell what you know. Who will care? Who will believe you, a minor Priestess, against me when I am Bishop?"

Sylvia's answer was to raise her right hand. She held a cicada shell.

Everyone present knew about the ritual that carapace implied. They all understand that insects would appear if Beatrice denied her offspring.

"What do you want?" Beatrice asked, her voice low.

"I don't crave power, actually. Not the transitory, political kind, anyway." The sorceress' voice was shy. "What I want is tolerance."

Beatrice straightened and composed herself.

"Of course," she said. "Your... liberal notions."

"Liberal compared to Solomon's. Mainstream by the standards of New Orleans. I don't know if you're aware, but the Lancea Sanctum is the *dominant* covenant in New Orleans."

"Without Solomon," Beatrice began, her tone revealing in two words her instinct to defend the man.

"Without Solomon we would be larger and stronger and freer," Beatrice said, without anger. "As long as he bears the mask, our covenant is his, as are we. Without him, we have the chance of making the covenant ours."

"Then we should… what? Cast him aside?"

"You're the one plotting to depose him. I don't give a fig what happens to Solomon Birch. I care what happens to my religion, to the faith that guides my existence."

"You'd let us reproduce wildly and douse ourselves in Kindred blood? You'd have every night be an Indulgence and let the Kindred breed out of control?"

"I would have us respond to the world as it is, not as Solomon Birch wishes it to be."

Beatrice put up her hands. "The ceremony is about to start. This sort of verbal play is fit for the fencers of the Invictus, not the bearers of the Spear. I will give you a place at the table, Sylvia. I will let you in. I will listen and give you the respect that Solomon never did, the respect you are due for your learning, if nothing else."

"If nothing else," Velvet repeated, rolling her eyes. Beatrice glared.

"It's better than you'll get ruining my bid, better than leaving Solomon in power. It's me or him, Sylvia. Understand that. Use your sight if you must and tell me if I'm lying."

"I know exactly the truth of what you speak," Sylvia said.

Walking down the hall, Sylvia produced a cell phone and began composing a text message. She trusted Beatrice's political judgment more than her own and was confident that what the woman had said was true. That no one else could challenge Birch, that the fundamentalists had made sure Sylvia was locked out. She was equally sure that Beatrice had baldly lied about accepting Sylvia's 'liberal' opinions.

Her text message read "B. GO."

Then she stopped in the middle of the passageway, her eyes not just distant but vacant. Her hands dropped to her sides and the phone clattered on the stone floor as a vision carried her out of the corridor, out of herself, out of time.

Then she blinked, smiled and picked up her phone to send another message.

Meanwhile, back in the chamber, Beatrice was headed toward the door when Velvet put a hand on her arm.

"Why?" the musician asked.

Beatrice stopped.

"Was it just like you said? Politics? Wanting a musician? Is that all there is to it?"

Beatrice almost shrugged her off, almost ignored her, but… but her emotions were running high. It was her big night, and lying to Sylvia had made her feel strangely uncomfortable.

"Does it matter now?"

"It does."

Beatrice looked her childe in the eye. "I thought… I thought I could make a difference," she said.

"What?"

"I thought *you* could make a difference. To us. I thought… I don't know, I thought that somehow, having you, a musician… a great musician. I had heard you and it…"

She trailed off.

"A great musician?" Velvet asked quietly.

"I hoped you would humanize us."

The three women barely made it back to the Temple for the excitement.

The rites commenced with the ringing of a sonorous iron bell. As its tones faded, the iron braziers flanking the altar were lit, one by the Bearer of the Mask, the other by the Bearer of the Claws. At this sign, the congregates began their chant.

It was a low, droning incantation, a minor-key rumble of Latin vowels, softer in the back of the Temple, where the young members were confined, their voices quiet as they fumbled over the syllables. Some of them didn't even know the meaning of their chant.

Longinus, striker of God's flesh, born on this day, we revere you.

The sounds became fuller among the middle ranks, those dead for a decade or more, those who were striving for comfort in their damnation or at least some kind of equilibrium. There was a greater density in their section of the Temple, and some of them had half-grins as they craned to see the entry of the Bishop.

Longinus, the darkness that illuminates, wielder of the Spear, we invoke you.

At the front, leaning up against the wooden rails that separated the pews from the altar, were the devout. These Kindred had made their peace with their condition or even reveled in it. Some were only a few decades past their deaths, but had been quick to comprehend their new state—had needed, perhaps, to be quick, to stave off madness or suicidal despair. Others, the truly old, had been in vampiric stasis longer than they'd known life. At least one had trouble remembering her Embrace, though she would never admit it to her fellows.

Longinus, bring us truth. Make us merciless. Make us selfless.

Longinus, forge our wills into implements for God's plan.

Longinus, refine us into the perfect curse on the living. We implore you.

Then, emerging into the fitful red light came a golden visage, tall atop dark robes, the Bishop. Solomon Birch stepped forward into the view of his followers, his bronze-clawed hands swept up.

"Solomon Birch, cease and desist."

It was not the Bishop's voice. It was not low and magnificent, it was clear and thin and plain. Birch stood motionless behind the altar. The heads of the faithful craned and cricked as they turned to the speaker.

"By my authority as Inquisitor, I deem you unfit to perform this ceremony."

"Xerxes," Solomon said, his voice low. Then he stopped. What else was he going to say? Any threat would sound preposterous and empty unless Xerxes backed down, and the Inquisitor would not have made such a public announcement if he had any intention of recanting.

Xerxes Adrianopolous was in the front section. He'd chosen a seat near the aisle and now stepped out and moved forward. He stopped right past the rail. Wisely, Xerxes was not inclined to get within reach of Solomon's claws, but realistically knew that the Bishop could close on him with fierce speed.

"How dare you!" This was Emily Morris, breaking position by the brazier and striding toward the Inquisitor until Solomon, with a gesture, stopped her.

"It is the law," Xerxes said.

"Not covenant law," Emily said.

"No, but Temple law. In 1893, the priest Andre Shackleton was stripped of his office due to vinculum. There's precedent. I'm sorry, Solomon. No one respects you more than I do—"

"I find that somewhat hard to believe," Emily retorted. Then a voice cried out, "Hold it, Chet!"

At that point, many of the spectators realized that they could not see Chet Berman, Solomon's claw bearer and sometime personal thug. He could do that, cloak himself from view. But not, apparently, from the view of Benjamin Blume, Xerxes' right-hand man. Blume stepped up on the rail and aimed an imposing rifle at what might be empty air between the altar and his boss Xerxes.

"It's all right, Chet," Solomon said gently.

Then the Bearer of the Claws was visible, his revolting face twisted with anger, glaring at Blume. "Put the gun up," he rasped, and Blume complied, aiming at the ceiling but keeping his gaze alert.

Many Kindred in the middle section started edging toward the back. Some of the old ones up front did, too.

"Upon the removal of a Bishop, it is traditional for the Bearer of the Mask to officiate until an election can be held," Emily said.

"No," Solomon replied. "I refuse!"

"Solomon," Xerxes warned.

"This is unbearable!" Chet bellowed. "This disrespect

of the Bishop before the entire church is nothing short of blasphemy!"

"The law is clear."

"Is it?" Solomon asked. "A minor law invoked once, decades before most of us were in the church—myself included? Applied with equal force to a Bishop as to a Priest none of us know? Announced without context, without debate or discussion?"

"I'm not a juror, I'm an Inquisitor. I'm not subject to review or reprimand, Solomon. It's my judgment, and this is my decision. You're bound. Your will is not your own. You are unfit to lead."

"And that makes him unfit to be treated with dignity?" Emily demanded.

"He had his chance." This time, it was Beatrice speaking. She stepped around the rail and flanked the altar—not moving straight toward Solomon, but definitely separating herself from the rest of the audience.

Though, given the rate at which they retreated toward the back of the chamber, she had little crowd from which to emerge.

The movement was not universally a retreat, however. For every four or five who stepped back, one or two came forward. Most were passionate devotees of Solomon's fundamentalism, but there were a few who had supported Sylvia's more moderate views, either openly or quietly. There were even a few who stayed out of Lancea politics and who just wanted a good view. Not many of those last, though. Most of the vampires gathering had a passionate stake in the conflict.

"We offered him an opportunity to step down quietly, to retain his dignity, to keep a position from which he could support a successor meaningfully. I believe the Solomon Birch I *knew*, the Bishop I once respected, would have seen the wisdom of that course, would have done what was best for the church."

"Beatrice..." Chet said, edging toward her, his tone full of threat. She ignored his warning.

"Not this man we see before us. He clings to power desperately, as if afraid to relinquish it. Is it merely a personal lust for authority? Or is it more?"

"That's enough, Beatrice." Chet was now four steps away.

"Has he been *ordered* to remain in office, no matter the cost?

Has he been compelled by a false friend, an Invictus officer who is artificially more important to him than the church? *Is Solomon Birch our Bishop solely at the command of Prince Maxwell?"*

That was it.

Chet swung with bone-breaking force, but Beatrice was just a blur—in front of the strike one moment, off to his side the next. Chet had missed clean, but turned for another punch as Beatrice raised her hands.

Emily pulled a curved knife from under her robe and charged Xerxes. A loud gunshot from Benjamin slowed her, but did not stop her.

Xerxes raised his arms, stepping back on dwindling legs as his body changed within his clothes, and then the clothes changed, too, darkening and shrinking into leathery bat-flesh.

Beatrice didn't strike Chet. She was no pugilist. She raised her hands because she knew he'd glance at them. She met that glance with her own and then unleashed *her* weapon, a battery of the mind and not the body. *"Be gone!"* she shouted. Snarling curses, he fled the chamber.

Standing behind Chet, she saw Solomon. He'd torn the mask from his face and shouted, "You want this? Come get it!" With that, he flung the mask among the coals of the brazier and Beatrice knew this was her moment, her gesture, her time to step from the shadows and take her rightful place.

Death does not come easily to the Kindred... except by fire. That is the bane of the race, and their instinctive fear of it is overwhelming. But Beatrice, driven equally by selfish pride and a selfless need to save her church, beat back the fear. She could sense the hush as she reached into the flames for the golden mask. It hadn't even gotten too hot. She could take it right from the fire and press it to her face.

As it passed in front of her eyes, Solomon said, "Take the claws, too." Beatrice had only a moment to feel lurching fear in the pit of her stomach, and then the agony of the 10 sharp points plunging home overwhelmed her.

"Aiiiiiieee!" she screamed, and slammed the heavy gold mask onto the top of Solomon's head. There was a loud crack, but he had his fingers in her wounds. He'd dug into her and reached up under her ribcage on each side. She heard the boom of Benjamin's rifle again, shouts, the crack of small firearms, the thud of bodies and clash of metal on stone, but her focus was on Solomon. He lifted her like a barbell and slammed her down onto the iron bowl of coals and burning oil.

Flames poured out and anyone who wasn't actively fighting ran from the Temple.

Solomon saw the fluttering halves of a butterfly knife, saw the blade coming at him and was vaguely aware that a dark-haired woman was trying to stab his face. Swinging Beatrice as a bludgeon, he knocked this new attacker aside. Beatrice struck him again on the head, and he flogged her against the edge of the altar like a washerwoman beating laundry.

His focus on the usurper was intense, only a fragment of his attention was alert for other attackers—for anything, really. He didn't see Xerxes the bat flutter away into darkness, but Sylvia Raines caught his eye.

Maybe it was because he hated her, or maybe because she wasn't fighting, just watching. She was watching him beat Beatrice to death with an eager, ghoulish grin. He had never seen her smile so widely, and suddenly he realized he was about to *kill one of his fellow Kindred.* He was about to murder in the Temple. It took every ounce of his inner strength, but he stopped. He turned and straightened his fingers, letting Beatrice drop off him onto the floor. He was bloodied to the elbows and she'd lost the mask somewhere. He couldn't see it in the half-light. It was gone in the tumult of violence.

Wordless, he walked away, not even sparing Sylvia a second glance, not even trying to see who'd tried to come to Beatrice's defense.

In the hallway, he saw Chet trotting back, a short spear clutched in his hands. It was a ceremonial weapon, but still dangerous.

"I fuckin' be-goned," Chet muttered. "But you didn't say anything about staying away, bitch."

"Leave it," Solomon said. He let the gauntlets slide from his hands and clatter to the floor. "Help me with this."

Chet blinked. "With...?"

"He was put into my custody. Mine, not the Sanctum's. I'm leaving and I'm taking him."

Solomon pointed at the massive bar to Cass' prison.

———

Weakly, Beatrice grabbed the edge of the altar and pulled herself up. She began to stagger out of the Temple, back toward her car. With each step she sent the blood within her to knit her wounds. She'd gotten to the edge of the chamber and was invoking the two reliquaries she carried—mystic objects that crumpled into ash after giving up a store of magically hidden blood, like the pistol Solomon had fed from, like the heart he had given Cass. In Beatrice's case, it was a belt and the robe she wore. It was enough for most of her wounds, but she was still weary and sore. Ravenously hungry, as well.

"Are you all right?"

She turned to see Velvet. The musician took her arm to steady her, and Beatrice shook herself free.

"I'm fine," she snapped. Beatrice hadn't seen Velvet attack Solomon, what with being swung through the air and slammed and stabbed. All she saw was a mistake she'd once made.

"I've... I have a car, if you...?"

"I've got my own vehicle, thank you. Maybe you should go see if your friend *Sylvia* needs any help. *I* can take care of myself."

"Fine," Velvet whispered, but she didn't go. She watched Beatrice limp up the hallway until she turned a corner.

———

In the Temple, things were calming down. Sylvia was long gone, poking a fresh text message into her cell phone and admiring the golden mask that had landed not 10 feet from her. It just barely fit in her purse.

Beatrice emerged from a secret door into an underground parking garage. She was trying to figure out what had happened, what it meant, if it was bad for Solomon (probably) or if it was good for her (probably not).

The flare of a small flame caught her attention and she jerked her head up. Her eyes widened at a figure standing by the stairwell.

Then there was the chatter of a machinegun and Beatrice felt bullets slam into her, much harder than they should have. She intuitively knew what was happening. She understood and tried to shout, tried to do anything, but the pain was too much. She was empty of the blood that could save her. Her flesh slackened from its previous strength. It felt like being alive again, like the kind of weakening pain only mortals were supposed to feel. She fell to the floor, trying to call on the blood, her only salvation, but there was none left.

She had time to understand, and then she was ash.

Aurora Graham gave a shaky exhale and dropped the empty machinegun. Black had called her at last, told her it was a go, had talked her through what she could only imagine was an elaborate set of defenses, and now she'd done it. One more mission accomplished. She climbed into her car, turned the key in the ignition and got the hell out of there.

She could see streetlights through the exit before a huge man stepped right in front of her. Seven feet tall at least, blonde and broad, he pointed a huge gun at her and shouted, "Police! Freeze, muthafucka!"

For a moment, she instinctively obeyed. Then she saw his fangs in the flash as he opened fire.

Chapter Nine

Aurora flung herself sideways in her seat as the windshield exploded. She floored the gas, hoping to hit her attacker. She heard gunshots, even through the ringing in her ears. She felt the car's nose dip, felt the axle scrape, and instinctively popped up to look.

Through sheer, blind luck she'd made it out onto the street. She kept the pedal down and listened to her tires scream as she turned, making for the highway. The acceleration was all off, though. The car wasn't responding right at all, and when she glanced back she saw the giant pursuing her.

He was gaining. Even with the accelerator pressed to the floor, he was getting closer, and then she heard another shot.

Something tickled her ear, making her jerk aside, and she realized it was the stuffing from her car seat. One of the bullets had hit the seat. The hole was just inches from her, and that did it. She swerved into an alley.

Earth Baines was getting his angry on.

The Sanctified had been real pissy about him wanting to work security for their friggin' Temple, so he'd told the Bishop he wanted to go to church and that was something else altogether. Instead of going in, though, he'd just wandered around outside, keeping an eye peeled for crazy shit, and he'd found some, hadn't he? He hadn't seen the whole thing—just flickers of muzzle flash from an automatic ripping. But when a car came tear-assing out and he saw a red-haired woman driving, well, he'd made up his mind.

Keeping up with a car was no treat, not even one all fucked up from miles, age and a few bullets in the motor. The blood was burning through him, but burning out, and then he saw her turn.

Nowhere to go.

He slowed down to the corner, and good thing, because a couple bullets chipped the concrete wall as he peeked around it.

But if she's shooting, she's not running.

He'd gotten the layout in his quick glimpse. Short alley, dumpsters, her car parked diagonally to block it. Sheer brick rise at the back, no exit.

He ran his tongue over his fangs, just for the sting and tingle. He raised his gun—the .50 caliber AMT Automag he'd taken from that Watts chump. You could stack bitches like her five deep and it would shoot through them all. He popped a couple rounds as he made his last burst of speed to her old shitwagon car.

Crouching behind the engine block (just in case *she* had something high caliber), he listened.

Nothing.

Baines thought about peeking, but then had a better idea. With his left hand, he wrenched off her side mirror and used it to look up over the hood.

BAMBAMBAM!

Okay, she's still watching.

But she hadn't hit the mirror before he could jerk it down. Slowly, he raised it again. This time she didn't shoot.

Probably fired before she thought. Now she's low on ammo. But speaking of low… Baines could feel the hunger inside starting to rumble and growl. He'd asked the Beast inside him for a hell of a lot of favors tonight—speed, strength. He'd have to pay up soon. If he caught the redhead he could just top off from her, but it wouldn't be smart to gamble on that. What if he emptied his belly chasing her, and she got away? He'd be in a sorry state, the cops would be there soon, and if the hunger took him he might do something really stupid.

Probably.

He saw two dumpsters, dim light, trash and no woman. That meant she was probably in one of them or hiding behind it.

Piece of cake.

If she was counting on a gun to put him down, the Bishop and everyone had given her too much credit. It would be a little sting, sure, but to him, nothing worse than getting sacked playing football.

He took a deep, unnecessary breath. Then he vaulted over the car, gun held sideways like in a DMX video, shooting wildly, a 'spray and pray.' He hit the ground, vaulted into a SWAT roll and was on his feet next to a trash bin, pressed against it.

Nothing. Again.

If she's in one of them, she won't be able to shoot me through the metal. If she's behind it... He grunted and pushed the dumpster against the wall, hearing metal scrape. Not behind it, not on the other side, not between them.

Okay then. Inside.

Without aiming, he raised his gun and fired a couple shots into the trash. He heard the first ricochet and actually saw the bin's rusted wall twitch and deform as the bullet exited. He moved to the next one and repeated the process. Then he looked in.

Lots of smelly, nasty, dirty stuff... but no red-haired vampire huntress.

What the fuck?

For a moment, Baines just stood there, baffled.

Then his ears cleared of the gun's roar and he heard a little shuffling sound. He looked.

He'd thought there was no exit from the alley, but he'd misjudged. The two buildings—one gray concrete, one brick—were very close, but they did not actually touch. There was a gap between them, in one corner, maybe a foot wide. No, not even that. Nine inches, tops.

No way. But seeing no other option, Baines approached.

If she's in there, and strapped, why didn't she shoot me in the back? He looked.

Aurora looked back, her eyes wide and desperate. She was

wedged in, face scraping across the bricks and feet sideways as she inched her way along. When she saw Earth, she started pushing harder and faster. She was making very little progress.

Baines laughed. "Outta ammo?" he asked. "That's a fuckin' shame." He pointed his AMT at her, took a moment to sight on her head and savored the thought that his gun must look about the size of the Space Shuttle to her... then dropped his aim to her leg and pulled the trigger.

His reward was the click of a dry fire and a muffled sound of fear from her.

"Oh for the love of... awright, reload, shit. Don't *go* nowhere." He reached in his pocket for his spare magazine and slapped it in.

Or in any event, he tried to.

"Son of a *bitch*." When he'd helped himself to Watts' stash, now kept loose and rattling around in his vehicle, he was certain he'd taken a second Automag clip, but damned if he hadn't grabbed the wrong one.

"Goddammit!"

He'd thought about taking a 9mm, too, but that was a popgun to vampires. He didn't think he'd need it.

Now really pissed, Earth turned and simply reached in one ape-long arm to grab Aurora, but his massive chest wedged into the gap and kept him from following. He felt his fingertips brush her denim sleeve, just barely stroking her shoulder. She shuffled away from him, her sobs now oddly tinged with giggles. Hysterical giggles, true, but the bitch was *laughing at him*.

"Hey FUCK YOU!" he bellowed, and then turned away to look for something—anything—to use as a weapon against the woman. He was searching with no luck when he heard three beeps from the gap.

"Police? Help me, I'm—there's this guy chasing me! He's got a gun. Blonde, at least six-foot-ten, he's, he's wearing a blue FUBU coat and a Kangol hat!"

"You ain't calling the cops?" Baines snarled, standing to look in on her once more. "You got more sense than *that*. We own the cops. They can't save you anyhow and you got all the drive-by shit in your car."

"He's got a big gold medallion shaped like the letter 'I' and… where am I? I'm, I'm around the corner of…"

"Oh, fuck this!" Baines said. He whipped his empty gun at her in total disgust and would have pegged her right on the head except that she got an arm up. She gave a little yelp, but most of the hit was absorbed by a tacky, beat-up, fake-silver bracelet.

Pausing only to tear the steering wheel off Aurora's car, Baines headed back to the parking lot. He told the punk 'Temple Guardians' where she was, but figured she'd be long gone by the time they got there.

"By the sufferings of all the saints," Solomon whispered through gritted teeth.

"I'm still not clear on what happened," Cass said, his voice suffused with glee.

"Be silent, you!"

"Or else what, exactly? You'll twist my arms broken? I suppose you could try to compel me, if only you could meet my gaze." Cass' grin was incongruous under his empty, scab-encrusted eye sockets.

"Put him in the lockdown chamber," Solomon said. Chet and Ian Brigman hastened to obey, though the latter was somewhat hesitant to touch or be near the defaced-yet-animated corpse that was being hustled into his home, still in torturous confinement, strapped to a wheeled dolly.

Ian was so distracted that he almost ran straight into his daughter.

"What are you doing down here?" he asked.

"Mom asked me to get a merlot out of the wine cellar," she replied, hoping he wouldn't check the lie. He seemed distracted by… by whatever it was he'd brought in through the attached garage.

"I'll grab a bottle," he said, looking over his shoulder. "You should definitely stay out of the basement for… uh, for the time being."

"Okay, Dad," she said. Then, "Are you okay?"

"It's probably a good idea to stay away from Mr. Birch for a while, too," Ian said, still looking back at where the vampires were. He focused on his daughter long enough to kiss her forehead and say, "I love you Margery. You know that."

"Of course," she said, and watched him go, wondering what it all meant. Wondering what secret had been buried under her home.

She heard heavy footsteps and just had time to duck into the triangular closet under the steps before Solomon turned the corner. She could see him through the cracks of the steps, bellowing into his cell phone, with one of his creepy yes-men lagging behind muttering into *his* cell phone.

"Who did it?" Solomon demanded. "Who dared defile the...? *Me?* They suspect me?" He stopped, turned to the wall and slammed the phone into it, hard. Then he started talking into it again.

Only the best for Bishop Birch. His cell was titanium and rated as 'bullet resistant.'

"Tell those ignorant brutes that if I'd wanted to kill her, I'd have finished the job in Temple!" Then he shut the phone and asked his follower if they'd found Xerxes. Margery didn't hear the answer, just their footsteps in front of her face and then rising above her head.

───

"Cash okay?" Aurora asked the man behind the counter.

"Legal tender," he said. "All debts public and private. Can I see some identification?"

She made a show of looking through her purse. "Shit," she said. "Where did I? If I left it in my other wallet, that means..." She sighed. "Look, I've got a... a Blockbuster card and, um, my phone company long-distance card in here..." She rummaged. "I've got an old insurance thing out in the car, I think."

"No, it's okay. That'll be fine."

"Thanks."

"Have a nice rest, Ms. Barclay," the attendant said. "I hope your car gets fixed soon."

"Well, my husband will be in town tomorrow. Everything will get straightened out then." She kept her left hand in her purse so that he wouldn't see she had no ring, and kept her right hand moving so he wouldn't notice how badly it was trembling.

———

"You seem troubled," the Prince of the city said. Velvet blinked and continued to put away her violin.

"Do I?"

"Yes." He smiled at her. "It affected your performance."

"Please forgive me." She bowed her head and inwardly cursed herself. A command performance for the Prince was nothing to screw up.

"Don't be. Don't assume it made it worse." They were in his home, his den. A fire crackled in the hearth behind glass screens—a daring affectation for Kindred. Maxwell had sat in an overstuffed chair, eyes closed, listening, his left hand dangling to caress the black fur of an utterly silent, utterly alert puma. It had panted at Velvet once before Maxwell spoke to it, stroked it. Then it had purred. Now it was still and quiet as a statue.

"I hope the music pleased you."

"Do you think I should declare an Indulgence?"

"M...my Prince?"

He smiled—a little cruel, but a playful cruelty. He said nothing.

"You asked me this before," she said.

"Yes, and received nothing that even resembled a satisfactory answer. I'm not used to being frustrated. So you will answer me tonight."

"It would be very... unpredictable. You've always seemed to... defend stability, I guess."

"Is the stable situation what you really desire? Your covenant is slowly withering, losing its position to the Carthians, the Order... and, of course, my own Invictus comrades."

"The Lancea doesn't Embrace," she said automatically. Maxwell smiled.

"Is that true?"

Confused, she looked away.

"There was chaos before you," she said. "Most of us don't want to go back, whatever banner we follow."

"That was normative chaos. This would be only a little break from the routine. There's always value in changing things up, keeping people on their toes. Perhaps I'm tired of being staid and stodgy," he said, his voice almost petulant.

"If you..." She paused, wondering if she was being too bold, but something drove her on. "If you want things to change in the Sanctum, you don't need to go so far as an Indulgence. There's already—"

"Yes," he said. "I know."

"Do you think there would be more Embraces or more... more acts of revenge?"

"In sum total, I think there would be a balance, and that the numbers of each would be far smaller than either the detractors or the supporters of the Indulgence believe. I think we'd get about... five. Yes, five of each. There would be sound, and fury and 10 total events. Ten isn't so many. And the rest of us would spend the night hunkered down and trembling with fear."

"Solomon Birch wouldn't like it."

"Solomon is not in a position to cross me." He shrugged. "It's my understanding that not everyone within the church agrees on the ban on Embrace. It might be refreshing, invigorating, for those who like it to do it and those who hate it to have something recent to rouse their indignation. I have to keep my people *entertained*, Velvet. As a musician, surely you see the value of that. What is more diverting than a good political brouhaha?"

"Would you...? Never mind."

"What? Speak freely."

"It's a personal question."

"Speak freely! Thy Prince commands it!" His eyes were bright, merry.

"Would you... indulge?"

"Mmm. Well, my political opponents are fairly well stymied

at the moment. I can't think of any Kindred I really *want* to kill, and if I started on a list of the deserving, I'd have to declare an Indulgence year. As for the Embrace, well, that's out of my system. What about you? There's someone you're thinking of, aren't you? Someone *special*?"

"Maybe," she whispered.

The Prince stood and put a hand on her shoulder. "You're a good girl. A clean citizen. You won't when it's forbidden, will you?" He leaned in. "I do not regret Persephone. After... well, the temptation to sweep her under the rug was quite strong. I'm sure you understand. But even then, on some level, I did not *regret* what I'd done. I have regrets... your Bishop, or former Bishop, I regret the necessity—"

"He's your friend," Velvet said. "Isn't he? He hates the idea of the Indulgence."

"Does he?"

"He must have told you?"

"We don't speak anymore. Besides, I know better than to assume that what Solomon says, or even what he believes, is what he wants." He released her and went over to the fire, looking into it. "Solomon and I have done things to each other." He sighed. "Either we are such close friends that we know we can forgive anything. Or we are both the most black-hearted of traitors to betray one another so completely."

He gazed into the flames, then shook himself and turned to her.

"You still haven't answered me," he said.

"Does it matter?"

"I will abide by your decision."

"What?"

"If I feel like it."

"You're... you must be joking."

"Oh yes, but that doesn't mean I won't do it. A good joke can be spoken in words, but the best jests are always scratched into reality."

"I can't decide, not for everyone!"

"Yet as Prince, *I* must."

Backlit, his face was dim, except for a smile of white teeth in the darkness.

"Tell you what," he said, reaching in a pocket. "Heads, we do it. Tails, no Indulgence. What do you say?"

Velvet said nothing.

"Do you know which side you hope for? I think you do."

The Prince's quarter twirled through the air and bounced once on the carpet before resting at Velvet's feet.

Margery's heart beat fast, but she worked with it. She pretended she'd just run a hard race, that what she was feeling was exhilaration and not terror.

What is he afraid of?

She was barefoot. The steps were cold beneath her toes as she crept downward, feet next to the wall to prevent creaks. Even in the summer it was cold, until she reached the carpet at the bottom.

What is so awful that it frightens Solomon Birch?

She didn't want to know. Morbid, pathological curiosity— that was fine for other people. Margery had seen enough things that no one should, and she had no interest in learning more. Not just for the sake of mere *knowing*.

But she needed to escape from him. From her family, too, though she wouldn't let herself think about that too often or for too long. She'd pilfered money and copied down her parents' Visa card numbers. She had vague plans to buy a dozen airline tickets that left around the same time, during the *day*. She could use one and give the others away or just hope for confusion.

She knew, though, that Solomon would never give up. Not if Margery stole herself from him. Not if she stole the child.

Edging closer to the door, she heard... *Ella Fitzgerald?*

She tried the door and it was locked, but she'd expected that. She knew where her dad kept his keys. He had been asleep. Solomon had him working hard on something all day and he'd gone to bed early.

As she opened the door, the music became clearer.

"That's how I'd cry in my pillow..."

Before her, in a chamber of empty concrete, was a figure that had once been a man. In a glance, she took in the shattered limbs, locked in positions of painful contortion. She saw the face, double wasted, first by the pallor and stillness of undeath, and second by the scars of maiming fire.

She didn't puke, but she tasted it coming up and had to swallow hard.

That mangled face turned toward her.

"Who's there? Solomon?"

The head tilted.

"No," he said. "Not Mr. Birch. I'd have heard his clumping steps, and you walk softly. Who, then? One of his pawns, his playthings?"

"Yes," she whispered.

"Sorry? Hard to hear you over the music. Though I must say, I prefer this to some of the other nonsense to which I've been subjected."

Margery looked around and saw small speakers, their wires poking through crude patches in the cement. Not seeing where the wires led, she simply disconnected them.

"Who are you?" he asked.

"Who are *you*?" she replied.

"They call me Cass. I got on the wrong side of Solomon Birch, as you can perhaps gather. You? Give me a name at least. If not your own, some kind of place holder."

"You can call me... Jennifer."

"Jennifer. That's the most common girl's name these days, yes? I heard a report on it 62 nights ago, when the radio was tuned to WBEZ-Chicago, National Public Radio." He said the last words with a manic, compulsive rhythm. Then he cleared his throat. "Sorry. I've been confined with little company, and most of that *Solomon's*. He didn't send you, did he?"

"What did you do to him?"

"Oh, tried to kill him. Almost made it, too. What a shame."

"Why?"

"Do you really care? You're here without his permission, aren't you, Jenny?"

"What makes you think that?"

"I'm extremely clever. If you came with permission, you'd come openly, speak at normal volume, the music would have gone off smoothly and not with that barking sound. And I think that if you were truly enslaved to his will, you wouldn't have agreed that you were his 'plaything' with nearly as heartbreaking a tone of regret. So. You are here against your master's will. And given the sounds of distress that I barely heard over the music, you weren't prepared for what you found. This interests me greatly. What brought you here? Just wanted to know?"

"You want to escape, don't you?" Margery said, meeting question with question, trying to regain control of the conversation.

Cass laughed. "Oh yes. And I think... I think you do, too?"

"More than anything."

"Well then, we have much to discuss. I can help you a great deal. But first, you'll have to trust me—just a little, just a tiny bit. And you'll have to help me."

"What do you need?"

The ruined face creased with a smile, and she could clearly see his fangs grow long and dagger-tipped.

"Blood. Blood, of course. If I know Solomon, he's got a stockpile of it somewhere near to hand. I can find it... but first I'll need an eye to see..."

———

Solomon's phone rang. When he looked at the display and saw who was calling, his fingers started to tremble. He had trouble flipping it open.

"My Prince?" he said.

———

The first Sunday of the month and the Kindred went to Elysium, all except those who stayed away from fear, or principle, or fear disguised as principle. All except those banned, like Solomon Birch.

Earth Baines went, much more comfortable without his wire this time. Solomon hadn't asked him to wear it. Solomon had been distracted, hadn't been paying attention to Baines at all.

Baines didn't care that much. He continued to hunt for the woman, for Aurora, for the lucky almighty witch-hunter, but no luck. He'd tried to enlist a seer or two to help him, but they had zero interest. They seemed as distracted as Ol' Man Birch. Finally, he'd gone to his *other* allies, the ones who had to be spoken to with great caution, but they'd crapped out on him, too. One had deigned to go and sniff around. He'd followed her as far as an El station, and then shrugged.

Earth Baines, despite his position in court and his new, odd relationship with Solomon, had no idea that an Indulgence was imminent.

But it was.

An Invictus boss-chick named Zelda Markov had paid for the right to decorate, and she got her money's worth. It wasn't because the decorations were so smashing—blue and green lights and banners that played off the water and glass to create a shimmering, deep-sea mirage, tastefully understated, but nothing as impressive as the late Priestess Cartwright's melting Jesus. Nevertheless, people would remember the look, and her name, for decades, because that was where they heard the Prince declare that in four nights' time, they would be granted a vacation from his usual law of Tranquility.

Even among those who expected or hoped for an Indulgence, the timing was a surprise. Maxwell had declared this, what the Sanctified were openly calling a "holiday from reason" on the same night as the Feast of the Gauls.

So the Kindred gathered weren't discussing the decor, they were furiously speculating on *why that night?* The consensus was that it was a blatant snub of the former Bishop, that Maxwell was kicking Birch while he was down.

Those in a position to know insinuated that Solomon, when Bishop, had agitated for the Prince's removal and that the Prince was now just returning the favor, with interest, as one might expect from a vampire in power. Using an abeyance from his own law against violence—when it was violence that had gotten the Bishop in trouble, hence bound, hence unfit to be Bishop—well, that was just considered an exquisite twist.

The assembled vampires chattered and planned and worried about the Indulgence night, some hoping it would never come, others that it would never end.

Velvet and Baines were mostly silent, and that only until she drew him away, after the announcement. They went downstairs into a dim cavern where the main source of light was from the whale tank. A beluga swam by, its gray bulk soundless.

"You've been near Solomon," Velvet said. "What do you think?"

Baines shrugged. "I dunno. Everyone thinks this hurts him, but..."

"What?"

"I dunno. He's a sly ol' dawg. And the Prince, hell, he knows more tricks than a hunnert-year-old hooker."

"What's that mean?"

"It means, he's got Solomon bent over, right? Why would he let him go, kick him down in the dirt? Solomon's gonna agree with Maxwell no matter what. He gots'ta, so why not keep his dog in power? Y'know whut I'm sayin'?"

"Maybe he can't," Velvet said, but her brow was furrowed.

"He's the Prince. He can do any damn thing he wants."

Velvet was silent for a moment more, then, "Maybe he's doing it to... to be kind."

Baines blinked.

"Awright. But I think Solomon would rather put his nutsack in a blender than have someone be 'kind' to him like that."

———

"Yes, take it," the vampire whispered. "Fight for it."

Four men were struggling. It was a small room, bare, with an easily cleaned tile floor and metal walls corroded by age. Blistering hot by day and still sweltering at night, especially with four men breathing hard, working hard, fighting to be the one who would get the taste.

Harry had Hank in a stranglehold and didn't dare let go.

John and Leo were letting him take Hank down for them while they kicked and punched and slammed each other into the walls. When Hank went limp, Leo threw John on top of Harry and Hank and staggered over to the vampire, wrapped his lips around the open vein and drank, and drank and drank.

"The precious life," the vampire said, louder now so that they could hear him over their own panting. "It's everything you've ever wanted, yes?" He closed his eyes. "There's more."

Leo's eyes opened wide in shock.

"Mm hmm," the vampire said. "Now you've got a little of it *in* you. A little of my strength. A little of my death. A little of my eternity." Gently, he pushed Leo aside and gestured for John. "I lied. Some for everyone. All of you need my power. We have three days. She won't know what hit her. And whichever one of you fights her best... you'll get the *real* reward."

Harry drank next while Leo and John experimented with the new blood in them, used it to close the cuts and cool the bruises each had left on the other.

"Wake Hank up," their master commanded. "He'll want to hear about his chance to be with me forever."

"You don't really think Solomon will come for you?" He'd tried for bravado, but it came out worried.

Justine gave a little smile. "I don't think it's impossible. Him or someone else. Someone who hates me."

"How could anyone hate you?" Again, he tried to say it in a way different from how he meant it. He was big, the muscle-bound bodyguard who'd helped her face Solomon at the Discarded Image. He tried to say it as a charming compliment, but it came out disturbingly sincere.

He thought that he loved Justine more than he'd ever loved anyone while he was alive. That was not true. He loved her as much as he had loved his mother, when he was a baby, before he learned any words.

"People do," she said. "And on this night, I think a lot of old hates will come out. New ones, too. Best to sit it out. Stay home with a few select friends." She put a hand on his arm and he smiled. She smiled back.

"And a battalion of private security guards out front."

"It'll at least slow them down," she said.

———

Xerxes Adrianopolous fluttered through the night on bat wings, chittering to his nocturnal brethren in bat-speech. He just needed to get through tomorrow night, and he planned to do the whole thing in animal shape. Hard to spot, hard to chase, he'd worked his will on crowds of bats throughout the city. They'd flow around him at need, hear his call and come. The rats, too. All creatures of urban filth. Xerxes liked his silk suits and manicures, but when the chips were down, the beasts obeyed.

He was a survivor from a long line of survivors, and he just needed to get through tomorrow night. He could flee anything he saw coming.

He just hoped that Sylvia Raines didn't have anything she could turn on him. But then, if she did, wouldn't she have used it long ago?

Xerxes forgot about Raines, fluttering away, his thoughts returning to Solomon, always Solomon. The man was just scarier, and famously revengeful, and what the hell would stop him now? His position was gone. What else did Birch have to lose? The timing couldn't have been worse, and Xerxes spared a dour and angry thought for the Prince, who surely had reasons of his own for destroying the local Inquisitor through a Lancea Sanctum proxy.

Well, fuck it. Tomorrow night, Xerxes wouldn't be bothering with the duties of an Inquisitor. Tomorrow night's agenda was survival and nothing else.

Nothing would stop Solomon except Xerxes' ability to hide, escape and endure.

———————

There were murmurs at the Temple, far more muttering than usual. Only the most reverent held their tongues while others exchanged shreds of gossip and suspicious glances.

"Xerxes will be here."

"Xerxes won't dare show up."

"Maybe Xerxes is *already* here."

The assembled Kindred tried to hide bewilderment behind poise, tried to pass speculation off as inside information.

"Solomon didn't kill Beatrice, but he *had* her killed. He'll argue it was all kosher, that anyone who can't defend herself from a mortal deserves to fail."

"No, he repudiated that doctrine explicitly back in 1982. I remember the sermon. Mark my words, he'll show up with Sylvia and Xerxes and make amends now that Beatrice isn't around to compete for the mask."

"I heard the mask is *gone.*"

"No, Beatrice has it."

"*She's* gone!"

"No, she's just hiding. Once the Indulgence is over and Solomon's cooled down, she'll come out of her hole."

There was no ringing of the iron bell, no dramatic leap of flame from the braziers. The murmur died down quick when the congregation realized Solomon Birch was standing at his accustomed place behind the altar.

He wore no mystic robe, only a white button-down shirt, a black suitcoat, and no tie. Without his mask or claws, he seemed smaller, diminished, out of scale compared to the hulking stone table.

"My faithful brethren," he said. He looked out over them, his face unreadable except for a thin patina of sorrow. "My *faithful* brethren.

"How often has that phrase skipped lightly off our tongues? 'Faithful brethren,' a common greeting. 'Faithful' an oft-used description. 'Brethren' an honorific meaning little more than

'Kindred' or 'people' or any other term worn out through familiarity.

"But tonight… of all nights, tonight, it means more. Tonight, I look before me and I know I see the *truly* faithful, and it is you, you who have stayed the course, who I am proud to call my true family, my true… home."

It almost seemed as if his voice broke a little on the last word.

"Tonight, you could sin. Tonight, you could murder. Tonight you could give in to that burgeoning weakness that begs for succor in damnation. Tonight, you could Embrace.

"It is forbidden, of course. Church philosophy forbids it. Save on this night, the Prince's law prohibits it. The very core of our natures resists it, makes it a taxing and destroying task." His mouth eked just the ghost of a smile. "Or, at least, that is how I've heard it described."

The damp stone echoed with a few nervous titters.

"Yet this sin is known, more than known. It happens again and again. Each one of us here tonight, every Kindred we know, is evidence of that. Each of us exists thus, trapped in the twilight of the soul, because of some sire's weakness or lust or regret or simple callous calculation. There are as many reasons to Embrace as there are sires, I suppose, and ultimately only one. Every mortal adulterer is different, and all the same. Every transgression of the marriage vow is ultimately about selfishness, and the same is true of this essential Kindred instinct. Cloak it as they may, making arguments of need or loneliness or even, laughably, *justice*… Ultimately, each sire acts from selfishness. Each hopes that by sharing his curse, he can lighten it. He hopes that enlisting a second set of shoulders to his yoke will ease his burden, but in the end, most find their cares and woes redoubled. Embrace for love and you will see your love corrupted. Embrace from hate and you will see your hate become eternal."

He looked down at his hands, then back up at his listeners.

"Eternal, that is, until the mercy of self-destruction, or the accident of sun or starvation… or murder. For make no mistake. Murder is a common end to our kind. Perhaps the most common. Some fall to mortals, trampled beneath the hooves of the cattle,

and good riddance. But others... far too many others... fall
beneath the talons and daggers of their fellows in perdition."
He gave a thin smile. "Slain by Kindred. Or if you prefer, their
'brethren.'"

"Like Old John?"

Gasps.

The implied insult—that Solomon had been involved in
the murky circumstances of a prominently feared Chicago
vampire's demise—caused heads to whip around as everyone
present looked to see who had been so bold. Not only to interrupt
Solomon during a sermon, but to accuse him of violating his
own beliefs?

"Yes!" Solomon said, his eyes wildly sweeping the crowd.
"Yes, like Old John. I didn't kill him and I'm still not sure who
did. But it was one of three Kindred and I begged, pressured
and threatened all three of them to spare him. Not for any love
of that... that foul, diablerist wretch." The deposed Bishop's
words were infused with pure revulsion. "He was as low and
vile as any of us. And even *him*, as much a scourge on us as
on mankind, did not deserve the slaying hand of his Kindred.
We deserved him. Humanity, too, deserved the perverse and
corrosive influence of that monster, to the extent that they were
unable or unwilling to root him out. He gave them only what
they asked for. And us? We labor under the curse of *God*. What
right have we to pass the fatal, final judgment on others so
afflicted?

"But that sin, too, is permitted tonight. We have, in the
eyes of the *court*, license to kill one another as we prey on the
living. More, perhaps! Yes, discretion is expected with humans,
but with Kindred? We turn to ash! No body to hide! As long
as it's not done publicly, what remains to conceal?" He put his
hands on the altar and leaned forward, daring the onlookers
to meet his gaze. "I did it. I killed my fellows. You know, some
of you. You remember my wild days, my bad days, before I
became Sanctified. But not a night passes, not one night, that I
don't regret those crimes. I saw only the immediate, like a child.
In my blindness, I robbed God. I stole from Him weapons He
might have turned on the bodies and souls of sinners. Until the

Dark Messiah showed me the heights of wisdom, I could not see as Kindred ought—in decades and centuries. Who knows what 70 or a hundred years of growth and wisdom might have made of those callow brutes I murdered?"

He hung his head, paused, and raised it slowly.

"That is why I can *truly* call you my faithful brethren. Not because we know the same prayers or sing the same songs or come to the same Temple on nights of dark sacrament. Because tonight I know you have made my same choice.

"I could be out hunting Xerxes Adrianopolous. I could. I *want* to." He gave a thin smile. "I have what some might call 'anger issues.' Certainly the Embrace did nothing to calm me. So yes, I want nothing more than to spend this night reveling in fury, *indulging* myself, taking part in the chaos by taking apart those who have angered me. It's a long list. But I don't do it.

"I don't do it, just like many of you who feel the same wrath don't do it. Because it's *wrong*. Because we have made a decision to exist in some dignity, some accord with God's plan for us! Because we have chosen the Sanctified path! Because we have sworn to put God's will for the Kindred above our own, we don't do it! We have decided to comport ourselves by what we know is right and not what by feels good. Therefore, we are here. Tonight. Not out there, reveling and wild and squandering ourselves on *freedom*.

"Looking around, some familiar faces are conspicuous by their absence."

That started the whispers again, and Solomon paused. He let them whisper. He milked it.

"I can't speak for those who have chosen to abandon the Temple on this night. I can't guess at what they're doing or their motives. I would hope it's simple fear, or that they're bottled up in their havens with weapons and a good book, like survivalists waiting for the bombs to fall. I would not accuse any of the Sanctified—no matter how philosophically opposed to my own viewpoints. I would not accuse them of partaking in the Indulgence they've been offered. It is my hope that they would extend me the same courtesy."

He frowned.

"I hope... that you'll let me talk about myself for just a little bit."

The whispers and muttering took on an encouraging tone.

"I am... under the spell of the Prince. You know this, we all know it. Certainly some segments of the church have been eager to remind you all. But I swear to you upon all I revere, upon the Spear, upon the *Testament*, upon Longinus and the God behind him—I give you my word that my will remains my own. I have not laid eyes on the Prince since the night of my... violation," and this time his voice definitely broke. There was no whispering now. Everyone was spellbound at the sight of Solomon Birch showing *weakness*. "I have stayed away, because I know the danger of it, the peril in what he has done to me. I know my feelings are not trustworthy, however strong they seem." He took a deep breath, his posture straightened, and his voice emerged with renewed strength. "That is why I set my *feelings* aside. That is why, when instinct howled for me to slay Beatrice Cartwright, I resisted. As you saw! I resisted. I dealt her the first blow, but withheld the last! Tonight I still resist, when all expect me to cast away my beliefs for a sweet night of revenge. I came here because I believe. I believe even the lowest of us, most jaded and cruel, the weakest and most desperate, can set aside our passions and sins and *become Sanctified*. I hold out that hope even for those who have betrayed me, humiliated me, tried to destroy me. You know their names. Xerxes. Cass. Maxwell."

One more deep breath and he was back to the Solomon they knew, or perhaps even stronger, the air of casual command infused with new meaning, new purpose.

"All my false love for the Prince cannot make his actions right, and I know it. All the machinations of Xerxes Adrianopolous cannot make treachery into true dealing. We are selfish and vicious and cowardly by the nature of what we are, but with prayer and hope we can rise above. With will we can find purpose in what are otherwise endless nights of hunger and ego. I came here tonight because I have faith, and hope, and the strength they lend. The rest of you did as well." He looked around the hall. "I think we have a quorum. I think there are enough of us here to elect a new Bishop, one that indulgent Chicago sorely needs." He smiled. "Does anyone have a nominee?"

The service stretched on much longer, nearly until dawn, but the memory everyone would take away was that speech. That, and the deafening chant of "Solomon! Solomon! Solomon!" that followed it.

Sylvia Raines spent the night in her own church. She celebrated with her most stalwart followers, perhaps a dozen of them, maybe a few less. It was quiet, solemn and proper, and no one felt anything as strong as the emotions that rippled through the Temple with even Solomon's first words.

After the service, Sylvia asked her congregates to remain, and they did, but sensing that she wished to be alone they withdrew upstairs. She did not ask them to guard her, but they did. They knew she was a target, or that she could be.

Alone, in the basement, Sylvia knelt before her skeletal warrior and prayed.

When her prayers were said, she reached behind the skeleton and withdrew the golden mask. She was unaware of her smile as she caressed it, the intricate whorls of the hair, the stern line of the brow, the strong cast of the mouth. It lost some of its charm under the steady electric lights, some of the mystery lent by flames in the Temple, but it was still beautiful.

"Mistress?"

Sylvia lowered the mask, instinctively hiding it, and then relaxed. The speaker was one of hers, even more so than the Kindred above. A mortal who had tasted her blood, he had little will beyond serving her.

"Yes?"

"The perimeter remains secure. You wanted hourly updates." His tone and posture were diffident. He'd been an FBI agent assigned to the Chicago office in 1964. She'd come to own him in the '70s, and he'd stopped aging around 1981, thanks to the unnatural stagnation properties of her blood.

He'd been smart enough to discover vampires and dumb

enough to tell the truth to a law-enforcement organization that had refused to recognize the Mafia until the late 1950s, that hadn't been able to conceive that it might have homosexual agents until the 1970s. He'd been fired and ridiculed and had learned that his was a typical fate for police who learned too much. First rejection by authority, and then seduction by the enemy.

He was okay with it.

Aurora would have recognized him as "Agent Black."

"Thank you, Michael," Sylvia said. "You may go."

He nodded.

Sylvia was afraid for her existence. Of course she was. But not nervous. She had the Sight, after all. It couldn't protect her, but she'd see it coming. Then Michael, and her not-quite-a-dozen followers… at the very least they'd delay any attack until she could flee. Or fight back, for that matter. Her mastery of Theban rites was unparalleled in the city, and she'd had plenty of time to prepare her blood curses. Any of her expected enemies who came too close could be made to bleed, burn or suffer. All she needed was a line of sight and a moment of flame to make their hardy Kindred flesh as weak and soft as a mortal's. That's what she'd done to Beatrice Cartwright, to make her fall before Aurora's bullets.

As her servant departed, Sylvia spared a thought for Aurora. The girl had been lucky, and thus useful. She'd also been gullible, swallowing that ridiculous line about a "counterinsurgency." She'd followed directions admirably to get past the Temple defenses, exploiting Sylvia's knowledge to get her shot at Cartwright. A pity. But in Sylvia's experience it was crucial to know when to let go, even of a treasured tool. The Aurora gambit had worked better than she'd hoped. The destruction of that fool Cartwright would be a major blow to the conservatives, especially if people continued to suspect Solomon Birch. Yes. It was definitely time to ensure that no one traced Aurora to Michael and then to her. She'd hidden her tracks, with all her cunning and Sight.

For a moment she wondered if she could be sure Velvet would take care of it. But she dismissed the concern. She had bigger issues to contemplate.

Besides, wasn't God on her side?

No, despite the charge of danger invisible in the air, Sylvia felt quite safe. Safe enough to withdraw the mask and dream, to even dare to press it against her face.

And as her eyes matched with the empty holes she saw. Not the small church she had built, not what was before her, but the tumult in the great Temple, the shouts and rejoicing as Solomon was anointed anew.

"NOOOOO!"

She flung the mask to the floor and trampled it, seized it and struck it against the edge of her tombstone altar, battering it with all her unnatural strength. Although the gold should have been soft, she could not mark that immobile visage.

Velvet got into the room with ease. She'd worked hotels before, back when that was her method. Sylvia had told her the hotel, the address, even the room number. When Velvet asked how she'd found the girl, Sylvia just laughed.

Velvet had checked into the hotel herself the night before, taking her time, doing it right, getting the layout of the place and its routines.

It was child's play to find the housekeeping staff's master key.

When she finally found herself outside Aurora's door, she was surprised how tense she felt, how excited.

How alive.

Slowly, she lowered the key into its receptacle, listening for the tell-tale click.

As soon as she heard it, she slammed the handle down, launched herself in, knife unfolded and ready, but she was shocked that no one was there. It was early evening, Velvet had just risen and she could hear the shower running, see the tacky clothes strewn lazily on a chair, the cheap silver bracelet on the bedside table. It was definitely the right room.

Velvet lunged for the bathroom and heard the clatter of the

rings on the shower rod. She was there first and popped the door open before Aurora could lock it. The sudden brightness and warmth was startling. For a moment Velvet just stared at her naked prey, wet red hair dripping over her eyes and her body looking chunky and tired in the unforgiving light.

Instinctively, Aurora raised her hands in front of her, ready to ward off a blow. Velvet smiled. Wrong move.

The knife had a rhythm in Velvet's hands as she sliced the blade along Aurora's fingers, forward and back, like when a child runs past a fence with a stick. Aurora yelped and pulled her hands back. That was when Aurora stabbed in at the belly, turned the blade and pulled it out. Aurora crumpled and Velvet's next cut was at the back of the thigh, just below the buttock. The hamstring. To keep her from running. Aurora drew breath for a scream and Velvet put the knife tip to the mortal's temple.

"Scream," she said, "and it's your brain."

Somehow, Aurora stayed quiet. Velvet took no chances. She got Aurora's bleeding hands cuffed behind her back and then wedged a washcloth into her mouth before stepping out of the bathroom.

She called her own suite. When Steve picked up, she gave him Aurora's room number and told him to bring extra towels.

Epilogue

"How I tire of defiant women," Bishop Solomon Birch said. He was examining a spreadsheet prepared by Xerxes Adrianopolous that listed the crimes of the Indulgence night. Most of the Embraces were committed by women. Most of the murders, by men.

The chart was broken down by covenant, and Solomon was abstractly pleased that the Lancea had sinned fewer times than the others. But it was cold comfort, as he felt sure that many of the Embraces had been performed to swell the ranks of his rivals, putting the Temple in an ever more awkward position.

But no matter. Every newcomer was a potential convert. All had the chance to fulfill their destiny, by God's plan. The Lancea Sanctum could afford to be patient. After all, they were *right*.

And now, they once more had a strong and righteous hand upon the tiller.

"Are we certain that Sylvia Raines has the mask?"

"She's all but confirmed it." Xerxes was hesitant and diffident around Solomon. It wasn't like the Bishop to forgive an insult. Removing a sitting Inquisitor wasn't easy, but Xerxes had an uncomfortable sense that eventually, the shoe would drop. Yet, why wait? Solomon, patient in such a matter? It was a thought to chill the blood.

"And she expects us to deal for it like Arab horse traders?"

"There was some talk of concessions. Minor stuff, probably. Penny ante. She knows which way the wind is blowing."

"Perhaps a token moderate in my counsels would calm and please that... group." He said 'group' as if it was a cleaned-up substitute for a much more colorful word. "As a 'new Bishop'

I suppose it behooves me to be conciliatory and inclusive," he said, with a sideways glance at Xerxes.

"If it got out that the mask was lost while you were... um, that is, during the..."

"During the what, Xerxes?"

But Xerxes was spared from answering by a sudden slamming door. "She's gone!"

Solomon was on his feet, staring intently at Ian Brigman. He knew Ian would never interrupt him unless...

"Who?" Solomon demanded.

"My daughter," Ian said, and Solomon could tell he was fighting tears. "Cass... Cass got her..."

"Cass?" Solomon suddenly had a very unpleasant feeling somewhere in the vicinity of his unmoving heart.

"The guns—the gun room was pilfered... a car is gone... he..." Ian's breath began to hitch with shame. "He got an eye back somehow, he..."

"You met his gaze," Solomon said, and Ian burst into tears.

"I thought he was blind!"

"Once again, you fail me," he growled at Ian, shoving past him toward the stairs. The last time Cass had tried to kill Solomon, Cass had done the same thing, meeting Ian's gaze and stealing his will.

"Don't let him hurt my daughter!" Ian cried.

"Xerxes," Solomon barked. "The game's afoot!"

———

"Why?" the new vampire asked. The old vampire shrugged. They were sitting in a park, after the rain, watching the streetlights stain the wet grass and pavement.

"I thought you'd be good at it."

"That's no reason. Not enough reason to... to turn me into..."

"Hey, you had a choice. You didn't *have* to drink. You could have resisted the change. Lots of people do, you know. Dagmar Brock—I'll introduce you, but you won't want to mention it. During the Indulgence he tried the Embrace *twice* and *both* times it failed. They wouldn't drink. Wouldn't go through with it. They," Velvet said, leaning in, "decided they'd rather be dead than become what we are. But not you. So please, when you address me, rein in that accusatory tone."

"You could have given me any victim. Why...?"

"Why Steve?" Velvet shrugged. "It had to be someone. He wanted it, Aurora. Believe me. Once he knew about us... it was meant to be. The Lancea has that much right at least. At *least*. Some people fail the test and get corrupted. They *long* to be spoiled and perverted. Once he'd felt the bite, Steve wouldn't rest until he died from it. Some people are like that."

Aurora was silent for a moment, twisting her bracelet on her arm and glaring at her failed reflection in a puddle.

"What makes you think I won't kill you?" Aurora asked.

"What makes you think you *can*?" Velvet replied.

"Maybe not tonight, or this year, but..."

"If you're not doing it tonight could we drop it? Burn that bridge when we come to it. You'll see. There are a lot of Kindred more deserving of death than me."

"That's small consolation."

"You won't think so after you meet the Bishop."

Acknowledgments

Special thanks to the Naperville Writers Group (online at http://www.napervillewritersgroup.org/) for its insight and support. Bottomless thanks as well to my sons, Nicholas and Daniel. While you boys aren't able to help me with these books yet (or, indeed, read them), someday I hope you'll know I did these for you. In that vein, thanks to my own parents: Having become a dad, my understanding of what they endured has deepened immeasurably. Finally, as always, thanks to Martha. Everything works better with Martha.

About the Author

Greg Stolze started getting gray hair when he was about 16, which just might tell you something about the psychological outlook of horror writers. Or perhaps it's just a genetic quirk, like his poor eyesight and absurdly low body-fat percentage. Regardless, Stolze has cultivated his neuroses, focusing them into an absurd phobia of missing deadlines. He has never missed a deadline in 10 years of professional writing.

Curious about other Crossroad Press books?
Stop by our site:
http://www.crossroadpress.com
We offer quality writing
in digital, audio, and print formats.